Between the glitter of Bombay's Colaba Causeway and the teeming seafront of Apollo Bunder stands Causeway Court, built in the Raj, and home for Brit Kotwal. It was his sister Dolly's idea to call him Brit, short for brittle, because of his bones. Besides, Parsees don't like long names, and it pleased his mother Sera because it sounded so English.

Brit never could guess what she really felt about having a son like him. Who knew what lay behind the fierce defiance of her brave act? He could see why a sophisticated public school man like Father believed in miracle cures, but it was obvious the sex-crazed holy man Wagh Baba couldn't make Brit grow taller, or walk, or stop his bones from breaking.

Sometimes it was fun being different. None of the other kids drank powdered pearls in their milk, or had almond oil rubbed into their legs until the skin gleamed like Bangalore silk. Brit knew he could always get his own way with Dolly – even if it took a little blackmail . . .

It was not such fun when you reach eighteen and you're still the size of an eight year old, and Brit starts to try his own way of growing, as all who turn the pages of this irrepressible first novel will discover.

Firdaus Kanga lives in Bombay. He is a full-time writer and reviewer and is at work on a second book about Britain as he sees it.

Firdaus Kanga

TRYING
TO GROW

PUBLISHED BY PAN BOOKS

First published 1990 by Bloomsbury Publishing Ltd

This Picador edition published 1991 by
Pan Books Ltd, Cavaye Place, London SW10 9PG

1 3 5 7 9 8 6 4 2

© 1990 by Firdaus Kanga

ISBN 0 330 31776 8

Typeset by Hewer Text Composition Services, Edinburgh

Printed in England by Clays Ltd, St Ives plc

TO MY PARENTS
For Valour

Part One
The Brave Act

1

'HIS TEETH ARE like windows,' said Father to the old Parsee with the droopy white moustache, sitting next to us on the bus. 'You can look through them – see?' Father tried to hold open my mouth. I pretended my lips were sealed with lashings of Stick-Fast.

'A rather stubborn four year old you've got there,' snorted the old man.

'Four year old? Guess again!'

'Three?'

Father shook his head. 'He's eight,' he said. The doctor had forgotten to tell us I was going to be a dwarf. I mean, I didn't look like Sneezy or Grumpy or someone – I just forgot to grow.

'Where are you taking him?' asked the old man, a total stranger. Father liked talking on buses; it helped him forget his itch to walk it out.

'To a witch doctor,' said Father gaily.

'What?' quavered the old man, hastily snapping his middle-finger and thumb to ward off the Evil Spirit that's always ready to pounce on Parsees when they're not looking.

'I was joking,' said Father, laying a hand on his snapping fingers. 'I'm taking him to a holy man, Wagh Baba. Maybe he'll cure my son.'

'Shame on you!' said the old man, his colourless skin suddenly daubed with purple islands. 'Don't we have Parsee prayers for children like these?'

'Oh, I've tried those!' said Father. 'They don't work.'

'You haven't tried them for long enough.'

'For six months. The priest told me to say them at three

3

every morning. All they did was give me insomnia – listening for the stroke of three.'

'Shame on you!' insisted the old man. 'Educated, speaking English so well and going to a mumbo-jumbo Baba.'

Father laughed. 'If my old school friends could see me doing this they'd jump out of their tailored suits. So would I, if I didn't know how desperate a man can get.' Father smiled that rueful smile which always made women want to hug him.

'I have to get off here,' said the old man. 'Be careful of the Baba. If he asks for money, tell him you want a cure first, then talk about everything else. Some of these people can be real swindlers.' Shaking his large head he got off.

We went on till we came to a small pavilion painted a horrible blue, like an ink-stain that hadn't been washed away. Sam (Father's name rhymed with palm not Pam) scooped me into his arms and we climbed off the bus. He bounded up the steps of the pavilion to a verandah overflowing with weepers.

'I'm not going in there,' I whimpered, my heart lurching at the thought of the Wagh Baba and his merciless tortures.

'Wait a moment before you make up your mind,' said Sam. He approached a red-eyed young girl in a white sari and asked, 'What's the matter? Is anything wrong?'

She burst into movie-giggles and said loudly, 'He thinks we are all crying! Oh, no, no, sir! This is because of the honey that Wagh Baba has put in our eyes to keep them clear and sharp like the eagle's!' Across the verandah we heard titters; the weepers surged forward to take a better look.

'Let's go!' I said, terrified of the crowd.

'We can't,' said Sam. 'It's not so easy coming this far to Chembur. Are you going to cry and join these people?'

I shook my head and shut my eyes so tight I could see squiggly worms.

'Come, come!' the girl in white was saying. 'Wagh Baba will see you now.'

'What language does he speak?' asked Sam. 'Hindi?' The girl nodded. 'Marathi?' She nodded again. 'English?' Her head bobbed. 'Esperanto?' Up and down, her head jerked automatically. Sam grinned at me; I giggled. He kissed my hair. 'Here goes,' he said. 'Into the mouth of the Tiger Man!'

4

The room we entered was sticky-hot and smelt of jasmine-scented joss-sticks. True to his name, Wagh Baba was stretched out on a tiger skin. He was stark naked. A woman in white with heavy coils of black hair falling over her sari was rubbing a perfumed ointment into his right thigh. Wagh Baba had the biggest dong I'd ever seen. He was pulling on a long strip of green and yellow mango that slid in and out of his mouth like paper in a printing press.

His beautiful assistant whispered something into his curly beard and Wagh Baba languidly opened his green eyes. 'Wagh Baba is fasting today, so he cannot speak,' said the woman. 'He is very-very weak like a hungry bird.' I didn't see how he could be very-very weak with all those hairy muscles curving like hills over his chest and arms and legs. I looked at Sam who shut his eyes for a split-second.

Wagh Baba laid one mango-stained hand on my legs. I tried to busy myself with the tiger skin on which he slept. His hand was heavy and hot, and his lips were moving feverishly. The beautiful assistant smiled at me and dipped her fingers into the perfumed ointment. She began to rub Wagh Baba's thighs slightly higher up. He shut his eyes and moaned.

The woman motioned me away. 'The blessing is over,' she said. 'Now Wagh Baba will write instruction.' She handed him a large *peepul* leaf and quill. I couldn't believe people still wrote on leaves: that was something I read about in *Tales from the Panchatantra*. Wagh Baba threw down the leaf on his chest, exhausted from the effort. Sam picked it up. The handwriting was remarkably like mine. It said: 'Appli warm salt on legses.'

'He can't spell, he sleeps naked in front of women and young children, he's strong as an elephant and weak with lust — ' said my mother Sera.

'Lust!' I interrupted. 'Is that some kind of disease?'

'Some people think so,' said Sam wryly.

'Then I'm not going to Wagh Baba again,' I said, clutching the excuse tight. 'I might catch lust.'

'God forbid, my kitten! You don't know what it is.'

'But he will!' said my big sister Dolly. 'Soon as I tell him.'

'If you do that,' said Sera darkly, dropping her voice so I

wouldn't hear, 'I'll burn every single one you've kept there, under your . . .' Her voice faded away, leaving me insane with curiosity. 'Under your . . .' I began thinking of all the possible places – Dolly's cupboard, her dressing-table, her shoe-rack.

'Stop it, Brit!' shouted Dolly.

'What?'

'Trying to guess.'

'I wasn't. I don't even know what you've got hidden.' But it was too late. Pinocchio had his nose, I had my spreading blush. When I felt my ears go warm as if someone had suddenly covered them with mitts, I knew the game was up.

Sera looked at me sharply and said, 'So let's discuss this Wagh Baba. I think he's a positive fake, can't write a line of correct English – shows what kind of man he must be!'

'Oh, darling,' said Sam. 'I doubt Jesus Christ could write a line of correct Greek. And about the other thing, the ways of holy men are strange. Maybe he's trying to overcome his senses.'

'And not succeeding,' said Dolly. 'Because he moaned with pleasure. You *said* he did.'

'Stop that!' snapped Sera. 'It's not something to say near a child.'

'Look,' said Sam stubbornly. 'The only way we'll know he's genuine is if Brit stops breaking his bones, right?'

'Wrong! Absolutely, definitely, certainly wrong!' declared Sera. 'You know Brit's getting more cautious as he's growing older; he's had just two fractures in the last three years. And he's getting better anyway, no thanks to any Wagh Baba Faba Gaba.'

'Don't make fun of a holy man,' said Sam. 'It's not right!'

'Oh, bloody rot and poppycock!'

'Where did you pick *that* up?' whispered Sam, looking devastated. 'It's the kind of thing even I wouldn't say.'

'Every English soldier in Colaba used to say it,' laughed Sera. 'In the good old days when *they* were here.'

'Well, you are not to say it again.'

'As you wish,' said Sera briskly. 'I won't when you are around.'

'If I were a Hindu husband, I would have thrashed you just now.'

6

'My God!' howled Dolly. 'Such shameful prejudice! Imagine saying that about Hindus. It's a scandal! You haven't learnt a thing from the National Integration Campaign, have you? You went to sleep in 1947 and never woke up.'

'Marry a Hindu and see!' said Sam. 'Then don't come back crying to us.'

'Oh, don't put ideas into her head! Everyone knows good Parsee girls marry Parsee boys.'

'But I'm not a good Parsee girl. Remember what I've hidden under my . . .' And Dolly gave me a look for which I could have shaved off her curls. And then it struck me by wicked reasoning: The Place had to be Dolly's mattress. That's where no one would look; that's where Sera must have discovered whatever there was during one of her cleaning sprees. I wheeled myself out of the room as unobtrusively as I could and rushed to the bedroom that I shared with her. I tried hefting the mattress. I couldn't even lift the edges; if I tried harder, I knew I'd put Wagh Baba out of business.

Slowly, I slipped my hand, then my arm under the cotton wool mountain and groped about until I felt a silky sheet. I lunged forward to grab whatever there was and pull it out. I saw my first *Playgirl*. My heart was beating so hard my whole body was shaking. They'd come looking for me before the minute was out. I riffled through the pages and I stopped. Here was a nude, bearded man stretched out on a strand of beach, holding his dong in his hand and it was twice the size of Wagh Baba's.

'Caught you!' whispered Dolly, and I jerked so suddenly for a moment I thought I'd cracked something in my chest. '*Aaaee!*' I made a little boy's sound and dropped the *Playgirl*.

'What is it?' said Sera and Sam in unison. 'Is Brit all right?'

'Perfectly!' sang Dolly, packing the *Playgirl* back into bed. She hugged me. 'Don't worry, I'm not going to tell them! OK? So stop shivering.'

'Dolly, I'm not scared of Wagh Baba any more,' I whispered into her neck, 'because his, you know, his . . .'

'Dong!' said Dolly, nodding excitedly.

I giggled. 'Ya! His dong. You know, I thought it was like a giant's when I saw it. Now I know it's just like . . . like a Lady's

7

Finger!' That made Dolly launch into her pendulum laughing fit, swaying back and forth in a wide arc that slowly grew smaller as her mirth receded. Watching her made me shake with laughter until my ribs ached.

Then Father came in with a little muslin bundle which he started rubbing over my knees. 'Appli warm salt on legses!' said Dolly, and Sam had to drop the salt.

I had a Jewish mother. Sera had more than twenty centuries of Persian blood in her veins, but any little Jewish boy from Brooklyn would have recognised her as his very own.

Even her name, which was pure Persian, had the ring of Sarah to it. She was tall, with short-cropped hair the colour of iron-filings, deep-set eyes ringed with dark lashes, a nose which I need not describe, and a chin on which you could balance a toothbrush. But it was her mouth that made her. It was usually open: smiling, speaking, cajoling, commanding, correcting, complimenting, wailing, worrying. When it was shut it was that perfect cupid's bow which had made my father's heart shimmy when he first saw her.

The Girl Guide Movement had laid its mark on Sera's mind, like the indelible stamp on a ballot paper. For instance, she was terrified of the roaches that swarmed around our kitchen floor at night. But she would step in at midnight, switch on the lights and catch them with their pants down. Then she'd cry, 'Look at me!' and, giving the Guide's three-fingered salute, she'd begin a robust death-dance, stamping to the tune of 'John Brown's Baby's Got a Cold'.

Two years before I was born the Indian Government, delirious with nationalism, banned the import of all consumer items. Unfortunately, we hadn't learnt to make enough of the things we needed. So we used to have sudden shortages of cheese and toilet-paper, soap and butter, talc and newsprint. But thanks to Sera we were immune to the empty shop shelves.

One sunny morning, Sera summoned me from the magic painting book in which I was studiously daubing water, making pink bunnies and green grass appear from nothing. 'Come, darling!' she said. 'Won't you help Mummy make little dollies? You can't get them at the shops any more and we must be prepared!' I spent a couple of hours happily spreading out the swathes of gauze that Sera cut out, padding them with cotton wool for her to shape and tape into place. It wasn't till I was twelve and another shortage hit us that I realised I had joined a sanitary towel assembly-line when I was four.

That was nothing. As time went on, our two-bedroom flat began to look like a supermarket warehouse. On top of all the cupboards was roll upon roll of toilet-paper balanced like flimsy towers; when we opened our cupboards they bounced off our heads. More carefully stacked were tins of drinking chocolate, dozens of bars of soaps, a bristle of tooth-brushes; in the fridge were giant slabs of butter, the biggest Sera could find; in the kitchen were brown and white porcelain jars holding kilos of rice and sugar, pickles and jams, spices and condiments. People who came to see us would gape at the cornucopia as Sera would declare, 'We never run out of anything. And when I say anything, I mean everything.' The visitors would nod dumbly, but the next time they ran out they knew where to call.

By the early 'seventies, shortages were in short supply, so you'd think Sera would slow down on hiding acorns. But inflation decided to make its debut and off went Sera giving a mad chase to the galloping prices, returning from every shopping spree with bags clinging to her like a brood of kids.

When I was twelve, India fought one of her periodic wars with Pakistan. My mother only had to read 'War Clouds On The Horizon' bannered in *The Times of India* and she was off. All our jewellery (like all prosperous Indians we had plenty of that) was snatched out of the bank locker. Sera ripped open a plump cushion and buried the gold bangles, the diamond earrings, the strands of pearls, deep inside the silk-cotton stuffing. 'As soon as the air raid siren blows,' she said, emitting a terrifying imitation of the wail, 'my little baby will grab this cushion and slip it under his bottom on the wheel-chair, where no one will ever suspect what it hides. Right, baby?'

'Right!' I cried, always greedy for an adventure.

'The last Tsar of Russia gave me the idea of hiding the jewels in the cushion. Now you see the value of the history I've been reading?'

'But they pierced the pillow!' cried Dolly excitedly, ever ready to prick the balloon. 'The Reds pierced the pillow with their bayonets!'

'I am prepared for that,' said Sera, pulling out one of those tough sling bags which airlines give away. 'In case, God forbid and heaven descend upon earth, the cushion is discovered, we shall have our precious possessions safely with us – in this.' In went a change of clothes for each of us, a cake of Lifebuoy soap 'to kill the germs', talc in a puffer pack, 'to keep us fresh and sweet smelling, no matter what', a pack of cards 'to keep the children amused'.

'You call these our precious possessions?' said Father dolefully. '*This* is what we need.' He dropped a huge bundle of notes that must have contained at least ten thousand rupees into the bag.

'Rubbish!' sneered Sera. 'Money is no good in wartime. I've read what happened in Germany – you needed a pramload of cash to get a pound of sugar. Out it goes!' From the depths of the bag she pulled out a thick gold necklace hung with a dozen gold sovereigns. 'We will bargain for our freedom with this,' she declared. 'And who will dare deny the value of British guineas?'

'Those days are gone, darling,' said Father. 'No one cares for Britain any more.'

'Such disloyalty,' sniffed Sera. 'If you'd only been a Boy Scout you wouldn't talk like that. I took an oath with the Guides which I intend to keep; an oath to King and Country.'

'From which you are now released,' said Dolly cheerfully, 'because Britain doesn't have a king any more!'

'His daughter reigns!' proclaimed Sera, as if she had to remind us. They were everywhere, the British Royal Family, grinning at us from behind glass-fronted cupboards, looking out like dour prisoners from book case windows, splashed over my bedroom wall in a poster Sera had pulled out of *Woman's Own*. Every time we walked past the Gateway of India we were ordered to attention while she read in sonorous tones the brown inscription high on the arch: 'ERECTED TO COMMEMORATE THE LANDING IN INDIA OF THEIR IMPERIAL MAJESTIES KING GEORGE V AND QUEEN MARY.'

'Now,' she said, 'there's some room left in the bag, so each of us can take one precious possession. What about you, popsie?'

There was only one book that would last me the duration of the war: I carefully handed over my bright red *Chambers Twentieth Century Dictionary*.

'Sera, dear, do you think it's wise to take that along?' said Father.

'It's his choice,' said Sera, 'and none of our business to question it.'

'Oh, well; I'll travel light,' said Dolly, handing Sera a copy of *Playgirl* with a hirsute chap squatting on its cover, his huge fists between his legs. 'You think the sexy Paki soldiers will seduce us?' she asked.

'I'm prepared for that,' said Sera grimly. 'All you have to do is hit him *there*.'

'Where?' asked Dolly, shamelessly shamming.

'Nowhere, dear; no one's going to touch you as long as I'm around,' said Father, looking terribly concerned.

'They just might,' said Sera. 'This is where you hit him, hard as you can.' She tapped her first finger on the cover-boy's hairy fists.

Father dropped something with a clatter and a thud. Without batting an eyelid, Sera lifted it up. She asked, 'What is this, Sam?'

'That's one of my suits, dear. I'd never dream of going to the bank without one.'

'The days when you had to wear a suit to work are gone, Sam. The British left twenty-five years ago.'

'Dear, didn't you say we should remain loyal?'

Sera knew when she was beaten. She said, 'Well, you'll just have to put it on in a hurry when the bombers come; there's no room for that in here.'

The bombers never came. Night after night we waited. Three times the air raid siren went off; three times I popped the bursting cushion under me, three times Father put on his suit and knotted his tie, three times Dolly hefted the emergency bag, three times Sera led the way to the entrance hall of the building.

Things were rather lonely down there. Bombayites knew,

they just knew, they'd never get bombed. If Fate had it in for them, why had she spared them in every previous war? Of course, knowing that India was winning helped. All our neighbours remained at home, blissfully unprepared. We heard that the war was over on the BBC; it had lasted just a fortnight. Dolly and I wailed with disappointment.

Father smiled, crinkling his eyes. 'Thank God India's non-aligned,' he said. 'Imagine being perpetually prepared for the Third World War!' Sera reddened and hid her face in his chest.

The next time we visited Wagh Baba, the lovely lady told us he'd taken a vow of silence. He motioned us to come closer and I looked pityingly between his thighs. Blessing delivered, he scribbled on a leaf, 'Veri good bones soft — soft now.'

Father asked the assistant if he should pay anything. 'I'm very sorry, I forgot last time,' he said, shaking his head.

'No matter,' she said, beginning to anoint the strip of hair that ran down Wagh Baba's stomach like a pipe between his chest and his dong. 'Pay what you can. Each gives what he can spare.' She raised her eyes and looked pious. A bent old woman, hair askew, came into the room and dropped a handful of coins at Wagh Baba's feet. The assistant quickly scooped them into her lap and began counting. 'See!' she said. 'This poor woman has brought twenty rupees. So much faith in Baba!' To prove her point her hand swooped down till it rested in Baba's pubic hair.

'I think we must go,' said Father hastily. 'I hope this is OK.' He pulled out a hundred-rupee note from his wallet and put it on the tiger skin.

'I felt so terrible,' he said later. 'I should've given at least five hundred and one. But I didn't have that much on me.'

2

NOBODY WHO KNEW my father would believe that his father was the legendary Khanbahadur Kotwal, One-Oh-One, the Tigers' Nemesis, Forest Officer to His Highness the Maharaja of Mazab. I have an old beige photograph of him, shooting a rifle into the camera. He looks quite dashing in his native state togs: turban, huge pantaloons, muslin shirt and sleeveless jacket. His features have sort of blended away into the paper, but you can still see a moustache that rises lushly from his lips and a brace of eyebrows thick enough to plait.

My grandfather decided to get married, having slain one hundred tigers in the service of his princeling – in those days you became a forest officer to keep the tiger population down. His valiant achievement earned him the Diwan or chief minister's only daughter, a Parsee lady, rather long in the tooth but even longer in her listed financial assets.

On their wedding night he boasted he would give her a hundred sons, one for each tiger. Since his bride was almost forty, it's obvious he was ignorant of the menopause. But it doesn't really matter, because the morning after the nuptial night, the Tigers' Nemesis decided to go hunting in order to give his new wife a gift of his hundred and first trophy, a hundred and one being a number much loved by the Parsees whose wedding gifts always consist of white envelopes with a hundred and one rupees inside.

As it happened, it was the tiger who did the hunting, in the process bestowing the posthumous title One-Oh-One on my grandfather. 'That,' said my Father, 'was the beginning of the Curse, the collective curse of the hundred whom One-Oh-One had sent on their stairway to heaven.'

13

His widow was left with his roaring seed in her womb which, strangely, grew into my father, a man as mild as the Bombay winter. As soon as she decently could, my grandmother Cooverbai, or Kuku, as she liked to be called, packed off her son to one of those imitation Etons that are scattered all over India. She was in a hurry because she had become what Sera called the 'kept mistress' of a British good-for-nothing-but-sex in the Maharaja's service. She lured him away from the sorry little state of Mazab to the throbbing British Indian city of Bombay where she bought a love-nest in the posh southern end of town. But soon the Englishman, whose name was known only to Father who was determined never to let it dirty his lips, got bored with the second-rate theatre, opera and parties Bombay had to offer. Afraid of losing him, Kuku took him cavorting around the playgrounds of Europe from where she scribbled 'Wintering on the Riviera' or 'Taking the waters in Wiesbaden' which is where she popped it eighteen years after One-Oh-One. The jaunt to Europe had become a way of life for her and she died in the nick of time, for her assets in India had sunk to below freezing point.

Father was left with nothing – the Curse was doing its best – but the flat in trendy Colaba and a public school education. Which counted when he went for a job interview at the Imperial Bank, since depressingly re-named the State Bank. He got the job as assistant to the British chairman, and worked his way up until he became manager of the Colaba Branch.

Then came the fateful Parsee New Year's Day when Sera swam into Sam's sight. He was feeling terribly alone. Everyone else was celebrating with parents, brothers, sisters, *fui-fuaas*, *Kaka-Kakies*, *mama-mamees*, *masa-masees* and other kinds of relatives. So he walked sadly to the local fire-temple, which was crowded with the worshippers of stylish clothes and Being Seen in the Right Place. We Parsees don't take our religion too seriously; those who do are considered downright dangerous and a little mad.

There in the darkened hall, where no electric light ever burns, among the plump women smelling of Chanel No 5 and moth-balled silks, Sam saw Sera. Actually, he heard her.

She was staring at the priest in his long white muslin robes as he swayed before the Sacred Fire, and suddenly she turned to the girl standing next to her and said, 'Do you think he's got anything on under that robe?' The other girl clapped a hand to her mouth and turned away; Sera laughed a rich, full-throated laugh.

It was love at first laugh for Father. 'She was different then and she's different now!' he would say when he was feeling romantic. 'I followed her that day from the fire-temple and saw that she didn't live very far from where I did; her place was just behind the Taj Mahal Hotel. I discovered that she went swimming at the Golwalla Baths every afternoon – '

'And he would stare and stare like some dirty old man,' Sera would say, looking disgusted. 'You'd never expect a public school man to behave like that.'

'But that's what you fell for, wasn't it? My style. Especially when I sent you those Bombelli truffle chocolates for your birthday. Those were the best chocolates in town made by a Swiss confectioner. Of course, he stopped creating his goodies by the time you kids were born.' And so we lived, my sister and I, irrevocably deprived of the gorgeous, gooey past.

'Huh!' Sera would sniff. 'As if Bombellis were anything new to me! My father used to supply furniture to the Bombay Presidency.'

'I don't see what that has to do with chocolate. Do you know, children, even in those days Sera was prepared; she never came to the baths without an extra swimming costume, in case the one she was wearing sprang a leak.'

'That was quite likely, the way you stared as if your eyes would burn a hole in my swimsuit.'

'What could I do?' Father would say, stroking Sera's neck. 'You had Betty Grable legs.'

And then they'd kiss and Sera would say, 'Not in front of them!' while Dolly hurriedly wheeled me out of their bedroom.

I don't think Sera and Father were really in love, but they were crazy about each other's charm. I mean, they didn't talk all that much about things that were happening around them or God or abortion. They were happy to make each other happy. If Sera had Betty Grable legs, Sam was a Gregory Peck look-alike.

Things weren't always chocolate and swimsuits between Sera and Sam. She said it was because she was a Libran. There *had* to be times when her scales were out of balance. It would begin like this: 'Sam, darling, I'm feeling too lazy to get out this morning. Will you buy a bucket on your way home from work? The one in our bathroom is about to spring a leak.'

'Delighted to, my wife!' Six in the evening and Father arrived, tomato-red plastic pail swinging from one arm.

'What is this?' asked Sera, dangerously tipping.

'You asked me to get a bucket, remember?'

'I didn't ask you to get a red bucket. Red! My God! When everything in our bathroom is blue?'

'I thought it would liven up the room, like painting one wall in a grey room bright red!'

'Red! I can't believe this.'

'But, darling, you must move with the times. Contrasts are in!'

'Red! Do you know what red does to me? It makes me ill. Physically ill!'

'It also makes you want to fight, my bull!' Father could never resist a good line.

'Here I'm suffering and you laugh? My God! My own husband. And the two of you sitting there, why don't you say something? Tell him I'm a Libran, I'm sensitive to colour – I can't keep that thing in my bathroom, it will constipate me.'

Sera wasn't being funny: she meant it. And she wasn't being mean when she burnt the fish and chips that were for dinner that night. Nor was she being cruel when she swept my carefully constructed jigsaw puzzle off the dining table. She really wasn't. It was just the way she was.

It took some time and weight to restore her balance. A couple of days had to pass while she kept ominous silence, shed occasional tears in the kitchen, snapped at the butcher. Then one evening, Father would arrive from work with two tickets to a piano recital or perhaps a bouquet of crisp white carnations (no red ones) or a rare pressing of Chopin's *Waltzes* (any classical record not from Russia was rare in Bombay) and everything would be chocolate and swimsuits again. Sera would smile and say, 'Sorry, Sam.'

16

He'd hug her and whisper, 'Wish I could glue those scales into perpetual balance.'

'Oh! We wish you could!' Dolly and I would chorus.

'I'd never let you!' Sera would exclaim indignantly. 'If my scales didn't wobble, I'd never appreciate how lovely it is when they're steady.'

Sam didn't have scales that tipped but he had his passions. Aeroplanes were to him what sex is to a pubescent boy. He didn't know anything about aerospace engineering but he loved watching planes, reading glossies about planes, imagining he was at the controls of a hook-nosed Concorde. On bank holidays he'd take a bus to the airport at the other end of town. And when he came back he had the look on his face that I was shocked to recognise in the mirror the first time I made love.

Sam hid all his aeroplane magazines in a secret drawer that you could only reach from the back of his cupboard (this devious contrivance reflecting my furniture-making grandfather's ingenuity). Whenever we didn't see Sam, we knew he was fiddling with his beauties in that dark corner.

'Why do you hide them? Aeroplanes aren't pornographic, you know,' Dolly would say a million times. She wouldn't listen when I told her it was the secrecy that Sam found so exciting. 'Nonsense!' she'd say. 'It's quite straightforward. Aeroplanes are a symbol of the escape he longs for, from that stodgy bank and his crackpot family. He feels guilty about it and he hides the evidence of his guilt!'

Maybe there was something in that because it could explain his other passion: walking. Like one of those dolls which lucky children got from America; once you wound them up they wouldn't stop. Sam stepped into his walking shoes when he got out of bed at five in the morning. His morning walk would take him to the seafront where he'd stroll past bunches of Europeans taking their constitutionals before the sun grew too hot, and fat Indian ladies who wanted to slim without browning their upper-class skins.

He took me with him once and through sleepy eyes I saw with surprise the number of people: servants snarling at the dogs they had to walk and little children using the trafficless roads to ride their bicycles, sulking *ayahs* pushing prams so that their charges could 'eat' the clean dawn air. We stopped at a *narielpaniwalla* to sip the water from huge green coconuts and behind us was a queue of thirsty walkers. Sam turned to me and said, 'Doesn't it feel good to be out like this when there's no one around?' I smiled indulgently as children do at the creaky jokes their parents crack.

I found out what Sam was talking about a couple of years later. We had this elderly French lady, a pen-pal of Sera's, staying with us, when Sam had the weird idea of showing her the Churchgate Railway Station. So we went walking: this lady, Jacqui, Sera, Dolly, and Sam wheeling me; it wasn't that far from where we lived. We'd hardly arrived when, like her famous compatriot at the storming of the Bastille, Jacqui screamed, 'Riot! Riot!' rolling her 'r's like Peter Sellers playing Inspector Clouseau. And I, ever the show-off, gave Rochefoucauld's reply, 'No, it's a revolution!' Battalions of men and women surged towards us, faster and faster; even from a hundred yards away we could smell their sour sweat.

'Let's go!' shouted Jacqui, quite hysterical, stamping her feet.

'Let's not!' I said. 'This is my first riot.'

'And if there's a baton-charge it will be your last,' rolled Jacqui.

'OK. Break it up,' said Sam. 'You know as well as I that this is only the rush-hour crowd making for the trains. People come to South Bombay to work and in the evening they hurry north where they live,' he explained to Jacqui.

'I can't believe it!' she said. 'There cannot be so many commuting every day.'

'Not so many,' said Sam. 'Just a couple of millions use the trains. Another million or so go by bus.' That was when I knew what a million must look like; there would be a million stars in the sky when you couldn't see an inch of black.

In the evenings, Sera and Sam would stroll up and down the Colaba Causeway which, like a mighty river, slashed through the southern tip of Bombay island. Along its banks rose buildings with names like Elysium Mansions and East and West Court, unshakeably smug in their middle-class certainty.

Like great rivers everywhere the Causeway could take it all: the disappearance of its European residents and restaurants, the coming of the rich refugees from Sind with their gaudy sari shops, the march of the hippies and the Arab invasion, the whores who chased them like camp followers. With every tributary the Causeway sparkled and glittered, more cosmopolitan, more gay than any street in India.

We lived in a building at the confluence of the Causeway and one of the graceful lanes that streamed out of it to Apollo Bunder where the Taj Mahal Hotel stood, staring confidently at the ship-rich sea. We reached the second floor of Causeway Court by a lift that hissed and shuddered but never went out of order. It was made in the Raj. On our door was a nameplate that still read 'Kuku Kotwal' in solid brass letters.

Our flat was furnished like a period movie set – late Victorian. A grandfather clock growled the time, carved sofas upholstered in old-gold waited for visitors (and the toothbrush that Sera wielded through their dust-filled crannies); four-poster beds slept in the bedrooms and tall wooden cupboards stood like ebony slaves in every room. None of the furniture was rare or beautiful – an antique-dealer would have laughed it out of his shop – but it was good wood and careful craftsmanship and home.

Out strolling the Causeway, Sera and Sam would window-shop everything from garlic and ginger to the foreign cheeses and chewing-gum that the smugglers sold in little folding trays, and they would meet everyone who lived in Colaba from our next-door-neighbour to Dolly's sports coach on whom she had a crush.

If Sera was off-balance some evening, Sam would go walking alone. Sometimes he'd follow the rail-tracks from Churchgate Station till he felt walked out; other times he'd stroll over to the Hanging Gardens suspended on a hill, miles from where we lived. 'Just so I can see those gay lights floating below me,' he'd say dreamily.

'And fool yourself that you're living in a beautiful city,' Sera would snort.

Sam would smile quietly. 'Those lights belong to Bombay like the slums do,' he'd say. 'And one day I'm going to cross

19

the Causeway with my eyes shut; I'm sure I can do it.' Which was quite an ambition because the bit of Causeway where we lived didn't have traffic signals or policemen waving their arms about and it did have huge red buses, wooden hand-carts and cars speeding in both directions.

'Sam! You are going to try nothing of the sort; if I wanted to be a widow I would have married a corrupt old man, not a poor public school boy.'

'Say what you like, my love. I'm going to do it one day. It's a *kusti* promise.' And Sam would fish for the three-stranded sacred thread round his waist which he invariably forgot to wear.

'Where is it, Sam?'

'Resting between my shirts and socks, love. We all need a break sometimes.'

Sera would collapse into his arms and say, 'That is why I married you.'

'Thank God you didn't have that much on you!' said Sera, her voice trembling with excitement.

There was Wagh Baba resplendent on his tiger skin, his dong smudged out by the prissy editors of the *Evening News of India*. But there was nothing modest about the blazing banner 'Sex-Crazy Baba Booked'.

'I'm going to read this!' crowed Dolly:

Wagh Baba, the miracle man who had seemingly laid a spell on Bombay's credulous citizens, was arrested this morning together with his beautiful accomplice Ma Shanti Devi on charges of fraud, cheating and indecent assault.

Police raided his ashram in Chembur after receiving complaints from the outraged parents of a seventeen-year-old girl who had been assaulted under the pretext of being treated by Wagh Baba. The Baba apparently claimed that he could diagnose women's diseases by feeling the shape of their breasts.

The father of the girl, one Ramdas Patil, broke down as he told this reporter that his innocent daughter, who suffered from asthma, had allowed Wagh Baba to fondle her breasts.

The Baba told her that her breasts were lemon-shaped and so she was to avoid all citrus fruits. But his hands did not stop there, said the numbed father. 'It was only when my daughter came home sobbing that we found out the truth.' Similar stories came from other devotees of the Baba who were questioned.

While Wagh Baba did not make any overt demands for money from his patients, his assistant had a sure-fire trick to extract cash from them. She had trained her old maidservant to enter Wagh Baba's room whenever a potentially rich devotee was being treated and shower the Baba with coins. The abashed devotee would then reach into his pocket to outdo the maidservant's offering which Ma Shanti Devi loudly announced as twenty, thirty or fifty rupees.

There is no record of any miracle being performed by Wagh Baba, although every devotee claimed he had heard of many cures. The strange aspect of the city's flirtation with Wagh Baba was that it affected people from every class and community. 'I remember,' said a devotee, 'a man who used to come with his little son. The man was dressed in a jacket, he spoke phin-phon English, he was as handsome as an American filmstar.'

Which only proves that the need for magic touches us all, rich or poor, ignorant or educated.

Dolly took a deep breath and said, 'Well, not bad, you looking like an American filmstar at the age of fifty-three! Hey,' she said, turning to me. 'What d'you think of all this?'

'I think it's fab!' I said excitedly. Fab was our 'in' word then. 'I mean, Wagh Baba was a real villain, not like the ones I've known.'

'You've known villains?' I knew we were jabbering to blot out the sound of silence. It wasn't often Sera and Sam were speechless. Made us feel spooky, like sitting around with sphinxes for company.

'Of course! I've known villains right from the Big Bad Wolf to the smugglers in *The Island of Adventure*.'

'Oh, those!' said Dolly. 'You and your books. I'm glad you've had this bite of real life for once.'

'Sure. Maybe I'll write about it one day.'

'And win the Nobel Prize for Literature.'

'They don't give the Nobel Prize,' said Sam, 'to writers who we can enjoy.' We were so relieved we just let our faces do what they wanted. 'I'm going for a walk,' said Sam. 'Don't keep dinner waiting, darling. I may be late.'

'Oh, Sam! You don't have to take it so badly. After all, you did mean well.'

'There she goes!' whispered Dolly. 'Trying to make up for proving right!'

'And besides,' said Sera, 'this has taught us a lesson – never to trust so easily again.'

Sam nodded. His eyes looked bright. 'Tigers are unlucky for us,' he said, and closed the door.

The only way a Parsee is going to be called by his name is if it's short and easy like Sera or Sam. We delight in stretching, snipping and squashing given names out of all recognition, with a view to making them roll off the tongue easily and, perhaps, even sound English. So boys who are named Faredoon become Freddy, Nowroji becomes Neville, Adi becomes Eddy, and everyone is delighted with his new name and what he hopes is his new image.

My parents went about it a bit differently when their first child, my sister, was born. They decided they'd like to call her Dolly, then they hunted about for a suitable Parsee name to put on the birth certificate. They discovered Daulat, which they thought was auspicious because it meant wealth, of which they didn't really have very much, what with banks paying rather badly to compensate for life-long job security. It was only Sera's inheritance, which brought in a couple of thousand a month, that allowed us to float in upper-middle-class pools.

Anyway, Dolly was never called what she was called unless we wanted to make her howl. Then someone would say, using her full honorific name, 'Daulatbanoo, is it true that you've failed in algebra again?' And sure as summer that would make her cry, not for the algebra test she'd flunked, she always flunked algebra, but for her hoary name that could rise like this just any time to mock her.

Oh, Dolly was a funny girl but the best sister a boy could want. She was always glad to play mother to me. Which came easily to her because by the time I'd left my pram she'd left school. For ten years Dolly was an only child and all that time she drove Sam and Sera crazy. Which wasn't difficult because they were already crazy about her. She was so sweet you'd want to cuddle her snapshots: chubby cheeks, dimpled chin, Shirley Temple curls, she had the works.

And she had her exploits which were repeated to shrieking friends so often in her presence that she learned them with her nursery rhymes. 'When I was three,' she'd begin, 'I was convinced that our huge table-top radio hid a man behind its gleaming dial. When I said that to Sera she just laughed and said, "What an imagination!" So, one night when everyone was asleep, I jumped out of my cot, crept to the radio and smashed in the front with my milk bottle. Oh, you should've heard the crash! Sera and Sam thought I had fallen out of the cot because they saw it empty, so when they found me there next to the radio they laughed and laughed and squeezed me and kissed me. I didn't do a thing.' (And here Dolly would give a remarkably sweet baby look even when she was twenty-five, you know, underlip pulled in, full-moon eyes.) 'I just said, "It *was* my imagination."' Which shows she was a pretty smart baby, unless, of course, this is one of those legends that families make up about themselves and can't stop believing and relating because it's so lovely and, in its own way, so true.

Dolly was the curse of her school teachers. She went to a very 'propah' Parsee school which specialised in producing goody-goody girls. But Dolly specialised in dirty tricks like gluing a page of erotic poetry into 'The Rime of the Ancient Mariner' because she couldn't stick Coleridge. And her prissy English teacher, Miss Lobo, read through a couple of stanzas before she leapt out of her Mariner-induced stupor. Dolly spent most of her time standing on the classroom verandah to which she was banished. She kept herself happy watching the busy road below her for victims. She would spit chewing-gum into their hair or, if it was raining, make white patterns on their umbrellas.

This state of affairs would persist for the better part of the year. Then a week before her finals, Dolly would sit down and swot, with the result that she would stand among the top three in her class. Even in algebra. You see what I meant about legends?

3

I DIDN'T JUST live with this bunch of weirdos, I also lived with osteo. Or, to give the devil his full name, *osteogenesis imperfecta*. I liked being different from most people. It tickled me. Though it didn't tickle me when I came into life howling with pain.

When Sera came out of her anaesthetic fog, she saw her Saint Bernard-faced doctor looking more Saint Bernardish than ever. 'I'm afraid I have bad news for you, Sera,' he said, looking down at his pudgy fingers. 'Your boy is born with bones brittle as glass. The ones in his legs are delicate as test tubes; I doubt he'll ever walk. He'll probably be toothless, too; his teeth will break as soon as he bites into anything hard.'

'Anything else, Doctor?' said Sera with a mysterious smile.

'This is no laughing matter, I assure you. Your son was born with a broken femur; his leg is in a tiny cast. In fact, the only silver lining is his disease will burn itself out by the time he's in his late teens. But he's never going to walk.'

'Then he must use a wheelchair,' said Sera.

'Yes, yes, of course,' said the doctor, terrified at the first signs of madness he saw in my mother. 'Call me if you need to talk.'

'I won't need to talk, thank you,' said Sera, and the doctor fled, his coat flying behind him.

Sam was whispering into her hair, 'You're so brave. When Dolly asked me outside about her brother, I couldn't speak. I just gave a thumbs-down sign. Darling, darling, are you sure you aren't just putting on a brave act?'

That's a question I've been trying to find an answer to ever since I could find answers. That Sera's behaviour was unnatural is undeniable. But are the responses we expect the only natural ones? Could it be that Sera really had the courage to meet the disaster that had slipped into her life? Or was it one of those blockades that we impose on our minds so that unpleasant facts are sunk like ships bringing sustenance to an enemy?

Because the next thing Sera said was, 'Sam, that was awful. He's our son, he's a boy like any other; only his body has problems. He'll cope with them more easily than you think; they'll just be a way of life to him. Now, will you call Dolly in to see her brother?'

'I love you, Sera,' said Sam, just managing a smile.

A nurse wheeled in my cot. 'Oh, Sam, he's beautiful!' said Sera. 'Look at that strong chin, just like mine! And that sweet sharp nose. His face is a perfect triangle!' Sera didn't know it but she was describing the telling features of osteo. When I grew up I didn't really mind the pointed nose and chin – they made me look Jewish – which was fine for someone who'd grown up on Leon Uris – but I did mind the inverted triangle. I even measured the angles of my face with a protractor – they added up to 180 degrees.

Dolly crept in, tear-smudges on her cheeks. 'Was the baby dead?' she asked.

'Dead! My God, no! Here he is alive.'

'But not kicking,' said Sam mournfully.

'He's so sweet!' shrieked Dolly. 'Oooh! I'm going to squeeze him.'

'Don't do that!' shouted Sam. 'You'll break him!'

'Is he some kind of doll?' she sniggered. 'I know babies are delicate.'

'But Daryus is different. His bones are brittle like biscuits; you hold him too hard, they'll crumble.'

'Really?' said Dolly, her eyes huge with excitement. 'Then we should keep him in cotton wool like an egg!'

'Now, don't be silly,' said Sera. 'We only have to be a bit careful, otherwise he's just like any other baby.'

'Look! He's opened his eyes, Hi! Daryus!' They had chosen my name straight after Sera's pregnancy test – Dolly and Daryus seemed to go together.

'Daryus!' said Dolly, wrinkling her nose. 'Doesn't seem right

for *this* baby. I'm going to call him – I'm going to call him Brit!
That's short for brittle!'

'That's very cruel,' said Sam. 'You don't call a mongol kid
Mong.'

'Being a mongol is different from having brittle bones. I
think Dolly's got a good idea. His disease is nothing to feel
embarrassed about and Brit with one 't' will sound rather
English, won't it?' In those days no one had heard of Britt
Ekland.

'But we will put Daryus on the certificate, won't we?'

'Oh, yes!' said Dolly enthusiastically. 'And then we can make
him cry just by calling him his name!'

'God, he's going to have enough to cry about without that,
Dolly,' sighed Sam. 'Do you know, he's never going to walk.
He's going to grow up toothless, and if he's lucky he'll only
fracture his bones a dozen times before he's five. Five. Just five.
Huh!' He laughed bitterly. 'You know what the doctor said?
He feels pain about four times as much as normal people do.'

'Sam, Brit is a normal person. He's just got a problem. Can't
you see it that way?'

'Normal? You call everything I told you normal?'

'Maybe,' said Dolly, always the ray of sunshine, 'maybe Brit
will die before he suffers all this!'

'Dolly,' said Sera, running her finger through the Shirley
Temple curls, 'do you want your little brother to die?'

'Of course not!' cried Dolly. 'I love him!' And to prove it
she dropped kisses all over my face faster than her lips could
pucker.

'If you do that,' said Sera, 'the child will die. You are
smothering him.'

'Like Othello smothered Desdemona!' cried Dolly, sending
Sera and Sam flying with delight.

'We were right to buy her that frightfully expensive book,
weren't we, darling?' said Sam.

'You mean that illustrated Shakespeare? I thought she'd never
read it but she obviously did!'

'Thank God for you!' said Sam, kissing Dolly on her forehead.

'Sam,' said Sera, staring with her long-lashed eyes into his.

Sam gave her a crooked smile. Then he bent over the cradle and, kissing his fractured hopes, he whispered, 'Thank God for you too.'

I saw to it that the doctor was proved right. I broke my legs eleven times before I was five years old. Mysteriously, the rest of me remained virtually uncracked.

I remember waiting in Sera's lap and her soft crooning while the doctors got ready to set a fractured thigh bone. I remember the dull weight of the plaster cast as if I had a wooden leg like Long John Silver. And I remember the smell of chloroform.

In spite of all the discouragement, my teeth appeared, translucent as lightly-frosted glass, and stayed on. They didn't decay, they crumbled. I'd be having a jolly time at a party when the hostess would offer me a beautifully wrapped chocolate. 'We just got these from Geneva, pure chocolate, nothing else!'

She would forget to tell me she'd frozen them solid before serving. My teeth would battle with the chocolate. The chocolate would win. 'Excuse me,' I'd say, spitting a chip of tooth into my fist and dropping it into the plate on my lap.

We never really learn our lessons, do we? Because deep inside we don't think we've done anything to deserve them. That's what Sam felt. It wasn't wrong of him to trust Wagh Baba, it was heartless of Wagh Baba to go around feeling apple- and mango- and lemon-shaped boobs. Actually, Wagh Baba was just one of Sam's flings with magic. A couple of years earlier someone in his office advised him to feed me powdered pearls. A lot of people take them as medicine, and in some shops you see bottles of the gleaming white powder sitting below the glass counter, humble as aspirin. I was awfully proud to be the only kid in the building who drank pulverised pearls stirred into his milk. Unfortunately, the month I started guzzling them I broke two ribs.

It happened at this sleazy restaurant called the Madras Café which served South Indian yummies; rice-cakes and paper-thin pancakes rolled up like giant calendars. Parsees have this nauseating habit of slumming when they want to eat *Indian* food, which means non-Parsee food, since we are reluctant

Indians. My family happily spent four hundred rupees at the Taj Mahal Hotel on an English meal, bland as an ulcer diet, but when it came to trying out some tongue-scorching, tasty food they made a bee-line for the cheapest joint they could sniff out.

'It's very simple,' said Sera once. 'The Indians are a poor people so the best place for genuine Indian cuisine has got to be cheap.'

'And dirty food is always tastier,' said Sam. 'I mean, nothing can match the flavour of a sweaty palm.'

'Don't!' said Sera impatiently. 'You're making my Brit sick. Daddy's only joking, sweetie. You eat what I order for you and you'll be fine.'

So there we were at the Madras Café sitting under the fluorescent lights next to cabbies and peons from the nearby offices. A waiter holding four stainless steel glasses in one hand (a finger in each did the trick) plonked them on the greyish laminated table. 'On the house!' he said, flashing a Colgate smile.

'Look at his teeth!' hissed Sera. 'Thanks to all the tamarind they eat. And the amount we waste on Colgate.'

Dolly had taken a sip from one glass. She made a circle with her forefinger and thumb. 'Have it!' she mouthed across the table.

I was short, but my arms were long. I snaked one out and snatched a glass. Three gulps and three hiccups later I found I'd swallowed some of the legendary pepper water.

'Why did you do that, Brit?' groaned Sera. I wouldn't have given away Dolly if I could have talked but it was easier because I couldn't. The hiccups were leaping out one every five seconds. Soon my chest began aching; I lay back in Sera's arms. Father ordered a glass of water. We tried all the 'cures': taking seven sips without drawing a breath, sipping with my eyes shut, drinking from the opposite side of the glass. Nothing worked.

'Let's go home,' said Sera.

'Let's!' said Dolly. 'Maybe he'll feel better if he lies down.' The lunch was forgotten.

Two hours later I was clutching my chest and sobbing with

each hiccup. At midnight the hiccups stopped; I was paralysed with pain. The next day an X-ray told us about the ribs.

'There goes the pearl powder,' said Sera. 'Straight into the dustbin.'

'Maybe,' said Father, 'maybe the man cheated us and they weren't real pearls.'

But the almond oil he rubbed into my legs every night for a full year and a half was a hundred per cent genuine, fragrant and thick. It made my skin the envy of my female neighbours. 'Brit, let us feel your legs!' they pleaded, the teenagers who lived upstairs. 'Ooh! Like Bangalore silk. Look! He's winking at us. Give me your eyelashes, Brit? You seven-year-old Casanova!'

Have you ever tasted the bone-marrow of a goat? It made me sick, the black and white jelly I ate by the plate. Nobody believed me when I told them that bone-marrow had nothing to do with brittle bones; it produced blood cells. I read that in the *Reader's Digest* when I was ten. I went on strike. I refused to swallow another mouthful of the spit-worthy stuff. Then father saw a winking light bulb in a bubble over his head. He began rubbing the marrow into my bones. 'They'll absorb it better that way,' he said.

The Breathing Generator came into my life when I was twelve. She was a dumpy little woman, placid as a holy cow. Her name was Rutty Regina. 'Sera, dear,' she said on her first visit, 'I have the power to conduct electric currents from my body to my patients. It is a rare gift for which I have been called the Breathing Generator by none other than – ' She named some Parsee top brass in the army. 'I have worked wonders with wounded soldiers.'

Sera declared her a fake that very day. Oh, how she cursed old Madame Defarge for getting her over! Defarge was our nosy neighbour, swollen with sound advice: she and Sera were the best of friends, the worst of enemies. 'I'll break that stupid woman's knitting needles,' Sera threatened through her teeth, knowing that would destroy poor Defarge whose whole life was held in the wool between her needles. 'As for that Generator! She has the least electric presence I've seen in my life.'

'I think,' murmured Dolly, 'she is a dead current.'

'Will you give her a chance?' said Sam. 'She says she can make Brit grow; isn't that something?'

'That's nothing!' said Sera. 'Of course he'll grow; he's at the growing age. The doctors say he'll grow till he's four feet tall.'

'Four feet short,' said Sam mournfully.

'It's the heights you reach that count,' said Sera, tossing her bob, 'not the height you are.'

'Absolutely Churchillian, Mother dear!' said Dolly, tapping her thumbnails in a donkey clap.

The Breathing Generator came at three in the afternoon. 'Excuse me,' said Sera. 'But Brit and I sleep from two to four. Couldn't you make it in the evening?'

'So sorry, I can't. It's the afternoon heat, you see; makes me absolutely pulsate with charges that I have to conduct into someone. Or my whole body tingles.' She giggled shyly, covering her mouth.

'She ought to be paying *us*,' said Sera to Sam when he came home from the bank that evening. 'Brit is relieving her of her tingles and on top of that we pay her ten rupees for every session!'

'Be patient, darling. Let's try her out for a couple of years.'

Sera's eyes opened wide. 'Two years without my siesta,' she whispered.

For two months the Breathing Generator came and stripped me naked. She rubbed her hands until they were hot with the friction and laid them on my spine, my feet, my neck, my thighs.

'You should tell her she's left something out,' said Dolly, shrieking.

'Oh, no! That wouldn't do,' I laughed, heady with the secret of my twelve-year-old hard-ons.

'You mean that cow could actually turn you on!'

'I don't know,' I said dubiously. 'I dare not find out.'

'Come on,' spurred Dolly. 'Give it a try, Brit!'

But Sera, with her weird sense of timing, never gave me a chance. The next afternoon the Breathing Generator came she rubbed and rubbed her palms, shaking her head with frustration. 'It's the sweat,' she grumbled. 'Blocks the electricity. This May weather!

'Why is the fan not working?' she continued angrily, looking at the stationary blades. She jumped up and tried all the switches. Nothing worked. 'Oh, no! Load shedding, I suppose.' She saw Dolly in the passage outside our room. 'Load shedding again – did you notice?' she called.

'I know! Such a pain!' said Dolly, keeping her mouth taut so I knew she was trying not to laugh. 'Hey! Aunty! Do you think you could generate some power – just enough for our flat?'

I bit my thumb. Dolly saw me and her mouth collapsed as she cackled and roared and shook like a laughing Buddha. That set me off in sweet revenge against Wagh Baba and almond oil and goat's marrow and all that might yet be in store.

The Breathing Generator turned to Sera who had appeared in the doorway. 'You have the rudest children I have ever had the bad luck to meet,' she said, her voice thin and sharp like a sliver of ice. 'I am going, never to return!' She pushed past Sera and stamped down the passage, her sari swooshing behind her.

'What a pity!' said Sera, smiling sweetly. The Breathing Generator whirled around in hope. 'This is the first time I've actually seen the sparks flying from you.'

That really extinguished her. Mouth agape, she walked backwards all the way to the door, shutting it in front of her silently like a thief.

'Dolly, darling,' said Sera, 'will you go and turn the main switch on?'

4

I WAS SCARED of the way handicapped people looked. You know, the hesitant gait and robot-stiff movements of the blind, the lolling heads and strangulated speech of the spastics. Whenever I saw them I wondered if I must seem as ugly and pathetic. I'd shudder and turn my mind away.

Not from Tina though. Tina was my cousin, Jeroo's daughter. And she was as deaf as a hearing person with ear-plugs on. But she was more fun than a dozen birthday parties. Tina and Jeroo, who was a widow, used to spend weekends with us. Of course, I could talk sign language with my fingers as fluently as Tina could, which was very useful. Tina and I never had to wait to post mortem a party till it was over. Bobbing her black-fringed head she'd draw my eyes across a crowded drawing-room, then say with quick little movements of her hands, 'Stay far from Ronnie. He's stinking!' or, 'The cutlets taste like number two!'

In the middle of the laughter and shouting she would smile sweetly, her eyes round and black like little records and, pointing a little finger at the toothy lady sitting next to her in a froth of frills, she'd say, 'A mouse in fancy dress, right?'

Someone was always watching us in fascination and they'd beg, 'Tell us! Tell us! What did she say just now?'

How could I tell them we were discussing butts? I had to invent something sufficiently deafy on the spot. 'Tina's so delighted to be here. She just wants to laugh with happiness.' And they'd nod understandingly, faces glowing with sympathy while I hoped they'd confuse my blush with their glow.

Dolly had a tough time, taking Tina and me around. She had to push my chair and keep an eye on Tina so that she wouldn't get run over by an exasperated motorist tired of honking. But we went everywhere – to the movies where Dolly and I took turns signing the dialogue to Tina, to the zoo where Tina drove the monkeys crazy imitating their doings like a mirror. She didn't hear things, so she watched them about ten times more intently than we did.

In Bombay, wherever you go, before you can say Urchin you are surrounded by about fifty-five grey kids – their clothes, their hair, even the look in their eyes is grey. Everything attracts them – a Toyota, a Dalmatian, perfumed Sindhis, sexy in their silken saris, and kids like Tina and me. I couldn't stand them because I always thought I'd catch mumps or measles or maybe (sweat of sweats) TB from them. So Tina and I had a trick. Now, Tina could speak pretty well. Her voice was guttural as a German general's, but once you got used to that you could understand her perfectly. Anyway, she could emit strange growls and shrieks, sounds that you and I could never produce. So, when the urchins came closer and closer, I'd mouth (with Tina we always mouthed, it was no use troubling our larynxes), 'Now!' And out of Tina's throat would leap a roar that would put a samurai to shame, and the urchins to flight, their mouths sucking on their hearts.

It was a pity Tina was stopped from going out with anyone but us. Her mother was terrified she'd end up in a molester's arms. Jeroo was gentle, soft-spoken, beautiful and frigid. With her brown hair styled in shining waves around her regal fore-head, green eyes and baby-pink lips she looked heart-racing even in her fifties. She didn't have a Parsee nose and she was fair like a white rose, with the slightest hint of a blush. Men horrified her. 'What do men want?' she once asked.

'Love,' I said.

'Food, of course!' snorted Dolly.

'A firm hand,' said Sera, smiling grimly.

'Money!' spat Defarge, bitterly twisting her long nose between finger and thumb.

'Wrong!' said Jeroo. 'Wrong as a moron's answer sheet. It's sex, sex, and more sex!'

'Now, do be sensible,' Sera whispered fiercely, at bridge. Jeroo and I against Sera and Defarge was our Thursday table.

'So sorry!' said Jeroo. 'I forgot about your son. You understand, when I say men, I mean – men. Not someone like you, Brit.' I wasn't male. Not to them. The magic mirrors of their minds had invented a formula: osteo = sexlessness.

She gave a little shiver and pulled down the sleeves of her blouse at the thought of all those wolves waiting to make a meal of her. 'The other day,' she went on, 'I went to visit Polly, and her husband came and sat next to me in nothing but shorts. My! I could have died; all that hair and muscle like some animal. I could feel the hunger in his – '

'Serves you right for going to visit these English *mudums*,' said Defarge enviously.

'What English *mudums*? Polly's my cousin Piroja, a Parsee born and bred!'

The horror began one morning, when Jeroo was eighteen. She woke to find her elder brother sleeping with his arm on her stomach. He was fully clothed in a striped pyjama suit. But in those sad, glad days Parsee girls didn't discover the facts of life till they got married. (One day, I found *What Every Young Lady Should Know*, a wedding present to Sera from Jeroo. It told you everything you wanted to know about Tolerance, Humour, and Gentle Affection.) When Jeroo saw that hairy arm, heavy on her stomach, she screamed so loud her brother has been slightly deaf in one ear ever since. 'I'm pregnant!' she howled. 'By my own brother! What will I do? Oh, God! I'll jump off the Rajabai Tower!' That was the University clock tower, in those days the tallest building in Bombay and the most tempting place on earth for every student who flunked his exams.

'Don't be silly,' her brother laughed in a nasty superior sort of way. 'Why would I want to make you pregnant?'

'Because you are – you are not normal!' sobbed Jeroo.

As it happened, Jeroo's parents were in Simla, it being May, so Jeroo trudged, heavy with the fruits of her imaginary incest, to Sera's place. Sera, being slightly more sensible, though no more enlightened, summoned the nurse who lived next door.

'So what's up?' said the nurse, looking thoroughly un-nursish in her curlers.

'I'm in trouble,' mewed Jeroo piteously.

35

'Who's the young man?' demanded the nurse, her long snout getting the better of her ethics.

'My own flesh and blood brother!' wailed Jeroo, letting her head fall to her knees.

'Why!' said the nurse. 'Then I must call the police. This is a criminal offence!'

With a leap, Jeroo made for the windows which were shuttered against the heat. 'Wait a moment!' said Sera. 'Tell me, Sister, can an arm make you pregnant?'

'What?'

'Her brother's arm. Could it have made her – '

'Don't say that word!' howled Jeroo. 'I'm not guilty, I swear I'm not. I was sleeping through it all.'

'Sleeping?' said the nurse. 'What kind of joke is this? How can you be sleeping while you are being pierced?'

'Eeeeaaagh!' screamed Sera and Jeroo like twin ghosts.

The nurse realised she'd gone too far. 'You are definitely not pregnant,' she said. 'That's all I can say. Now I must hurry or my curls will crinkle.' As she left, they saw her holding her mouth tight, her cheeks blown out as if she were trying to swallow an outsized bite of laughter.

When Jeroo had her daughter she decided to protect her ignorance as long as she could. Tina wasn't allowed to see movies rated 'Adult' till she was an adult. She was the only person in Bombay, apart from me (and that was because of my size), to have waited that long. Jeroo tried to accompany Tina to every movie so she could clap a hand on her eyes each time someone kissed. Indian movies were the safest. The censors didn't allow smooching at all. Furthermore, Tina wasn't allowed to read perverted writers, which meant Oscar Wilde, Thomas Hardy and E. M. Forster but excluded Harold Robbins, since Jeroo hadn't heard of him.

She didn't know that Tina could have beat Masters and Johnson at a sex quiz. Thanks to Dolly and me. We invented the most odious signs to explain things to her. After that, we couldn't do the most simple things like lick an ice-cream cone without collapsing into shrieks at the thought of what it meant in sign language.

'I know it's terribly sinful,' said Jeroo, putting down her cards and slapping her cheeks in perfunctory penance, 'but it was such a relief when Jimmy died. We were only together for two years and of that I was free for the nine months I was carrying Tina and for the forty days after that, till my purification bath.'

'Do you mean,' asked Defarge, always lusting for sex-talk, 'your husband was voracious?'

'Disgustingly demanding,' said Jeroo, putting two fingers to her cheek in distressed memory. 'Sometimes, he even wanted it again.'

Defarge hid her raddled face in her sari in sham embarrassment; actually, she was afraid we'd see her excited flush.

'Twenty-two times I have endured it,' said Jeroo.

'Enjoyed it, you mean,' said Dolly from the corner where she was reading *Stardust*.

'Huh! You'll know when your time comes,' said Jeroo bitterly.

'I can hardly wait!' said Dolly, her voice shimmering in the evening sunshine.

'It's you behind that newspaper, isn't it?' asked Sam one Sunday morning. I was eclipsed by the outsize *Sunday Special* I was reading. 'How d'you do it, Brit?'

I emerged: his giggling, twelve year old. 'How do I do what?'

'Live.' He turned his head to see if Sera was around. 'You seem to be quite happy. Are you?'

'Of course I'm happy!' I said indignantly. I mean, if you weren't happy, it was like flunking your exams.

'Or is it just your brave act? Smiling face, weeping heart. Y'know, like that movie we saw last week about the circus clown, how he was always putting on his comic act while he was really having a rotten time.'

'That was a movie. A *Hindi* movie.'

'So? Oh, you mustn't be snobbish, Brit. That only means you aren't big enough yourself. Oh, God! I'm sorry! I didn't mean BIG enough. I'm really sorry.'

He lifted me gingerly on to his lap. I was always sitting on people's laps: at the movies when a tall bald man or a fat, fuzzy-haired lady took the seat in front of mine (finally, I started buying the seat in front and keeping it empty), in motor-cars

37

so that I could see the passing view, at parties where there was a shortage of chairs.

'Happy?' said Sam, looking like a suspicious lover. 'After everything you've been through? After knowing what life's going to be like?'

I was squirming like a puppy in his arms. No one likes being asked things like that. Stalling, I asked, 'What do you see in your crystal ball?'

'Well,' he said, and his eyes were sad as death, 'fractures for a few more years. Then I suppose you'll study but you won't get a job. You know, it's very tough getting a job these days. I see the young boys who come to the bank with their applications. Some of them have their MAs and they're healthy and good-looking; they're trying for a job that'll pay them eight hundred rupees a month. And they don't even get that. Then you're going to need girls; you're going to get really frusty when you can't have them.'

'But I have girls; all my best friends are girls. There's Tina, and there's Ruby in the flat below, and Indu and Usha who want my eyelashes.'

'I don't mean having friends who are girls. I mean – '

'I know, I know,' I said. The last thing I wanted was sex education. It would have been like sitting through the fourth standard, when I really belonged in the eighth.

'Are you happy in spite of everything? Only, the pain you've been through should've been enough to put you off life for ever. This doesn't sound like discouragement, does it? Sera and I love having you around, whatever you are. I just hope you aren't running away – '

'I can't run, remember?'

'OK, smarty-pants. I don't want you to escape from what you are. It's no use pretending, if you *are* pretending, that everything's all right. Because it isn't.'

Did he have to remind me? I know he meant it kindly, but did he really believe I thought everything was all right? When everything meant something like this: playing bridge, slamming my way to victory, gathering the cards, bending to pick up one that had fallen on the floor, staying bent because I'd broken a thigh bone and couldn't move, not because of the

38

pain but because of the terror, worse than facing a murderer with a blood-stained knife.

Bone-deep fear stays. Of the pain. As if that murderer had dipped his knife into my blood again without bothering to finish me off. And I would drag myself through that trench of pain saying, 'Four times worse than anyone else's. Maybe this time it will kill me. Maybe.' Then I'd cry for thinking that way. Because it was so futile.

The nights were the worst. Sleeplessness drove my thoughts recklessly round the craziest bends. And the flat was lifeless around me. No one to divert me with whispers: Dolly and Sera and Sam sleeping like an insomniac's envy, as exhausted as their broken child. Then someone would wake to ask if I wanted a sip of water and I'd say yes even if I didn't want any, because doing something made things seem better. I'd ask inane questions: 'What is the time? When will the milkman come?' I'd take the weary answers, the grieving kiss, and crawl back to the torture-house alone.

In the morning the pain slinked away, and things got worse. I'd begin thinking of the tough time ahead, starting everything from sitting in my wheelchair to taking a bath as if I'd never done them before. The boredom of not going out for six weeks. After that, waiting for the next time.

A week later, I'd laugh, really roar to think how crazy I'd been. Pain loses focus so quickly. The anguish I had squeezed into my plaster-hard leg – what was the fuss about? It made me sort of brave: knowing I could get over something so terrible and still smile.

But just now I stuck out my jaw to throw Churchill into Sam's mind and I said, 'Please don't worry, Father. I'll get over it all. You'll see!'

'You deserve a medal!' said Sam and I knew the histrionics had worked.

But they had worked too well. Once we were at the People's Supermarket when Sam spotted a boy on crutches, about as old as I was. He had a disgustingly martyred expression on his face. So Sam walked up to him with me in his arms – wheelchairs were too bulky for crowded stores – and said, 'Lad, put a smile in those eyes. Look at my son! He's going to run in the

Olympics one day.' Of course, that drove the kid horrifyingly close to tears, while I tried to count the number of different colours in which you could get toothbrushes.

'Get off Daddy's lap,' said Sera. 'Come on! Stop basking in his smile.'

'Do you mind?' said Sam. 'Haven't you heard of son-worship?'

Sera smiled grimly. 'Madame Manekshaw will be here any moment,' she said.

A swirl of French perfume announced the arrival of Madame Manekshaw dressed in the latest styles painstakingly imitated from *Vogue* by her impoverished tailor. She was so slim her ivory bracelet slipped right up to her elbow when she lifted her arm, and she was so rich she never dreamt of charging us for teaching me French and maths and English and whatever else Sera and Sam couldn't manage.

When she lit her Gauloise with her Cartier lighter, you might have thought she'd come straight out of a mansion on Avenue Foch, but Meheroo Manekshaw was as Parsee as they come. It was just that she'd married this millionaire who was one of those eccentrics with which our community abounds like the Arabian Sea with ships. Dinshaw Manekshaw lived for his stamps which occupied the top floor of his two-storeyed villa on Warden Road. The stamp collection was worth a million rupees which represented a tenth part of his wealth.

The other nine parts were at Meheroo's disposal. Now, Meheroo had been rather badly off before she married, living in the Grant Road with her widowed mother in one of those dying buildings where you had to lock your door and walk fifty yards down the common passage to reach the loo. So when Dinshaw proposed to her she said yes before he could finish his question, although he was a rather shabby fifty-one and she was seventeen. After that a lot of envious people called her 'Seventeen Threes Are' – but Meheroo didn't give a damn. She settled down to capturing a Bachelor's degree in French, grabbing a Master's in English, then switching to commerce and taking another degree. Degrees became the substitute for all the toys she never had as a kid.

Charity came very hard to Meheroo. She just couldn't bear to give away money. She was so terrified she'd have to go back to the flat with the unattached loo one day. So she spent her time doing good works. Her face bore an astonishing resemblance to Indira Gandhi's (who wasn't a Parsee although she was the widow of one) with its hooked nose, pale skin and hooded eyes. Whenever she went to the villages to distribute grain or exercise books on behalf of one of the many societies of which she was chairperson, she would be surrounded by a hysterical mob of country folk screaming, 'Mother Indira!' in any one of India's seventeen official languages. Of course, she took great care to sport the long-sleeved cotton blouses, and white saris with colourful borders draped over her head that the Prime Minister wore on her village expeditions. She took even greater care to streak her hair white in the same place as Mrs G. even though she was a quarter-century younger.

All this made her a formidable figure when she first came to teach me, a seven-year-old kid. 'Do you mean,' she demanded of Sera, 'that this child has not had a proper teacher all these years? When Jeroo told me about him I knew I had to rush here, like a firefighter, before it was too late!'

'But,' said Sera, looking outraged, 'my husband and I have taught him conscientiously, every day. You can test him if you want. I bet you anything in this house he knows more than most children his age; he certainly reads more.'

'I won't take that bet,' said Madame Manekshaw. 'Firstly, because there's nothing in this house that I covet, and secondly, I don't care how much your son knows. Parents are not meant to be teachers. Especially when they're Parsee parents and the pupil is their only son.'

'OK!' said Sera. 'Let's see if you can get him into Campion School. If my son is to be attached to a school – he's not going to attend, that's for sure – I don't want friendly slaps and pushes and cracks and fractures. If he is to have a school to call his own, it shall be Campion and none other!'

'Such poor taste, Mrs Kotwal,' sniffed Madame Manekshaw. 'That Catholic school with its shuffling priests and cruel discipline. And no girls, just boys – most unhealthy for Brit's budding sexuality.'

41

I held my breath, hoping they'd forget I was there so that I could find out more about my budding sexuality. But Sera crushed such talk like those cockroaches in the kitchen. 'Let's not discuss such rubbish. My husband went to a boys' school and he's perfectly normal. As for Catholic priests, may I remind you that the priests at Campion are all foreigners, Spanish or Irish – '

'So?' said Madame Manekshaw, raising one high-curved eyebrow.

'So? Did you say so? They are foreigners so they're good. That's what!'

'Gosh!' laughed Madame Manekshaw pityingly. 'Parsees and their craze for foreigners.'

'Did you say Parsees? What are you? An Englishwoman from London town?' shouted Sera.

'OK, OK, don't lose your composure; I'll get him into Campion.'

'Without paying a penny in donations?'

'Oh! You mean you want to get entrance on merit?'

'What did you think? That I'd pay five thousand rupees like all those Sindhis and Gujaratis do?'

'Shame on you, Mrs Kotwal! If this is the kind of communal attitude you've been teaching your son, I fear for his mind.'

'What's communal about that? Is it or is it not true that Sindhis and Gujaratis get their children into school by giving fat donations?'

'So would the Parsees, if only they could afford it. But they can't because they don't have the guts to make money; all they want is a nine to five job and their trifling three thousand a month.'

5

So THERE I was, small and seven, waiting outside the Principal's office at Campion, watching the black door so sternly shut, willing with a child's intensity that he should be a kind, gentle priest, maybe a little like St Francis of Assisi.

The door opened and a finger like a piece of chalk beckoned through a crack. Sam hoisted me into his arms, I hoisted my *Tales from Toyland*. 'It's very important,' Madame Manekshaw had told us, 'that the Principal should get to know that Brit is mad about reading, which is why he must go armed with a book, to keep away the boredom of waiting for the Reverend Father.'

'Ho!' said Father Ferra, who happened to be a twin of Friar Tuck. 'Huat is thees?'

'He's my son,' said Sam. 'I'm Sam Kotwal. This is Brit, uh, I'm sorry, his name is Daryus. He . . . he . . . is . . . a cripple.' Sam's voice vanished in a whisper. I knew he'd remembered Madame Manekshaw's warning: 'Cripple, cripple. That's our key. These Catholic priests will do anything if you are crippled.'

'Sit heem on my laap,' said Father Ferra, patting his plump thighs. 'So light!' he exclaimed as Sam plonked me down. 'I haaf read your aaaplication form, Daryus. You want to study in our school?'

'Oh, no!' I said, horrified at the thought of leaving home. 'I just want to come here and pass exams, so that people will believe I really study at home.'

'Ho! Ho! Ho!' he laughed, and I felt his stomach against my back, soft as boiled custard. 'Do you studee or do you read *Tales from Toyland*? Huh? Answer me.'

'I only brought this along so you'd know I love reading and

43

you'd think I was clever. I really do love reading, especially Enid Blyton.'

'A child speaks weeth the tong of angels,' said Father Ferra, joining his hands and looking at Sam who was desperately groping for a handkerchief to wipe the sweat-beads off his face.

'You like Blyton? Fatee and Bets and Peep and Daisy and the doeg Booster?'

'You mean Buster,' I said.

'That ees huat I said, Booster.'

'Brit, the Reverend Father must be tired,' said Sam. 'Let me leeft – lift you off his knee.'

'I like your son, Mr Kotwal. If he passes the tests I shall take heem like thees!' Father Ferra punched the air above his head. 'And huan more theeng. I shall charge no fees.'

'Oh! But you must!' said Sam, looking horrified. 'We can afford them very well.'

'Neverrr!'

'Please, please!'

'No ees no!'

'But this sort of thing is not done!'

'Een your publeck schools eet is not. We are Catholic. We are deeferent. We are betterrr!' Sam was stunned into silence by so immodest an assertion.

A week later, I went for the entrance exams. That morning I woke to the sound of my heart beating fast and furious with the erratic rhythm of a *tabla*. My mouth felt parched as the *papads* Sera put out to dry in the sun. I didn't speak a word while I was bathed and dressed. Actually, I took a bath by myself every day but whenever we had to go somewhere important Sam washed me. It was safer. As for dressing, no one would believe it, but till I was fourteen I came out of my bath naked and lay down on a bath mat, spread over my bed. Then Sera or Dolly would sprinkle me with talc all over, cooing, 'Now lift your arms. Turn on your stomach.' Then they'd tuck me into my clothes and brush my hair with a baby-blue baby's hairbrush. I was perfectly capable of doing all this myself. But you know how it is, when you can't do some things people feel you can't do anything.

At breakfast I squeezed a couple of slices of toast through a tiny slit in my mouth. 'Oh, cheer up!' said Sera. 'You're looking like a goat at the butcher's.'

'There! I can feel his horns,' said Dolly, ruffling my hair which had to be neatly parted all over again.

In the taxi, Sera said to Sam, 'Have you noticed he hasn't said a word since he woke? What if he doesn't answer the questions they ask him?'

'Never mind,' said Sam, 'it's a written test. Do you think something might be hurting him? You now how he keeps his pain like some precious secret.' He shook his head. 'Like that time I lifted him off the piano when he was banging his hands off and he struggled violently. And then he went silent for hours until we found he'd cracked a rib.'

'Don't talk like that! He'll get upset; then he won't do well.'

'But why doesn't he tell us when something's wrong? We don't scold him when he breaks something.'

'Maybe he doesn't want to give us trouble. That's the only sane explanation.'

'Life is rarely sane,' said Sam.

I smiled secretly. It was simple. I didn't speak about pain as long as I could take it; that way I didn't have to admit something broken inside me. When my secret was out a cyclone hit my life raining tears, grief, guilt, defeat.

The taxi stopped and I clenched my teeth till I thought they'd break against each other when I looked up at the red and white, blood-on-snow school building. About sixty boys stood around us staring, their mouths open. I saw them all but not for a moment could I look at any one. I'd never felt worse about my body.

'Velcome!' said Father Ferra, and I let out my breath and unhunched my shoulders. 'For you, Daryus, there ees a special room for thee tests. Not veedh thee rowdy leetle stoodents of mine – but alone! Small table, small chair, see! Your tongue ees in your stomach? Haf you swallowed eet?'

I shook my head and pretended to smile. I was aware of the other boys clustered around me, hands on their firm little hips, ties swinging across their strong, straight chests.

'Weel you walk eentoo my parlour,' said Father Ferra, smiling and pointing to the brass plate on a door. It was marked 'Parlour'. The narrow room had two rows of sofas facing each other, green with dust-filled ribs. At the end of the room, below the window, were a doll's chair and table.

'Parents out!' said Father Ferra, clapping his hands. I slid from my wheelchair into the little pink chair. Sera and Sam kissed me, one on the left cheek, the other on the right.

I knew I was going to cry; it felt worse than a fracture. 'Thees,' said Father Ferra, 'ees Mees Peento. She weel take your test. Good luck!' Miss Pinto was black as the hair she wore in curls round her head. She was thin in a bony sort of way, her eyes were sunken like her cheeks and her teeth protruded, large and yellow. She was dressed in an A-line frock of blood-red cotton. 'Write!' she squeaked. 'In figures. Five crows – '

I opened my mouth to say Pardon? but what came out was quite different. I can't forget the horror on Miss Pinto's skull of a face, the relief that left me crazily happy, the grey vomit held in her red lap like a grotesque bowl of soup.

'Help!' squeaked Miss Pinto. 'Oh, Jesus Christ, help me!' But no one appeared. She began to cry as the vomit started crawling down her legs in thick streams.

The door wooshed open. "I thought I heard something,' said Sera. 'Oh, God! What have you done, Brit? Don't move till I call someone.'

I sat there, smiling, thinking irrelevantly: One, two, three, four, five, six, seven, All good children go to heaven. That's what I felt. As if the gates of Paradise had swung open and I'd wheeled myself in.

Father Ferra came in and said, 'Oh! Huat a naughty boy you are, Daryus. Mees Peento, pleez stand up.' With a *plop* the vomit fell to the floor. A gaunt *hamal* hastily smothered it with sawdust. Sera cleaned me up. 'Daryus,' said Father Ferra kindly, 'you haf to geev your test steel. Dhees time your teacher is Mrs De Souza.' Who was plump and dark like a Christmas cake. She smiled a big smile and said, 'Naughty boy! Put on your thinking cap!' Which made me giggle so much, I sort of floated through the test. When it was over, Mrs De Souza said to Father Ferra, her face solemn as a priest's, 'He's a s-m-a-r-t one.'

'Am I?' I asked, tumbling with joy. Mrs De Souza ruffled my hair; I kissed her hand. She made me feel so good. Just like I felt at home.

To celebrate her success, Madame Manekshaw took me to the elegant Sea Lounge at the Taj Mahal Hotel for a snack. 'Look!' she said. 'You feel as if you're sailing in the Arabian Sea, don't you? Now, if it were a clear day you'd see the shores of mainland India.'

'But that's geography!' I said sharply. 'You aren't supposed to teach me that. It's Father's job.'

'Brit! You're getting precocious and there's nothing as disgusting as a precocious child. You know what precocious means?' I shook my head angrily. 'It's a boy who's so busy showing off his brains he ends up making a fool of himself.'

'I like being s-m-a-r-t,' I said. 'It makes me happy.'

'I know,' said Madame Manekshaw, resting her beautiful tapered fingers on my hand. 'And it's lovely that you have a good mind. But you mustn't lean on it to feel good about yourself; it's as silly as those vain girls who say I'm so beautiful, I'm superior to everyone else.'

'I'll never be able to say *that*,' I said, looking soulfully at the sea.

'Of course not,' said Madame Manekshaw simply, leaving me a bit stunned. 'But you should be glad you know that right from the start. It's so much worse for people who are beautiful and then something happens, an illness or an accident, and they're suddenly ugly.'

'So what? It's not so bad being ugly.'

'It is for them. Because they've learnt to depend on their looks, to get their own way, to get admiration, even to feel happy!'

I nodded and stayed silent.

'Do you like this place, Brit?' she asked, looking around the Sea Lounge which had soft green armchairs and sofas arranged in groups around coffee tables like so many little sitting-rooms.

'Very much,' I said grinning. 'Thank you.'

'What d'you like about it? The triple sundae you're spading through?'

'Oh, no!' I said. 'It's the people. They don't stare like the people at the movies and at Campion do.'

'Perhaps they're selfish,' said Madame Manekshaw. 'So engrossed in themselves, they don't want to spare a moment thinking of your problem.'

'Then I like selfish people. They make me feel comfortable. I think they've got better manners.'

'And harder hearts – '

'But,' I said quickly before I lost the thought, 'if you're rich it's not so hard not being able to walk, is it? I mean, you would have a servant to take you everywhere and do things you couldn't do. It wouldn't even be trouble having a son in a wheelchair.'

'Hmm,' said Madame. 'There may be something in that.'

'Of course there is!' I crowed. 'Rich people feel nothing when they see me. That's fab!'

When I went for my terminals for Campion a few months later, Father Ferra mournfully explained that I'd have to write my papers unsupervised. 'Mees Peento, she has told one and all of her unfortunate experience with thee child so no teacher ees prepared to sit weeth heem. Therefore, we weel leave thee parlour door open.'

'What about Mrs De Souza? She liked me,' I said confidently.

'Alas! Mrs De Souza ees weeth her Heavenly Father now.'

'She's dead?' I began feeling the way I had the last time I was sitting in this green, dusty parlour.

'Daryus,' said Father Ferra, laying a hand on my head. 'No one dies. They only go home.'

I nodded and shut my eyes. I could see Mrs De Souza saying, 'Naughty boy! Put on your thinking cap!' When I opened my eyes, the vomit was spread like a tablecloth with tattered edges over my tiny desk. Father Ferra crossed himself and hurried out of the room to send in the *hamal*.

After that, it became a kind of tradition for me to throw up on the first day of the exams. 'Just have some milk, pupsie, so that you don't make too much of a mess,' Sera would say. Sometimes I thought it would be shocking if I *didn't* throw up, like an actor forgetting his lines. Because there was the *hamal* waiting outside the parlour with his broom and dustpan, and Sera with my fresh shirt and towels and Tata's Eau de Cologne.

Which might make you think I was always lurking around the deep-end of my class, waiting for someone to do worse than me. But that wasn't true. I won prizes all the time for everything from moral science to general science. Once I even won a prize for nothing.

It was my first Annual Prize Day and Father Ferra was giving his speech when I heard my name and froze in my cotton shorts. 'Daryus,' sang Father Ferra, 'ees only eight but he ees so brave and hardworking that he haas stoot feefth een hees class weethout attending a seengle day of school. For heem, there ees an Especial Prize!'

Around me the applause burst and swelled like some orchestral climax while I grew smaller and smaller in my seat wishing I wasn't there, wishing Father Ferra hadn't talked about me, wishing I hadn't got this prize for having legs that didn't work.

6

'THAT'S JUST THE view from one window, Brit.'

'What d'you mean?'

'You can look at a scene from a thousand different windows and you'll see something new every time.'

'So what's that got to do with Father Ferra giving me that prize for nothing?'

We were in Madame Manekshaw's drawing-room on the second floor of her house at Warden Road. Like giant pages in a book, huge plate-glass windows were alternately open and shut on three sides of the room. The view was an aluminium sea and ebony rocks. Nothing else. But Madame Manekshaw was right: from every window you got a different view – the rocks took a new shape, the water changed shades like strips of metal in the sun.

'He was looking at your prize from a different window. He saw it as a shining reward for your being so strong. You felt he was giving it to you for being weak and handicapped.'

'Different windows,' I nodded. 'Let's look in; there's so much to see in your home.'

Madame Manekshaw laughed and threw her bracelet up to her elbow which it threatened to slip across.

'Look at that vase. It was made eight hundred years ago when the Sung Dynasty was ruling China.'

I gingerly touched the delicate porcelain gleaming in a breathless curve. 'What if I pushed it?' I teased.

'It would shatter into unrecognisable pieces.'

'Like me,' I said, laughing.

'Yes,' said Madame Manekshaw, hesitantly touching the silver streak painted into her hair. 'Precious things are brittle, aren't they?' She smiled a rueful smile. 'I'd like to squeeze you,' she said. 'But I'm terrified I'll break something.'

'You probably will,' I said quickly. I mean, Madame Manekshaw was great to be with but I wouldn't have felt quite at home in her fleshless lap. 'Do you think I'm brave?' I asked, more to change the topic than anything else.

'What a silly question. You've got to know yourself!'

'But I'm only eight – '

'So what? What do you feel inside you?'

'Not brave,' I said, looking up at her.

'That's brave! Being able to say you're not.'

I shrugged my thin shoulders. 'I don't think so. I'd be brave if I didn't cry when I broke my leg.'

Madame Manekshaw laughed with her manicured hand over her eyes. 'Oh, Brit! That's absurd. You'd be a real crackpot if you didn't cry when you broke a leg. Why, soldiers cry when they are injured.'

'The brave ones don't.'

'Oh! What a romantic you are.'

That night I told Dolly. 'Madame Manekshaw said I was romantic. What did she mean? I'm not crazy about her. How could she say I was getting romantic?'

'Maybe,' danced Dolly in a whirl of duck-yellow nightie, 'she can spot your hidden feelings – all your sexy desires.'

I pounced. 'What are sexy desires? Tell me, Dolly. Tell me now.'

'When you find out, Brit, you'll wish you never had.'

'How can you be so mean? I'm your only little brother. Please tell me. *Please.*'

'It's not something I can tell. When you know, ooh! Boy! You'll know.'

'I'll tell everyone about the *Playgirl* if you don't tell me.'

'Don't, Brit; jut your chin out like that. It's pushy enough as it is.'

'Shall I tell everyone? Shall I? Or I think just Father will do.'

'Then he'll know you've had a peep and you'll get a spanking.'

'No!' I squealed.

The last time I'd got a whacking was when I chucked a brand new bar of Camay soap (bought from the smuggler for the price of two movie tickets) into the toilet bowl and flushed it away just to see the splash and the foam foreign soap left behind. Sam had been really mad, his eyes frighteningly large and white with the black irises jumping about crazily. And then he spanked me and spanked me and I was cheeky and said, 'Is that all? I'm not scared, you know.' I really wasn't because a spanking was to a fracture what a firework is to the A-Bomb. Besides, I wanted to laugh, because every time Sam brought his hand down he hesitated, looking for a target that wouldn't crack. Finally my skin began to sizzle so I shut up and Sam stopped. Luckily it was all in my bathroom and there wasn't much noise.

But when I came out and Sera began sprinkling talc on me she screamed. 'What's wrong, darling? Did you fall?'

'No,' I said, beginning to feel warm around my ears.

'Did you bump into something? Don't keep shaking your head like that. Talk, will you!'

'Father spanked me because I flushed away the Camay.'

'Don't try to fool me, Brit. Tell me what really happened.'

'He's right. I did give it to him.'

'You did *what*?'

'He was behaving like a brat, so I tried to make him stop.'

'By bashing him up so he looks as if some cannibal has broiled him alive? And what about his bones? God knows what must be lying cracked and broken in his little body waiting to be discovered by the X-rays.'

I was lying on my tummy, my head on my hands, and suddenly my hands were wet and I was crying and shaking all over.

'See what you've done!' said Sera.

'See what *you've* done!' said Sam. 'He was taking it like a man and you've made him feel sorry for himself.'

'That's not true. He's crying because he's hurting.'

'How come he wasn't hurting all this time?' said Sam with a smile that wasn't too sure of itself.

'Of course he was. He was just trying not to show it; you know how he doesn't like to admit it.'

'But we have to discipline him sometimes or he's going to be a horrible little thing when he grows up.'

'I won't be little when I grow up,' I sobbed into the bath mat.

'You know that's not what I meant,' said Sam wearily.

'You could've done it some other way,' said Sera. 'Stopped his supply of comics from that sleazy library down the road or something.'

'*That* would be cruel,' said Sam. 'It's one of the few things he can enjoy – '

'Stop pitying the child,' said Sera through her teeth.

'You're pitying him, I'm pitying him, he's pitying himself. So what?'

'So let's take him to the doctor, that's what.'

'Listen, Brit,' Sam whispered sadly, 'are you really hurting? Do you think you might have broken something?'

'I haven't,' I said, feeling guilty about all the wounds I'd bled.

'Then why on earth were you crying as if . . . as if you'd fallen from your chair?'

'I felt that way,' I said.

Dolly was watching me. 'You didn't like the idea of getting a spanking, did you?'

'Huh! That was bad!'

'Not half as bad as blackmail,' said Dolly, wagging her finger.

'That sounds exciting – what is it?'

'What you were doing to me. Threatening to tell Sam about the *Playgirl* if I didn't tell you about your sexy desires.'

'I don't have any other way of getting it out of you.'

'That's no excuse. A blackmailer is about as disgusting as a bottom-pincher.'

Poor Dolly, if only she knew that a bottom-pincher compared with a blackmailer like the tooth fairy to Lady Macbeth. I should know, because that was just the beginning of my career as a big-time blackmailer. For some funny reason, there were things in our flat that were kept out of my reach. I don't mean the family jewels or stuff like that – ordinary things like the earthenware pot in which we kept our boiled and filtered drinking water; it perched on a brass tripod about five feet tall. Or the set of encyclopaedias I loved dipping into; they stood red and gold on top of the polished brown book case. Or the Girard-Perregaux gold watch I'd inherited from old One-Oh-One that I loved to sport; it was tucked away in the top shelf-locker of Sam's cupboard. It wasn't as if they wanted to keep me thirsty for water or knowledge or time. It was just how things were kept. If I yelled and demanded, 'Why can't I keep my watch in *my* cupboard?' Sam would say, eyes crinkling with puzzlement, 'But, Brit, you just have to ask. We're always here to help.' Which made me mad. I didn't want someone always to be there.

And it wasn't as simple as just having to ask. Because if there was one thing about which Sera and Sam were firm and frank it was about not letting me treat them like bonded labour. 'He's not going to order us round, that's for sure,' Sera told anyone who met me and was worried I'd be spoiled rotten, staying at home like this.

'Certainly not,' said Sam, looking self-conscious instead of strict. 'Dependence is very bad for a growing boy's character. He mustn't have everything as soon as he demands it.'

And, of course, everyone feels lazy sometimes. Like the winter's morning a swoop of tiny brown birds flew into the scarlet almond tree that looked into our window and I knew, I just knew, they were migrants from Siberia I'd read about in the newspaper that very day.

'I want my binoculars,' I shouted. 'Quick! Quick!'

'I'm too tired to go rummaging for them in Sam's drawer,' said Sera.

'But I've got to have them right now. Those birds from Siberia are here!'

'They'll be here for the rest of the winter; you can watch them tomorrow or the day after.'

'I can't.' My voice broke in desperation. 'They've been mis-directed to India by unseasonal air currents. They'll fly off as soon as they realise their mistake.'

'Stop bothering me, Brit!' snapped Sera, glaring at me. 'Remember to ask Sam for the binoculars and watch with your eyes just now.'

I rushed to Dolly, fast as I could wheel. She was painting her nails with a frown of concentration on her sweet, round face.

'Dolly, please, please give me my binoculars from Father's top drawer. I need them quick – '

'I know: to look at the birds. I can't at the moment, Brit. My nails aren't dry.'

'But the birds won't wait for your nails.'

'It's not that important, Brit. Stop making a fuss.'

'Look,' I said, changing my tone and tune. 'If you don't give those binos to me before I count sixty I'm going straight to the phone to tell Parvez Mody you are crazy about him.' Parvez, who looked like the matinée idol, Rishi Kapoor, all pink and baby-faced, only had to know that a girl was interested in him and before the week was out he would have her. No one was sure what 'have' meant, least of all me, but it was something terrifyingly pleasurable to Dolly and the girls in her first year arts class.

'You wouldn't dare!' said Dolly incredulously.

'Sure I would: 212136. I even know his number by heart.'

Dolly gasped and bit one freshly painted orange fingernail.

'Don't waste time,' I said. 'Here goes! One, two – ' Before I reached thirty the binos were in my hand and the unwilling visitors from Siberia in front of my eyes.

Slowly it became easier. When Parvez Mody left college, I was at a bit of a loss, but then something awful happened to poor Dolly. A band of lice made their home in her hair. Not that she was dirty or anything, in fact Sera was always grumbling about the bottles of shampoo she was emptying. But she had a girlfriend in college whose hair teemed and when they put their heads together to study *Hamlet* – well. Like the housewife who discovers bed bugs and keeps them in her heart, a shameful secret from her neighbours, Dolly kept her lousy friends from everyone but me.

So whenever I wanted a glass of water in a hurry, I'd just have to remind her about the lice. I felt good about what I was doing. I mean, a kid has a right to his Scrabble game or his *Big Book of Kings and Queens* and if they're tucked away out of his reach he's got to use everything he's got to get them – quick. I felt I was kind of enforcing my rights. That's all.

But it soon gets difficult to tell your rights from your pleasures. Suppose Sera piled my plate high with French beans, which I couldn't stick. There was no reason why I *had* to eat them. When she went to the kitchen for a moment, I tipped the green stuff on to Dolly's plate, softly murmuring, 'Lice, lice.' I went on to nastier things like making Dolly walk to that corner library to exchange comics for me even when she was feeling dead beat after a tough day at college, or forcing her to come with me to old Alfred Hitchcock movies though they gave her screaming nightmares.

When Dolly finally managed to wash those lice right out of her hair while Sera was away one evening, I found something else to blackmail her with and after that still something else. The funny thing was Dolly never stopped telling me her secrets, because she was a disbeliever. She couldn't quite digest that I'd use that bit of information she was telling me with such excitement or pleasure.

One day I blackmailed her into not going to her long-awaited college social because I wanted her to take me to a fair; it was the last day. When I woke from my afternoon nap I saw Dolly biting her pillow and sobbing her eyes out so the pillow-case was one dark soaked patch of blue. I kept watching from the corner of my eye; when Dolly saw me she sat up quickly, turned the pillow over and gave me a smile. 'Yuck! I had a horrible dream; all funerals and tears,' she said, rubbing her reddened eyes. 'Come on, Brit! Stop staring like an owl and get ready. The fair's going to be awfully crowded if we're late.'

I slid on to my wheelchair, went into the bathroom and shut the door. I held out two fingers and tickled the back of my throat. The vomit gushed out and down the toilet bowl.

'What's up, Brit?' shouted Dolly. 'Don't tell me you've been sick. Exam time is two months away, you know.'

I washed and fell back in my chair. 'Your ribs, Brit?' demanded Sera. 'Are they OK? How many times must I tell you to call me when you're going to be sick so I can hold you and you don't get a jolt.'

'I want to sleep,' I murmured. When Sera went to fetch the Tata's Eau de Cologne I said to Dolly, keeping my voice weak as a puppy's, 'I can't go to the fair today, Dolly – I'm feeling too weak.'

'Oh, Brit!' she said. 'Don't feel sad. We'll have fun at home. You can teach me honeymoon bridge – ' Honeymoon bridge was bridge for two and Dolly had resolutely refused for a whole year to learn anything so boring. In fact, I'd been planning to blackmail her into it.

'No!' I howled. 'I don't want to do anything today. I just want to sleep.'

'OK,' said Dolly. 'Sleep as long as you like. When you wake up we'll have fun.'

'So what did you do?' said Madame Manekshaw.

'What could I do? I pretended to doze all evening, that's all.'

'Oh, well! You had a good lesson. I guess that's the silver lining.'

'But it's awful,' I said, 'so horrible that Dolly loves me like this. It's weird. I mean, it's not – it's not normal.'

'Oh! Ho! Normal! When did you start saying things like that?'

'I'm grown up now. You know, I'm almost thirteen.'

'Oh, dear!' said Madame Manekshaw with a weary laugh. 'I still don't feel grown up and I'm almost forty.'

'That's old!' I said and bit my tongue so hard I had to swab it with glycerine that night.

'Yes,' said Madame Manekshaw, touching her hair. 'And soon this silver streak won't have to be painted in.'

'Does that scare you?'

'Yes,' she said, making a face. 'It does. Especially when I think Dinshaw won't be with me much longer.'

'You really love him?'

'I do. I married for something else but I changed. Soon he'll be gone.'

'So what? You'll still have your lovely house and things, and friends like me.' I winked to make it feel real.

She shook her head. 'Enough! Enough about me. I say, did it scare you to know Dolly loves you so much she doesn't mind taking quite a bit of hurt from you?'

'Sure it did. Because I don't think I love her back that much.'

'Makes you feel guilty?'

'Ashamed.'

'Of how you treated her? She shouldn't have let you do that.'

'She did; without ever loving me any less.'

'It's not always right to love people, no matter what they do. You've got to draw a line somewhere.'

'A line? Between what?'

'Loving well and loving wisely.'

'That's something!' I said, impressed by Madame's originality. I hadn't read *Othello* then.

'You think I'm a wise old woman, don't you? Like a psychiatrist. You know what he does? Makes his patient lie on a couch and talk and talk until he finds a way to walk into the patient's mind and help him sort out things inside.'

'That's what I want to do when I grow up. I love knowing why people think like they do.'

'So you can help them? Or just to know?'

'Just to know,' I said. 'It's such fun: better than any book I can buy!'

'I don't think you can do it, Brit. People are going to find it very difficult to trust you to solve their problems.'

'Why? Do I look stupid?' I said indignantly.

'To a lot of people you seem stupid because you are so short and, I know it's absurd, because you can't walk.'

I nodded. In my twelve years Sera and Sam must have shaken their heads to at least a thousand questions like, Is his brain damaged? Is he severely retarded? 'I can't blame them,' I said. Somehow it was easy to be brave with Madame Manekshaw.

'Still, you feel sad that this is one door which is shut to you. You shouldn't, you know. Feeling sad won't open it. We haven't studied much today, have we?'

'What fun!'

Madame Manekshaw winked. 'It's what you learn that counts, not what you study.'

'I learnt a lot today,' I said, not very easily.

'Yes,' said Madame, nodding. 'You learnt something so important you can use it as long as you live.'

'That a blackmailer is a crook?' I said, grinning like crazy because I was feeling all hot inside.

'That when you do something awful to someone you end up doing some worse to yourself.' Madame Manekshaw rose and moved to the door. I followed her, hardly feeling the wheelchair under me. I thought how good the Catholic children must feel after their Saturday powwow with the Father Confessor.

7

'I'M GOING TO be an air hostess!' said Dolly, whirling around the drawing-room, *The Times of India* with its 'Air India Wants Smart Lady Graduates' ad wrapped around her waist like an apron.

'You might as well say glorified *ayah*!' sniffed Sera. 'Picking up vomit bags and dishing out trays. It's no profession for a daughter of mine. We didn't make you a graduate for this!'

'You didn't make me a graduate, Sera darling; I swotted like a Fulbright scholar to get those first-class honours.'

'I just don't like the idea,' said Sera, her pale cheeks turning brown with annoyance. She stirred the prawns cooking on the stove till they sizzled. The white tiles in front of her gleamed in the December sunshine.

'Darling,' said Sam, drawn by the delicious smells, 'what's cooking?'

'An air hostess, that's what!' said Sera. 'Can you imagine?'

'You're joking, aren't you, Dolly?' said Sam, looking amused.

'Why would I joke about what I want to do with my life?'

'But, darling, there's so much you can do. Why, when you were little . . .' Sam wrapped his arms around Dolly's waist. 'We thought you'd grow up to be a lawyer. You argued so well! Even better than your mother.' Dolly snorted impatiently.

'If you don't like the smells in the kitchen, you can move out,' said Sera.

'And then,' said Sam, ridiculously handsome with that starry look in his eyes, 'when Brit was little we thought you'd become a teacher, maybe a professor, the way you sat so patiently with him while he drew all those upside down 'e's and 'f's.'

'Let Brit become a teacher or whatever. He's the bookworm. I want to fly! That's all.'

'You can't fly,' said Sam. 'You think I don't know what it is to love planes? I'd love you to fly but you can't. You mustn't.'

'Why ever not?' said Dolly. She could deal with Sera; maybe cross her will. But not her Father: him, she always had to convince.

'I know a lot about airlines, the kind of people who work with them. And it's not the kind of life a girl like you would want.'

'Oh, Daddy! You've been reading all those "come, fly with me" kind of novels, haven't you?'

'What on earth are they?'

'They're about air hostesses getting laid like whores and they're rubbish.'

'Oh, my God!' said Sam. 'I didn't know it was that bad!' And, of course, Dolly could have plucked out her tongue with bare fingers right then. 'But,' said Sam, 'I had heard of pilots threatening young girls with bad flight reports if they refused to flirt. I never thought – '

'It's settled!' said Sera, banging the lid shut on the prawns.

'Oh, let her do what she wants!' I said. The thought of Dolly, Airline Stewardess, made my mouth flood: blue tins of Kraft cheese, chunks of tender pink Danish ham, moist brown bars of Tobler chocolates.

'It's not so simple, Brit,' said Sam. 'She must also do what's right. It certainly isn't right for her to fall into dangerous hands.'

'But she wants to. She likes the idea of the handsome pilots chasing her!'

'Bloody rot and poppycock!' said Sera, quite forgetting Sam's admonitions. 'Has Dolly been telling you such rubbish and corrupting your mind?'

'Your son is a sex maniac if ever I've known one,' said Dolly, glad to get the heat off her.

'How dare you say such things!' howled Sera. 'You shameless hussy!'

'Now, don't shout!' shouted Sam.

'Let me become an air hostess,' screeched Dolly, 'and I'll stop shouting.'

'You won't become an *ayah*!' howled Sera, stamping her foot so hard I felt the vibrations through my wheelchair.

'She's right,' said Sam, and Dolly burst into tears, because she knew now she would never stand at a jumbo jet's door and say, 'Welcome aboard.'

To make up for his refusal, Sam soon found Dolly a job – an airline job. Only she had to work in the airport instead of the aeroplane. For Sam it was a big thrill having a daughter working at the hub of his fantasy life. He'd wait every morning for Dolly to return from night-duty with a tongueful of stories. Like the one about the veiled Arab lady who sat through a flight from Jeddah to Bombay cradling a baby in her lap. The air hostess found it very suspicious that the baby didn't wail or wake even once, so she alerted the customs officials who discovered the baby was dead, had been dead for the past so many hours. 'But,' said Dolly, leaning across the breakfast table, 'that isn't all. They found the baby's tummy slashed, and lying inside its tiny entrails was a little packet of the purest diamonds.'

Sam choked on his fried egg but that evening when he returned home and saw the story splashed across the *Evening News*, he smiled smugly, his lower lip protruding. 'Gave the chaps at the bank a scoop today,' he said. 'Really impressed them!'

Father often spoke then of the chaps at the bank because he was close to retirement and he knew he was going to miss them. He'd been forty-five years old when I was born. Young Parsee men have this inbuilt resistance to getting married; when they're about thirty-five they suddenly panic at the thought of a lonely old age (the Parsee old people's home being a cross between a loony house and the Lubyanka) and get married. Sam had fortuitously fallen in love at this dangerous age. So he was fifty-eight now that I was thirteen and everyone in Bombay retires at that unripe age promptly to take a new job with some private firm that pays half the salary because you are a full month older.

'Daddy,' said Dolly one evening. 'Let's take a trip to shoo off those retirement blues.'

'A trip? Where to?'

'Round the world!' said Dolly. 'Remember the free tickets I get at the end of the year?'

'I remember,' said Sam, his voice shaking like the hand that was stroking his chin.

'And I get three, so we'll take Brit along as well.'

What with foreign exchange restrictions allowing us to take just eight US dollars each, we couldn't stay much longer than eighteen days. Though Father knew all the tricks of smuggling out money. One night, he returned from a tryst with the black money-changer, his pockets pregnant with dollar notes. We had to hide them in our luggage.

'Not in Brit's cushion – don't you dare!' said Sera. 'I won't allow you to put my little one at risk.' Sam had to agree with her to make up for not taking her along on the trip. Not that she cared. 'Papa sent me for a grand tour of Europe when I was five years younger than you,' she said, pointing a derisory finger at Dolly. 'And this time I'm going to have my first real holiday – since – since Dolly was born.' She smiled quickly, terrified at what she was going to give away.

'OK,' said Sam. 'Who wants to watch the Indian Note Trick?' He had flicked a toothpaste tube from Sera's Be Prepared stock; now he began squeezing the toothpaste into the sink.

'Alas! The madness is come upon him!' cried Dolly in deep thrilling tones.

'There's method in my madness,' grinned Sam, holding up the half-empty white and red tube. He skilfully slit the bottom with a penknife and prised it open. Slowly he pushed in a carefully folded hundred-dollar note until it disappeared completely. Then he rolled up the tube.

'Huh!' snorted Sera. 'No one takes half-used toothpaste abroad. They'll find you out like this!' She snapped her fingers.

'I can keep a note in my powder box,' I said. I couldn't dream of going abroad without the Nycil in which I was smothered every morning like a Swiss Roll in icing sugar. So we plucked out the plastic cap on the powder box, rolled up ten ten-dollar notes and buried the bundle deep in the white stuff.

One evening in Los Angeles when we were going back to our hotel, we got lost. So we stopped at one of the Shell gas stations – in LA we all said gas station though we knew the right thing, the Bombay thing, to say was petrol pump – and we asked for directions. Sam was explaining not very clearly where he wanted to go, so I said, 'No! We've got to go about three blocks away from the Lankasheim-Burband junction.'

The owner of the gas station, who looked like Bob Hope, exploded. 'You mean your kid knows English? Such good English? My! This kid is out-a-sight. A genius in a wheelchair – ooooff!' He jogged into his office shouting, 'I'll be right back!' over his blue-sweatered shoulder.

He came back with a huge box of candied fruit and of course Sam stood very straight and said, 'Oh, no! We can't accept this.'

And he said, 'Take it. Please take it; it's for the baby! – I mean the kid.' So we did and the last thing we heard him say was, 'Smart Ki-id.'

But I've never understood if he was astonished by my very ordinary remark because I was Indian or because I was handicapped. Dolly said, 'It doesn't really matter. To them, it's all the same.'

And one night in the subway in New York, when there was no one around but dope pushers and beggars with their tin cups, we saw a girl killing herself, smothering her head in a plastic bag, slowly sealing it shut by pulling the drawstrings tight.

Sam pushed us up a stairway before we could see any more but Dolly shouted in despair, 'Whatever happened to the America we saw in Honolulu and LA?'

'It died in New York,' I said, thinking that sounded great. But you don't learn till you're bigger that most people and things are a mix of the charming and the repulsive and the neither of the two.

It was also in the subway that I saw a black guy being pushed along in a wheelchair. He was about a hundred yards off and I politely turned away my glance as we rushed towards each other. But I was looking from the corner of one eye and what I saw made my heart stop. In the wheelchair sat the bust of a man, armless and legless, his head thrown back in a laugh. I couldn't believe it. Just couldn't believe my luck. I mean, a couple of years before there was this cyclone in East Pakistan and hundreds of thousands of human beings died, were left orphaned, widowed, homeless, and I was lying in bed with a broken leg and reading the awful news and seeing the devastating pictures and crying. For my broken leg.

I broke my leg again on the journey back to Bombay. We were waiting for the customs officer to clear our baggage when the new watch I was wearing, a flat gold Seiko we hoped to smuggle through, somehow came loose and fell down with a thud. I bent down double-quick before anyone could see when I felt my thigh go crack; I blacked out. When I came to, Dolly was grinning. 'The watch's safe,' she said. 'That's the good news. You've broken a leg, that's the sad news.' As if she had to say it.

When we went back home with my leg in a cast, Sera wasn't really surprised. 'The holidays are over, I suppose,' she said.

Imagine needing a holiday from your own child and all the time wishing you didn't feel like that, because you love him, and you don't need holidays from someone you love. So the question slides up into your mind: When I said that bit about really loving my son, did I mean it?

That's a question Sera fought all her life. And whenever she wasn't too sure of the answer, I could sense it like the crows outside my window could sense a monsoon shower. If there's one thing worse than doubting if you love your kid, it's being the kid in question.

8

'IT'S A SHAME!' said Defarge, clicking away at her needles, knitting a chunky red cardigan she hoped to sell at the next Time and Talents Club sale for self-employed women. 'Your daughter is twenty-four, five feet-six, graduate, earning, and you are not getting her married.'

'What do I do?' said Sera complacently. 'She refuses to let me arrange any boys for her to see. Anyway, it doesn't worry me. Love marriages are a tradition in our family. Like in all *good* Parsee families.'

'Very convenient,' said Defarge. She looked up slyly. 'Everyone knows the real reason why you are not getting her married.'

'What is that?' said Sera sharply.

'You want her to stay and look after Brit, don't you? You are worried he will be alone when, God forbid, you both are gone.'

'Bloody rot – ' started Sera.

'Then why are you so red?' laughed Defarge. 'It's natural. Everyone in the building understands how you feel.'

'What? Everyone's been talking about us? Really! These neighbours are such shameless gossips.'

'It's true,' whispered Ruby, my friend from the flat below, holding her pig-tails together in front to hide her mouth. 'My mummy and daddy were also talking and Daddy said, "One more Parsee spinster, so what?" Mummy said, "Yes: but it's so bad because Dolly is so pretty and such a nice girl – see how she looks after Brit?" Now, stop feeling embarrassed. I know it's not because of you Dolly is still unmarried. And who says you are going to be alone? After all, *we* are going to get married, aren't we?'

'Of course not!' I whispered fiercely, horrified at the thought of spending my life with the skinny, yellow-skinned twelve year old in front of me, never mind if I shared all my evenings and most of my secrets with her.

Ruby brushed aside my rejection. 'Oh, you're in a bad mood because of Defarge's talk. All right, let's play the Ice Game!'

We used to play these fantastic games right up until we were waist-deep in our teens. There was a game called Royal where I was the Prince of Wales and Ruby was whoever I wanted to make her, sometimes I was Henry VIII and Ruby was anyone from Catherine of Aragon to Catherine Parr. Then there was Lost in the Desert, which was an idea I'd stolen from a movie.

But our favourite was the Ice Game. It always started with us having a lazy swim in a lake we'd discovered, when suddenly the top of the lake froze leaving us trapped inside. But we found unused oxygen cylinders and scuba equipment, canned salmon and baked beans. Best of all, we found an underwater cave that was warm and dry. Here we made our home and we went hunting for food and the air that we breathed.

Our kooky games gave us huge open spaces to romp in, even while we sat in my drawing-room above the Causeway; they took me places I could never hope to go and let me do things I could only dream of doing. Best of all, they let me create all the stories I was too scared to put down in blue ink on white paper.

'You tell them,' Sera was saying to Defarge. 'You tell everyone who's talking about Dolly not getting married that when she finds the man she likes she'll get married like this! And then they can all sit and watch. Tell them that from me, Sera Kotwal.'

Sera called Defarge for a cup of tea the next morning. She came at eleven sharp in the brown Japanese georgette sari she'd bought for five rupees sometime in the thirties. Sera didn't give her a second. 'Look!' she said. 'Since you're so anxious to find a husband for Dolly I've decided to give you the job. You find a nice boy – handsome, educated, earning – and we'll get them together.'

'And if it works out?' asked Defarge, her voice cracked with cunning.

'Works out? They get married, of course.'

'What else?' asked Defarge.

'What else? Oh! Yes, yes, you'll get something from us. Don't worry about that.'

'Then,' said Defarge, 'I have someone in mind – are you sure he's not listening to our talk?' She watched me, hooked into my tape machine.

'No, no; not a beep goes through those earphones. Thank God! If Dolly gets to know, we are finished.' She didn't know I'd turned the volume off.

'Really?' said Defarge. 'You are trying to say she isn't anxious to have a man?'

Sera ignored her. She was proving her credentials and she couldn't care less about Defarge's little pokes.

'Then may I make a phone call?' said Defarge.

Now, Sam had got this brainwave, when we were granted a telephone (after being on the waiting list for seven years, because he refused to bribe the telephone company) of keeping the instrument in a neutral place that didn't belong to anyone. Both the bedrooms were out and so was the drawing-room which belonged to visitors. Finally, the phone was installed at the end of the long passage that ran the width of our flat. How I cursed Sam's choice as Defarge tripped away in her black velvet slippers to make her call.

She returned, exulting, 'It's fixed! It's fixed! Apollo Bunder at six tomorrow evening. They'll be there. His mother will be in a shocking-pink sari, so you can spot her at once!'

'But what is their name? What's he like? Where do they live?' said Sera, horrified at the imminence of it all.

'Vera is the mother, and your future son-in-law is Dinsu Dinshaw; they live at the other end of town in Bandra. Well off – you'll like them.'

'Yes,' said Sera doubtfully. 'But must we meet just like that at the seafront?'

'Of course!' said Defarge. 'Double advantage: after the first talk, the happy couple can go for dinner to the Taj Mahal Hotel just across the road.'

Hearing these words, I broke out in an icy sweat. It sort of made Dolly getting married and going away to live in far-off

Bandra like a pair of hands on my throat. I was terrified of Dolly leaving me. I mean, she really was my best friend: in the end, she gave me those binos to watch the birds. And anyway I was too small for my twenty-foot-square bedroom.

I had to stop Dolly from walking into the Apollo trap, epecially when I heard Defarge say, 'He's a handsome boy, a six-footer, and his body, he's built like a Mr Bombay, big-big thighs and chest dark with hair.'

I got the idea when I was about to slide into sleep that night. I shot up in my bed and intoned, like an oracle, just loud enough for Dolly to hear, 'Beware of Apollo!'

Dolly jumped up and asked, 'Why? Why should I beware of Apollo Bunder? Are you dreaming, Brit?'

'A nightmare awaits you,' I said, pitching my cracking voice low as I could. 'In the shape of Dinsu Dinshaw, your unchosen husband, Defarge's choice.'

Dolly jumped out of her bed and clambered on to mine. 'Wake up, Brit!' she whispered in my right ear.

I shook my head, opened my eyes and gasped, 'Was I talking in my sleep, Dolly?'

'Sure you were. About a husband for me — what's all this?'

I clapped a hand to my mouth. 'You weren't supposed to know. I wasn't to tell you. Don't tell Sera I talked in my sleep. Please, please — say you won't.'

Dolly wrapped me in a big-sister hug. 'Don't look so scared, Brit. Of course, I won't tell Sera. Now I know why she wants me to go for a stroll to Apollo.'

'Thanks,' I said in a small voice and grinned myself to sleep.

Apollo, where Sam took his morning walks, had a long promenade that unwound along a remarkably unworried sea — unworried because it had a sheltered life between Bombay island and the Indian mainland, which you could see as distant humps of mountains.

We made quite a procession that Saturday evening. There was Jeroo, who Sera needed for moral support; Ruby, who Sera needed for publicity value; and the four of us. Tina was left behind because even Sera had to admit that two handicapped children in one family was a bit too much. Dolly, much to my surprise, was dressed demurely in a pale-blue silky chiffon dress with long sleeves and a Chinese collar. She stood, leaning against the sea wall and gazing across the water.

Poor Dinsu Dinshaw must have been quite knocked over because as Dolly sighed at the end of that evening, 'My ears have not drunk a hundred words of his tongue.' Vera Dinshaw, in a lurid twinkle-nylon sari, was a hunchback in a queer sort of way. She wasn't bent forward but her body leaned to one side as if she were carrying a pailful of water. Sam winked at me and said, 'One all.'

'Shut up!' whispered Sera fiercely.

'Well, well! What a surprise!' said Mrs Dinshaw in a boom of a voice, as if she'd known us all her life. She paid little attention as Sera introduced us one by one. Her narrow eyes were digging into Dolly who in turn was making sheep's eyes at Dinsu who was certainly something to make sheep's eyes at. His thighs were heavy and muscular, even under his black terry-wool trousers, and he had a huge crotch-bulge. (I always saw people from down up; that was the view from my chair.)

'Look!' I whispered to Ruby. 'He has a hard-on.'

'Already?' said Ruby, and then we couldn't stop giggling so Ruby had to turn my chair quickly to the direction of the sea. 'Defarge was right; his chest is like a forest.'

'Terribly hot in the Indian weather,' I mocked.

'Sshh,' hissed Ruby. 'We're missing out on the elders' talk.'

'I hope you can prepare a good prawn curry,' Mrs Dinshaw was booming. 'It's the way to my Dinsu's heart.'

'I'll try my best,' said Dolly softly, and I swung my chair around in amazement. She was standing with her hands clasped on her skirt, her eyes watching the paving stones. My heart sank like one of those stones a little boy was hurling into the sea.

'And I hope you can stitch your own clothes,' said Mrs Dinshaw, pressing her advantage. 'Tailors are too costly these days.'

Dolly shook her head. 'But I learn quickly,' she said.

'Mr Kotwal, being a banker, I hope you've taught your daughter the importance of savings and investment. My son has no time for these things. He's a junior manager; he has no time for routine matters like filling in slip-books and changing light bulbs. Those are things for us women to do. After all, what education do you have, Dolly? I mean, really have. Nothing! Just an arts degree.'

Dolly looked up meekly and nodded in sad agreement.

'Now,' said Mrs Dinshaw, trying to sound careless with all the intensity of a huntress. 'You can chat with Dinsu, while your father and I discuss financial arrangements.'

'If you mean dowry,' said Sera, making a last ditch stand, 'that's absolutely against our principles.'

'Now, don't get upset,' cooed Mrs Dinshaw. 'I was only talking about – '

We were never to know what, because exactly at that moment Dolly stood tall so she could look Dinsu almost level in the eye, and said in gong-ringing tones, 'It's my turn, Dinsu ol' chap. Let's see what you know since you can't fill in a slip-book or change a light bulb.'

'Who! Who! Who said that?' stammered Dinsu.

'Never mind,' said Dolly lightly, swishing the sash at her waist across Dinsu's hairy arm. 'Now, tell me, what do you think of Kant's categorical imperative?'

'Must be a new group,' said Dinsu. 'Haven't heard of it; at least, it's not in the Top Ten.'

I didn't know what it was either but I hooted derisively as Sam and Sera turned away to hide their grins.

'I was talking philosophy, dear Dinsu, not music. OK, next. Do you think the paintings of Turner pointed the way to Debussy's music – '

'Hey! Hey! I know nothing about all this arty-farty stuff,' said Dinsu, shifting his weight from one foot to another.

'Arty-farty?' hissed Dolly. 'What sort of language have you taught your son, Mrs Dinshaw?'

But Mrs Dinshaw was crying at her son's humiliation as loudly as she had talked. She wept in words, like someone from a comic strip. 'Boo-hoo!' she sobbed. 'Boo-hoo-hoo!'

'Hey!' said Dinsu. 'Play fair and ask me some science questions. C'mon! Give a guy a chance.'

'OK,' said Dolly, serious as a schoolboy. 'How many light-years ago was the earth born?'

Dinsu shut his eyes and shot in the dark. 'Three thousand light-years back?'

'A light-year measures distance, not time,' said Dolly, sighing. 'I'm afraid it's no use, Dinsu, I'd probably die yawning after a couple of days with you.'

'What about a couple of nights?' shouted Dinsu angrily, thrusting out his pelvis.

Jeroo gasped. The sky went dark as the sun went out. 'It's time we went home,' she said weakly.

'Yes,' said Dolly, watching the ships in the harbour come to light. 'Dinsu has a lot of reading to catch up on.'

'Bye-bye,' we chanted, and strolled away. I turned back to savour the moment and I think I saw Mrs Dinshaw trying to climb the sea wall on her way to a plunge while Dinsu held on for his mother's life.

'That's that,' said Sera, wheeling me along.

'Let's go on to the Taj and celebrate!' laughed Sam, and we laughed with him, feeling happy and cosy.

'Defarge was right about your parents,' Ruby whispered. 'See how glad they are that it didn't work out!'

'It didn't work because Dolly didn't like that nincompoop,' I said stoutly.

'Thank God!' said Jeroo. 'As soon as I saw him, I shuddered. All that hair and those thighs and that giant – '

Sam laid his hands on her head and she shut up. 'Imagine!' he said. 'A man who expects his wife to fill in his slip-book.'

'And change the light bulbs,' shuddered Sera. 'I've never changed a light bulb in my life.'

'I have,' said Jeroo. 'It's better to change your own bulbs than have a man around who'll ask you to give him you-know-what in return. I just can't get that thing out of my mind.' She shivered.

'Neither can I,' said Dolly and shrieked; Sera hit her across her bottom.

'That last remark he made,' said Jeroo. 'What sort of a man must he be to say something like that with children around?'

'A bounder, of course,' said Sam.

Which settled the matter. That night when we were going to sleep like well-fed people, after our dinner at the Taj, Sera and Sam came to kiss us goodnight. 'Hey,' said Sam to Dolly.

'How did you think of all those questions – I didn't know half the answers.'

'As if I did; just looked them up in the encyclopaedia before we left.'

'Then,' said Sera, her voice low and excited. 'You knew you were going to meet a young man this evening.'

Dolly buried her head in her pillow from where she kept making 'I'm sorry' faces at me. I turned red as Rudolf's nose.

But Sera wasn't watching either of us. She was saying, her eyes lazily following the whirring fan, 'These modern tape machines are wonderful things, they've got tiny indicators that move up and down with the volume. When they don't move you know the sound is off; then it's time to speak!'

Dolly looked at her as if she'd gone mad. I saw her quite differently: as a saint.

9

THE NEXT MORNING we heard that Madame Manekshaw had killed her husband. She hadn't murdered him — there was no malice or premeditation — but she'd killed him sure as she would have if she'd plunged an antique Chinese dagger into his silk-gowned chest.

Sera explained to Defarge who had come to find out if she were in for a commission from the grateful Dolly and Dinsu, 'She was driving him in the Daimler to the Hanging Gardens for a breath of fresh air, when his door swung open, he fell out — '

'Like a bundle of old clothes from the *dhobi*,' I said, proud of my imagery.

'He fell out and Madame Manekshaw, who was watching the sunset from her side-window, drove right over him — '

'Squelching his neck under her tyre like some rubber toy.'

Thok! Defarge's hand hit my cheek like a hurled stone. 'Shameless boy!' she cried. 'Making fun of the dead. No! Don't open your mouth or you'll get another one so hard it will turn your face around.'

'What do you mean?' screamed Sera, rushing towards Defarge so she had to step back hurriedly. 'You know how his bones are; how dare you!'

'Spoil him, spoil him,' taunted Defarge, 'until one day he sits on your head.' She had this quaint habit of translating her native Gujarati idioms into English — like the time she had this chili-hot curry and asked for a sweet to repair her mouth.

'He can sit on my head, he can stand on my head if he wants,' said Sera.

'He can't stand,' said Defarge sweetly, and I thought Sera

would explode all over her in little bits of grey hair and superior nose.

So I said quickly, 'Tell her about last evening,' and Sera calmed down as if she'd had an Equanil.

'Yes,' she said. 'Yesterday.'

'Yes?' said Defarge, pale with anticipation. 'Yesterday?'

'Yesterday was a waste of time,' said Sera, and Defarge winced. 'Your choice, I'm sorry to say, is abominable. That boy was a moron if ever I've seen one, and his mother is a cry-baby.'

'But – but,' said Defarge, 'his body, his looks?'

'My daughter is looking for something more than looks,' said Sera. 'And that woman was looking for a dowry.'

'All men want money,' said Defarge bitterly. 'Why do you think I am like this, alone and old? I was pretty once; but I was poor.'

I turned away and pretended to look at the sun because I wanted to cry. I knew what Defarge had just said was maudlin and common but it was the first time I saw her as a person and not as a sort of cartoon who went through life looking for commissions. I thought how I'd made fun of her, even just now when I asked Sera to give it to her, when all the while I should've been doing something, anything, to make her feel better.

'See what a sissy you've made him,' said Defarge, peering at my tear-stained face. 'Fourteen years and he can't even take a slap on the face.'

'Oh, shut up!' said Sera. 'You must've hurt him.'

'I wasn't crying,' I said. 'The sun was making my eyes water.'

'A likely story,' sneered Defarge. 'Cry-baby!'

'I know what!' said Sera. 'You were crying for poor Madame Manekshaw, weren't you, sweetie?'

'Crying for her!' exclaimed Defarge. 'He was making fun of her just five minutes back.'

'That's his way of handling sorrow,' said Sera, her hand on her heart. 'Sensitive children use words to conceal their feelings.'

'I wasn't crying,' I said.

'Take him to the funeral,' said Defarge. 'That may make him cry.'

'Oh, no!' said Sera hastily. 'That would be too much for him. All those vultures and peacocks waiting to make a meal of poor Mr Manekshaw. Most unhealthy for a growing boy's imagination.'

'What do you suggest?' said Defarge. 'That we are burned to ashes, like those Hindus? Or chewed by worms like the Englishmen? I, for one, prefer to be eaten by vultures.'

'Don't talk like that,' said Sera. 'It's bad luck.'

The phone rang and I wheeled away to take it. 'Hello,' said a mock-Oxbridge voice, the kind that U-Parsees invariably affect. 'Could I speak to Brit Kotwal?'

'Speaking,' I breathed, trying to out-Oxbridge her.

'I'm Aloo Manekshaw and I thought I'd inform you that Madame – '

'Yes; we heard,' I said.

'Oh! You did! Terrible, isn't it?'

'Verra,' I said.

'Both of them, in twenty-four hours.'

'Both?' I squeaked.

'Hello! Hello! Am I speaking to Brit Kotwal?'

'Oh, yes,' I said faintly.

'Then you haven't heard of the sad second event. Madame Manekshaw slit her throat this morning. It was awful. Blood all over her Persian carpets – such expensive ones, too.'

She must be Madame's heiress, I thought, while my head felt like I'd just got off a merry-go-round. 'I'm very sorry,' I murmured.

'Thank you,' said the voice. 'And, oh, yes! The funeral, both the funerals, are at three this afternoon – Bombay time, of course.'

'I'll be there,' I gurgled. 'Thank you.'

I knew I wanted to break open and get rid of the awful smush churning inside me. I knew I couldn't do that once I told Sera the news. I went into my bathroom, locked the door and got ready to start.

I waited and waited. Have you ever cried after you've had a

cry? It's like trying to get an orgasm five minutes after you've just had one – all you get is dry heaves.

I tried everything. I thought of that first time I met Madame Manekshaw prematurely silver-tinted, when she said, 'Most unhealthy for a growing boy's budding sexuality,' and of that afternoon at the Sea Lounge; and of the time she threw my Parker 51 out of the window because I said the capital of India was Delhi, when everyone knows, or should know, that it's New Delhi: of the morning she wanted to hug me but was afraid I'd break like that Sung dynasty vase. It was no use. I came out, washed my face, because that's what I do after I've had a cry, even if it only consists of sounds, no tears, and I went and told Sera the news.

'Now,' said Defarge, pouncing, 'you have to take Brit for a last look.'

'Oh, dear,' said Sera. 'Yes, we'll manage that. But who's going to teach you now? We've got to find someone soon; it's your final year and you've got to do well.'

'We'll think about that when the time is right,' I said frostily. My teacher hadn't reached the vulture's belly and Sera was thinking of finding her successor.

Sam was called home from his office to help take me to the funeral. Then we remembered I didn't have the knee-length white muslin coat with bows down the front that Parsees are supposed to wear at funerals – and weddings. So we settled for my school uniform which was white pants and white shirt, and which I thought was quite appropriate for Madame Manekshaw because without her I wouldn't have had that uniform at all.

The afternoon was gentle, pale grey with clouds soft as silk-cotton blowing across the sky. 'Picnic day,' said Sam irreverently.

'Yes,' I said. 'Isn't it funny? All the novels we read call sunny days with blazing blue skies fine days – '

'Awful,' said Sam, shaking his head.

'Yes, and all we want is shade and cloud and cool breeze. Different windows, I suppose. I talked about that with Madame Manekshaw once.'

'You talked about a lot of things with her, didn't you?' said Sam. 'You're going to miss her.'

'No!' I said blindly. 'I don't intend to miss her.'

Sam looked at me and put his arm around my shoulder. 'Don't fight, Brit,' he said softly. 'If there's something you feel, you've got to be brave enough. Even if it hurts like – like a fracture.'

'Enough of that!' snapped Sera, fitting a red velvet skull cap on my head. 'We're in the Tower of Silence grounds.'

'Stop protecting him, will you?' said Sam. 'He's big enough to talk of death – and fractures. Don't treat him like a baby.'

'He is my baby,' said Sera. 'Look! We're skirting a forest. Isn't it lovely? Dark and mysterious.'

'It stretches for miles,' said Sam. 'Or at least it looks like miles. I saw it from a helicopter once, just a spread of green, almost touching the sea.'

'They should have a holiday resort here,' I said brightly, to prove I wasn't missing Madame Manekshaw one bit. 'Right in the heart of Bombay – it would be a smash!'

'Don't talk like that,' said Sera. 'This is sacred ground. It's our place where we can dispose of the dead like we're meant to – one last act of charity.'

I didn't answer. Madame would have loved my holiday resort idea; we would've had a wild time talking about it, planning the hotels, the nature trails, the boating-lake shimmering between the vermilion *gulmohurs* we were rushing past in the taxi.

'Stop!' Sera commanded the driver. 'There's the bunglee, Brit – where the funeral prayers are said.'

'Bunglee?' I sniggered. 'Is that a bungalow's wife?'

'I want none of your juvenile wit,' said Sera. 'Better be on your best behaviour, because I'm taking you in.'

'You can't take him in,' Sam protested. 'The men sit outside.'

'The children,' said Sera firmly, 'are allowed in.'

The bodies were quite a let-down because Mr Manekshaw, whom I'd never seen, looked, well, dead, and Madame Manekshaw looked exactly as she always did, a younger, slimmer Indira Gandhi. And she was all swaddled so I couldn't even see the slit in her throat.

Then quite suddenly I noticed I was sitting next to an old lady in a wheelchair wrapped in a white Chantilly lace sari.

When the priests finished their chanting, she turned to me. 'I'm Aloo Manekshaw,' she said in a rasping voice. 'The dead man's sister. You must be Brit. Your teacher has left this for you.' She gave me a small blue envelope.

'Don't open it just now,' whispered Sera. 'It might be something confidential.'

'Thank you,' I said. 'I'm sorry about – '

'Yes,' rasped the old lady, 'I'm sorry too. If this had happened ten years ago, I could have done things – seen Paris, dressed at Dior, had a little villa in the Nilgiris on a plantation; I love the solitude of the coffee hills. Now, what's the use? I resent the money – if I didn't have it I wouldn't mind so much being like this.' She touched the steel rims of her wheels. 'I'm only saying this to you because you also – '

'Yes, yes,' I said softly. 'But you can be in a wheelchair and still have a good time, you know.'

'*You* can,' she said, smiling enviously. 'Because that's how you've always been. I wasn't like this till six months ago.' Her voice faltered. 'Funny, isn't it?' she said. 'How things can come too late.'

They were taking away Madame Manekshaw to the vultures and I didn't know whether to think of her or the rambling lady next to me. I turned and she wasn't there – someone was wheeling her away.

'Let's go,' said Sera. 'There's no one here that we know.'

'But I want to go up,' I said, 'to see the well where Madame is going to be laid.'

'Rubbish!' said Sera. 'You can't see the well even if you follow the body: you've got to view it from some distance away. Look! even Daddy's not going.'

'But I want to go,' I said loudly.

'You can't. The road's too rough and your chair can't make it.'

'Someone can lift me in the chair.'

'Now, don't make a scene. What will people think of Madame Manekshaw when they see you behaving like this?'

That shut me up. But the next moment I heard a lady walking behind us say to her husband, 'Guilt, dear, guilt. She knew she'd always have to live with that and she chose the easy way out.

79

There could have been a criminal prosecution – after all, she was quite an heiress.'

'I'm sorry,' I said, wheeling round and pushing down my brakes so Sera couldn't drag me away. 'It's not true, what you just said about Madame Manekshaw. She wasn't afraid of stuff like guilt. She just didn't want to live without her husband, she loved him that much – I know.'

The lady, hook-nosed in a black silk sari, looked at me haughtily. 'Small mouths,' she said, 'shouldn't concern themselves with big affairs.'

'I'm not small, I only look that way,' I whispered, shaking all over.

Sera snapped up my brakes. 'I'm sorry,' she said, 'he's a bit upset – Madame Manekshaw was his teacher for years, you see.' The lady didn't deign to reply. She and her husband slipped into their ancient Morris Minor and drove away.

'I know how you felt,' said Sam, 'but strong feelings are no excuse to butt into someone else's conversation.'

'I knew we shouldn't have brought him,' said Sera.

'What d'you mean?' said Sam, crinkling his eyes against the sun and Sera.

'It's not a normal, healthy thing. A funeral, I mean. I've always tried to keep things normal and healthy. Oh, you know what I mean, Sam.'

'All right, all right,' said Sam, putting his arm around her shoulders as we went downhill to the waiting taxis.

But Sera's balance had been undone. In the taxi, she burst out, 'Sam, do you realise there's something we aren't prepared for?'

'Oh, dear,' he said, smiling. 'Here we go.'

'Don't joke, Sam. Suppose something happens to us like it did to the two of them.'

'It's bound to, darling – we're mortal.'

'Very funny. But we aren't prepared; don't you see? We've hardly saved anything.'

'Well, we're living pretty well on what we have.'

'That's not the point.' Sera was getting quite flustered, mechanically tucking her salt and pepper hair behind her ears. 'I mean, what about Brit?'

'What about Brit?' repeated Sam. 'I guess we leave him

80

whatever we have – the money you got from your father, my provident fund from the bank.'

'You think that's enough?' cried Sera. 'You know how money shrinks – '

'Like cheesecloth!' I cried.

'Yes! Quite right, pupsie: so what are you going to do? You must find a way of earning when we're gone. *Be* something – a teacher, a lawyer . . .'

'Don't be ridiculous,' said Sam. 'Life's tough enough for him as it is; I've said that a million times. How on earth do you think he can go out and compete with all those young men bursting with energy?'

'We're talking about holding down a job,' said Sera, 'not making an atomic explosion.'

'I guess Dolly can always help him out,' said Sam.

'We can't count on our daughter to provide for our son. It isn't right.'

'Umm,' mused Sam. 'I suppose Brit would find it a bit demeaning.'

'And besides,' said Sera, 'what if Dolly wants to get married? After all, she is a lovely child. It's hardly possible she won't fall in love and be loved right back.'

'Brit can find a rich wife,' laughed Sam.

Sera hit his thigh with her fist. 'Don't talk rot,' she said loudly. 'My Brit is going to be a bachelor boy, aren't you, darling?'

I wanted to shoot back, Certainly not. I mean, what guy of fourteen is a confirmed bachelor, unless, of course, he is still stuck in that all-girls-are-asses phase. I answered nonchalantly, 'I guess so.'

'Right!' said Sera, pushing the white wisps back from her forehead in relief.

'I suppose that's only sensible,' said Sam, 'considering Brit would find it rather hard getting a girl. On the other hand . . .'

'There is nothing in that other hand,' said Sera firmly.

'Oh, yes, there is,' said Sam. 'I think we would be totally wrong to confine Brit to a loveless future.'

'Who says it's loveless? I love him, you love him, Dolly loves him, Jeroo loves – '

'That's not what I meant. I meant it's not right making Brit believe from now on that romantic love is out for him.'

'It is out,' said Sera. 'Do you know that osteo can be inherited?'

'Well, he can adopt children.' I knew Sam probably agreed with Sera one hundred per cent but he wanted to argue.

'Parsees can't adopt,' said Sera shortly.

'He'll be childless then,' said Sam. 'So many people are, and happy too.'

'Please stop!' said Sera, her palms on her ears, 'I don't want Brit to hear any more.'

Sam kept quiet: I could only hear the swish of the taxi on the road. I remembered the little blue envelope the old lady had given me. It was still in my hand, squeezed into a ball. I managed to unfold it and pull out the soft blue paper inside. It was a short message my teacher had left for me: *Sorry I couldn't stay. Shall miss you up there, MM.*

And I'll miss you down here, I thought, my face screwing up though I was trying to keep it straight. Which was a bit like trying to walk.

10

AFTER MY FINAL exams at Campion I had a half-year of holidays, because the college term didn't start till then. That's when I became a sex maniac, making Dolly's words come true. Not that I didn't try to fill my hols with other things – I read like a man who had only six months to see, learned chess, refined my bridge game, started Spanish guitar lessons and gave up when I found the instrument larger than me.

Lurking below all these busy hours like some Loch Ness Monster I didn't quite believe in was my single-minded pursuit of lust. I woke to the anticipating hardness of a stiff cock and I fell asleep that way. I jerked off just any time I felt like it – listening to the BBC news, while solving a bridge puzzle, in the middle of a scale I was practising.

Feeding my daily explosions of lust were my thoughts, hot and bubbling like a volcano's magma chamber, of Tina and Ruby. They were both budding before me, and watching their growing feet and breasts and bottoms filled me with giddy delight. It was even better because I really cared for them both.

Tina was, for me, that delicious creature every guy wants – a sister whose body he can crave without a scrap of guilt. We were so familiar with each other, yet I could get a hard-on just watching the half-apples of her breasts as the sun tore through her thin dress. Or we'd sit together at the movies and, all the time I was explaining the story to her with my fingers, I could smell the swooning scent of her skin – part soap, part hormone. But I knew I didn't really want Tina. Not the way you want a girl when you're fifteen. Because then you've got to have everything just right – soft music and poetry and whispered somethings. And they couldn't have worked their magic on her ears. I didn't want a deaf girlfriend even though she was a gorgeous girl and a fabulous friend.

I knew I had to fall in love. Engelbert Humperdink and all the singers I heard were in love, the books Dolly read were love stories, and Tina and Ruby were in love (but not with me). I wanted to feel what everyone else was feeling – I was determined to have my knees turn to jelly (not that it would make much difference) and my heart pound like a jungle drum. I longed to pine away and lose my appetite.

So I turned to Ruby – she was the only one left and she was shamelessly sexy. Her figure was a perfect hour-glass (how quickly she'd changed from the bony little thing of three years ago) and she revelled in it, wearing hot-pants that clung to her as if they were wet, and brief little tops that were colourful glorified bras. Her eyes were light-brown and saucy like the stone in one of Sera's rings that no jeweller had been able to name. Ruby was in love with Alphonso Almeida, her English teacher at school, a dark and dashing Catholic, fresh out of B.Ed. class.

That didn't stop her from flirting outrageously with me. 'Hey,' she'd whisper, when we were alone in my bedroom, 'you're growing a fab moustache; it's going to be really thick in a couple of years.' She'd trace one soft fingertip over my upper lip, from left to right and back again, while I sat open-mouthed with lust trying desperately not to pant. When she'd had a sweet she'd pretend to stuff the wrapper in my pocket, at the same time rubbing my nipple with a steady stroke. That was enough to send me flying through the wall straight into Defarge's flat.

I paid her back as much as I dared. 'Wow!' I'd say, shooting my eyebrows into my hair, smoothing my palm against her leg from below her hot-pants to her knee. 'You've got such silky skin; bet you could be a model for Afghan Snow.'

Ruby would gasp and breathe, 'Don't do that! You're arousing me, you devil.' And we'd laugh our mouths off with excitement.

When she came in through the door, I'd drop the book I was reading and say, 'Could you pick that up for me?'

'Sure!' She'd get on her knees and bend over, taking time to brush her hair out of her eyes, lift the book, close it gently, dust it, while I stared down her blouse at the succulent strawberries and cream of her breasts. We both knew I could reach for that book from my wheelchair as easily as I could scratch my head.

One day Ruby asked me, just like that, 'Brit, have you ever French kissed a girl?' I said no, I hadn't. 'Neither have I,' she said, and giggled. 'A boy, I mean. Let's do it the next time your parents are out.'

'Sure!' I said, a bit stunned by my luck. 'But don't chicken out.'

As it happened Sera, Sam and Dolly decided to leave us alone the very next evening, because there was this movie *Klute* running which was 'adults only' and there was no way they could take a four-feet-short me. Sera had a thing about not leaving me alone if she could help it. What if there were a fire? How would I get into the lift on my own? She used to ask Defarge to keep an eye on me but I'd put a stop to that. An earful of her clicking tongue left me clawing at the drawing-room walls. Nowadays, Sera asked Ruby or Jeroo or someone. This time she picked Ruby.

Who came dressed to seduce in a silky-brown skirt that showed off her legs which were the colour of her blouse, a rich cream with a hint of rose. 'Bye,' said Sera. 'Be good.' She said that every time she left me. It was a sort of ritual; her way of making sure I'd remain unbroken till she returned.

They left, and we sat at the window, studiously watching the hesitant pedestrians and the wilful traffic below. We couldn't talk or look at each other. My heart was Zulu-dancing inside my chest. Then it fell dark and we watched the moon, full and bright as a street light over the Causeway. Ruby was kneeling next to me, blowing into my ear. I could see her eyes shine and her neck was the colour of the moon. She held my head until our lips were touching. Hers felt soft and swollen. I opened my mouth. Then my eyes. I waited for a second; as gently as I could manage I took her hand from my head and moved away.

'What's wrong?' she whispered. 'You don't know how?'

'Huh? Ya,' I said.

'Oh, boy! We can always try!'

'No.' I shook my head. 'I don't think so.' And even before I shut my mouth, I wanted to kick myself hard as a goat's hoof.

God! Why had I stopped? Was it because I was Sera's good little boy? Was I afraid I wouldn't be able to stop at smooching? Did I think I'd land up in a soggy love affair I didn't want? The fact was I just didn't want to kiss Ruby. But that was a bloody lie: I was dying to eat her soft lips and suck her tongue. But the truth was — and it was awful — I thought she didn't deserve a kiss from me.

We never talked about it again but our little games were over. We still met every day, Ruby still sighed over Alpho, we still played the Ice Game because it was the sexless one.

About six months later we were playing Monopoly one rainy evening; Ruby was staring at me as I counted out my money to see if I could afford Mayfair. Suddenly, she said, 'You know, Brit, you're awfully ugly. I mean, I could never had done all those things I did with you if I were some other girl. It's just that I've known you all my life, and I could forget the way you looked.' She laughed. Then she saw the colour of my face. 'Hey!' she said. 'Did that hurt? I don't mean your face is horrid or anything. Actually, it's quite sweet when you smile. I was talking about the whole thing — you know, your body, and your legs and — '

'I know!' I laughed. 'But I've got litres of charm to pour over all that. So it doesn't matter.' Ruby shrieked with relief; I smiled: my sweet smile.

But it was no use smiling that night when I was alone in bed. Because I thought: I'll be alone in here ten or even fifteen years from now. I remembered Ruby's hungry body that moonlit evening. And I kicked myself till I was black and blue all over.

I'd never sat on a see-saw but I knew how it felt better than any four year old. Because I was riding this huge see-saw for quite some time. I guess it must have been all the stuff my glands were pouring into me, because one day I was jollying around on my building's terrace looking out at glorious Bombay city floating on blue and white waves. The next day I was huddled up in the cellar, dark and closed and alone.

Like the time I got my school leaving exam results and I

found I'd missed a First by one mark. That's the sort of stuff you read in novels and snort about incredulously. Everyone around tried to make it better by talking about that one distinction I'd won in English. But that evening I got a note from the Principal that said, 'You're going to write; and make it big some day,' which sent me flying out to Pluto.

College life really wasn't very different from Campion. I didn't attend. Instead I took this ghastly correspondence course that the University ran and which was really good. Every week they sent you about ten carefully printed, detailed, lucid lectures with response sheets attached. And if you didn't write those and send them regularly you couldn't get into the exams. How I sweated under what Dolly called my Correspondence Cross. I kept wondering how Ruby, who was in the same class in a real college, always said she bunked almost every lecture except English because, well, English teachers were becoming a fetish with her.

I found out when I went for my first exams. There was this brown owlish girl sitting next to me who was clutching her hair at the temples and rocking back and forth. 'Would you believve?' she said, and I suddenly realised she looked like an owl because she had these dark circles under her eyes.

'Believe what?' I asked.

'That I hadn't read a word of this subject till last night.'

'How can that be? When you sent off your response sheets you must have read something.'

'Response sheets?' she shrieked. 'You mean you actually sent them off?'

'Didn't you? Then how come you're here? Maybe you've got influence. Nowadays, everything works with influence.' I realised I sounded just like Sera, off balance.

'I've got zero-influence,' shouted the girl, making a ring with her index finger and thumb. 'No one, absolutely no one ever writes out those response sheets. It's just a threat from the University and it works only on some gullible goons – like you.' And she went off into a cracker-chain of spluttering laughs.

That was nothing compared with what came next. Someone should've told me that moving from élite school tests to university exams is like shifting from a convent to a cabaret-joint – for the first time you meet sin, face to warm red face. Soon as the papers were given out, I heard a low buzz like the humming of a dragonfly on a warm night. Then there were rustles and whispers and sharp little calls. 'Hey, Raju! Shah Jahan died, what year?' And so on, for about half an hour.

I stared at the two supervisors – weedy young men who I knew were paid fifteen rupees for enduring three hours of boredom – they smiled back. One asked, 'Want more paper?'

'No,' I said, hastily returning to answer 4a.

The hum now was a buzz. 'Look!' cried one of the invigilators who was dressed in yellow pants and red sweatshirt with a clown painted on it. 'If you make noise, the senior supervisor will come and there will be serious trouble. If you cheat softly, everything will be fine. We will even help you.'

I told Ruby and she laughed. 'You old fuddy-duddy, Brit! Why d'you think there's such a rush into colleges? If people had to study to get through, they'd stay at home.'

'I don't believe that,' I said. 'There must be thousands like us who wouldn't dream of cheating.'

'Us?' said Ruby. 'I cheat, Brit. Not because I need to; just for the fun of it. And you've got to be careful with some of the students. If they want your paper you've got to give it to them.'

'Otherwise they kill your horse and leave his head in your bed?'

'They send you to Coventry and it gets awfully lonely there after a while – especially if you are a chatterbox, like me.'

I smiled. 'I'm glad I don't go to college,' I said.

'That's a dumb thing to say. It's like wishing you were dead because people fall ill sometimes.'

'Very profound,' I said.

Ruby ignored me and looked at her platinum watch, a gift from her parents for leaving her alone while they took a second honeymoon on the beaches of Greece. 'It's five-thirty,' she said. 'Tina will be waiting.' She took the handles of my chair and we walked over to the old house in the tree-filled lane where Jeroo and Tina lived on the top floor. It was a beautiful house, the kind you saw in books about European capital cities, with a generous balcony that Jeroo had filled with plants she could talk to since, living with Tina, her voice tended to fall into disuse. The balcony had a black wrought-iron railing, cast in an incredible pattern of lions, unicorns, crowns, shells and scrolls. I never grew tired of admiring it though it usually meant a stiff neck the next day from looking up that long.

From the days when I had been light enough to carry up, I remembered that the flat had about six bedrooms and a maze of passages in which we had to hunt for Tina every time we wanted to talk to her; she wouldn't hear if we called.

Tina emerged with Ruby from the building's entrance. If they had been frozen into a painting, Ruby would be the beauty made of wine and roses reclining on a gold silk couch, while Tina would be floating near the top of the picture, pale and lovely as an angel, soft brown hair blowing in an ethereal breeze.

Our evening walks at Apollo had become a great adventure. Every evening at exactly six o'clock we reached the massive Gateway of India, its four gigantic arches brown with neglect, its huge hall slippery with piss and shit. Not that we cared about anything like that. Because this was where we met Rohit, who was handsome as a Hindi filmstar, white-toothed and curly-haired. He was Tina's boyfriend.

Actually, he lived in a boarding-house across the street from her window. It had started one Diwali evening when they were both watching the rockets and fountains of light with which the children were celebrating. Then this huge string of crackers, extra-loud so they were called atom-bombs, went off and Rohit, who was sticking his fingers into his ears, marvelled at the lovely girl opposite who was smiling through it all. He thought she was smiling at him and he waved. Then they started talking and because of the street dividing them it was to be all lip-reading and signs.

Rohit didn't discover that Tina was deaf till he met her, which was almost six months later because of Jeroo not allowing Tina out alone. Finally she resorted to Ruby and me, and that's how her romance took off. Rohit said it made no difference to him whether her ears worked or not. He liked the feeling that talking in sign language gave him; it made him feel they were still the boy and girl divided by the tree-filled street.

For Ruby and me, waiting under the Gateway while the lovers took a leisurely stroll, it was better than watching a James Bond movie. That was saying a lot, because we both had a crush on 007, collected pictures of Sean Connery and Roger Moore, tore out articles, pasted them in a huge scrap-book that we destroyed with great ceremony when we turned eighteen.

The excitement bubbled for us, because we were doing something so heinous we knew we would be punished in the worst possible way if Sera or Sam or Jeroo ever found out we were leading Tina astray – they would stop us from meeting again ever.

There was also the romance of the star-crossed lovers to keep us going. Because Tina and Rohit's love was as surely doomed as the court dancer Anarkali's passion for Prince Jehangir. We knew Jeroo would never, not on her frigid life, allow Tina to marry Rohit, though he was handsome, rich, working in his uncle's business, had a house in New Delhi. Because he wasn't a Parsee. When life came to solid things like marriage, everyone, even Sera and Sam, forgot how modern they were.

'But we can't just throw up our hands,' said Ruby, holding her nose to keep out the Gateway stench. 'We've got to do something for poor Tina. If she loses Rohit, she'll probably never find anyone else. You know how it is for handicapped people.'

I looked at the sea.

'So-rry,' said Ruby. 'Why don't we have a party for Tina's birthday next month?'

'They'll smell something fishy. We've never done it before.'

'This year it's different; she's eighteen.'

'Right! And then?'

'And then we call Rohit, as a college friend of mine. Even Jeroo doesn't mind Hindu *friends*. She just might get charmed.'

'Yes, she is her daughter's mother.'

Ruby laughed gleefully and we planned the party down to the last slice of cake.

We saw Tina crossing the pigeon-filled square with that abstracted look she always wore, as if she was really living somewhere inside her head. And with long-distance signs we told her about the party. She turned and explained our plan to Rohit, who took her in his arms, right there outside the Gateway, and kissed her with his red mouth open against her shell-pink lips. Though Ruby and I had read about hundreds of kisses, we almost died seeing him devouring her mouth like that right in front of the *narielpaniwalla*, the snake-charmer and the man who rented out his telescope to curious eyes.

'Let us go to the studio and take out a photo!' said Rohit. 'We will always remember today.' He had a funny sort of accent that sounded as if he were speaking Hindi when he was speaking English. 'It's a good thing Tina can't hear him,' Ruby whispered. 'It might have turned her right off him.'

We went to the Mona Lisa studio and Rohit said, 'Take out our photo in colour, please – I don't mind the expense.' Ruby made a face at me and we all lined up to say cheese to the camera; the shutter clicked and Rohit tripped over his feet.

'Oh! It's spoiled!' squealed Tina with her hands.

'Sorry!' said Rohit. 'But I can't afford price of two colour photos.'

11

'SHE'S GONE! SHE'S eloped!' wailed Jeroo, standing outside our door, her beautiful face contorted as if a child had crumpled it angrily.

'Calm yourself at once!' commanded Sera, holding her by the shoulders and shutting the door so Defarge wouldn't hear.

But Jeroo began screaming and tearing at her cream-soft arms with her nails. 'My only child is gone – gone with the wind!'

'Nonsense!' said Sera.

'Nonsense!' said Ruby and I, but we couldn't hear our own voices.

'I am born to misfortune,' wept Jeroo. 'I should have jumped from the window twenty-five years ago. I've been raped and widowed and betrayed. Oh!' she sobbed. 'Let me go through that window. I beg you, have pity, pity, *pity*!'

Sera slapped her cheek and Ruby started crying. 'Call the police!' said Sera.

'It's no use,' I said. 'Tina's eighteen today: she can do what she wants.'

'She is not,' said Sera, hitting her fist into her palm. 'It's her *roj* birthday today. She's not eighteen for another five days.'

All of us had two birthdays: there was one that we celebrated on the date we were born, and the other, which stepped back one day every leap year, was by the calendar we'd carried across from Persia.

'By Jove!' said Sam, who had been stunned into silence till now. 'You're brilliant, Sera, my love. So who's she run away with?'

'I don't know,' said Jeroo. 'She doesn't know a single boy

92

– except Brit. And he's here,' she added accusingly, as if she wished I had taken Tina away.

Ruby crooked a little finger behind her and walked into my bedroom. I wheeled after her. 'What shall we do?' she whispered, fiercely wiping the pink paste of tears and blusher off her cheeks.

'We can't tell,' I said. 'They trust us not to.'

'Rot!' said Ruby. 'They didn't trust us enough to tell us. Why should we keep their secret now?'

'They expect us to. And think what they (I shot a thumb at the drawing-room) will do to us.' Ruby shuddered and her breasts bobbed up and down, inspiring me. 'I know what!' I shouted, and Ruby hurriedly clapped a sweaty palm to my mouth. I shook her hand off. 'Listen, Ruby, in law there's the concept of legal immunity. Know what that means?'

Ruby shook her curls. 'This is no time for showing off, Brit. Tina may be catching a train to Kashmir right now.'

'OK. There's this idea. We promise to tell Sam and Sera eveything; in return we get them to promise us no punishment.'

'Let's go!' And Ruby swung into the drawing-room.

It worked. When we told them of our proposition, Jeroo and my parents reminded me of hungry puppies rolling on their backs at the sight of a dog biscuit, though by the end of our story, Sam had to hold Sera's twitching hands between his own. 'Darling, please, remember people like us don't break their word.'

'Then call the police!'

'No!' shrieked Jeroo. 'I've lost my daughter, I don't want to lose my reputation as well.'

'I think she's right,' said Sam. 'Let's investigate on our own. If we can't manage, we'll call in the police.'

It was unpleasantly easy. Rohit had left a forwarding address at the boarding-house where he lived, with strict instructions to the receptionist to keep it secret. She quite forgot them when Sam gave her a bouquet of red roses with a hundred-rupee note curled among the petals.

Night was falling as we drove into the Falkland Road which was lined with dirty-green little cafés with signboards that read: 'REAL MUGHAL BIRYANI AVAILABLE HERE, FIT FOR A NAWAB!' and 'HOT FRIED CHICKEN WHOLE!'

Suddenly the street grew darker and the shops on either side began selling flesh instead of food. I watched the whores, heavy and shapeless, or emaciated into skeletons, dressed in long skirts that they hitched up and tucked into their waistbands, and short *cholis* bursting at the seams, bare flesh oozing out between the skirt and blouse like rolling-pins. They were scratching their heads and looking at their fingernails to see what they'd found in their scalps. They shouted lewd invitations in hoarse voices to the passers-by who seemed to be window shopping, sauntering slowly past, their hands rubbing between their legs.

'Stop the taxi,' I cried, wrestling with the door which had its handle missing. Flinging myself across Ruby's lap as the cab slowed down, I was sick till I felt my guts in my throat.

'Are you OK?' said Sera and Sam from the front seat where they sat together though it was quite a squeeze, what with the driver and all.

'Yes,' I gasped and shut away the whores with my eyes.

We drove on, our hearts beating in a sort of collective thump so that if a doctor had held a giant stethoscope to the cab he'd have gone deaf.

'Here is your address,' said the driver, rushing out to open the dicky and take out my wheelchair. Ruby held the door open and Sam heaved me into the chair. I looked up and saw a narrow grey building just the width of a room across. We found the entrance at the back and filed in, Sera holding Sam tight around the waist, Ruby clinging to the handles of my chair as if they were her English teacher's arms.

'Thank heavens it's the ground floor,' said Sam. 'Or with Brit – '

'Shsh!' said Sera. 'I hear music.' It was a lilting song from a Hindi film, the same one that we'd heard blaring from the bazaar all night, last Diwali. When Tina had smiled at Rohit.

I looked at Ruby. 'Are you going to be sick again?' she asked, and crouched next to me. Sam pressed the doorbell and the ring merged with the music. Then silence fell like darkness.

The door creaked, then swung open. A plump, smiling, fortyish lady reeking with *attar* of roses stood with hands folded in front of her as if she were praying. 'What can we do for you?' she asked, her voice sweeter than home-made fudge gone wrong.

'We want our daughter, Tina,' said Sam, his voice shaking.

The woman rolled her eyes. 'There is no Tina here,' she said.

'Oh, yes, there is,' said Sera. 'We know that Rohit Gupta lives here and he has taken her away – '

'And she is a minor,' I said, trying to keep my voice gruff. 'So he has actually kidnapped her.'

'What are you saying?' said the woman, wrinkling her huge Plasticine face in puzzlement. 'Someone has given you the wrong address.'

'The police will soon find that out,' Ruby cried. 'Give our Tina back to us or you'll go to jail, you ugly whore.'

'I will call the police if you don't leave my threshold,' spat the woman, her charm falling away like a scab. She took a step forward and grabbed a curlful of Ruby's hair. 'And if you threaten me ever again, I'll take you in and lock you up, there with the other girls.' Ruby turned pale as ice while the madam held her head like a triumphant Perseus. She let go and stepped back into the brothel, bolting the door in our faces.

'They've taken her away,' breathed Sera, 'somewhere deep in India.'

'The police will find her,' said Sam. 'I'm sure they will.'

'Oh, no, they won't,' said Sera. 'D'you know how big India is? Endless forests and as many villages as – as the stars up there. God! We've lost her.'

Seeing Sera like that, Ruby began to tremble, and we went home to the sound of sniffles. The taxi-driver didn't say a word. When we arrived he refused to take a paise of his forty-rupee fare. 'Fate has robbed you of enough,' he said. 'Should I take away more from you?'

'The secret,' said Jeroo, smoothing her new red-and-yellow-printed sari as she sat down, 'lies in forgetting. Forgetting that I once had a daughter I loved, that she is now a prostitute who is raped day and night by fat men smelling of sweat, that she will die soon of a disease she catches from them and that I will not see my child again – in this life.' She smiled a smile that was

95

made of tears. Sera, Sam, Dolly, Ruby and I sat and listened to her as we did every evening.

'Swamiji says,' she went on, 'I must remember that my daughter was deaf and dumb – '

'She wasn't dumb,' I said.

Jeroo looked shocked, as if I'd ruined her spell. 'She was dumb,' she insisted. 'Only *we* could understand what she said. So she was dumb to the world. And, after I had gone, her life would have been a perfect misery. No money, no love; she would have felt like she is feeling now. So, nothing matters. What is, is. Swamiji said that.'

We looked at each other. 'I would like to have a television like yours,' she said brightly. 'I can't afford it, but . . .' She shut her eyes and began to pray, jabbing a finger at the TV with every breath.

'What are you doing?' cried Sera. 'Have you gone mad?'

'When I get a television, not just any, but a Japanese set, you'll know if I am mad or sane. Swamiji has given me very powerful mantras; they always work.'

'Then,' said Dolly, 'I can think of one way you can use them – '

'To find you a husband?' said Jeroo, smiling as if she weren't in the room.

'To find Tina.'

'I don't *want* to find Tina,' whispered Jeroo. 'She is not mine to find; she is not mine to love; she is not. What is not is not.'

I shivered. Jeroo got up and floated to the door. She opened the latch, stepped out, stepped back, put her right foot carefully over the threshold, moving her lips quickly, turned her head, smiled graciously and left.

'She's off her rocker,' said Sera firmly, as soon as we heard the latch click.

'Stark, raving mad – alas!' cried Dolly, her hand on her heart.

'So would you be if your worst fear came true,' said Sam.

'It's her fault,' said Sera. 'If she hadn't kept thinking of rape and things like that, they wouldn't have happened to her.'

'I think she's dealing with it pretty well,' I said. 'I mean, if something like that happened to Dolly, Sam would've died.'

'I would,' said Sam quietly.

'And it's all helping her, isn't it – the stuff the Swamiji tells her?'

'What is is. What is not is not – God! What bullshit,' said Ruby, shaking her head.

'Ruby!'

'I'm sorry,' said Ruby. 'I'm so used to talking like this with Brit.' My face turned hot as an April day.

'With Brit?' said Sera. 'Thank God he had the sense not to imitate you. What do your parents have to say about it?'

'My parents hardly ever see me,' said Ruby matter of factly.

'About Jeroo,' said Dolly, winking at me. 'I think what Swamiji says makes sense.'

'Of course it does,' said Sera. 'But we all know that what is is, and what is not is not.'

'But we don't believe it,' said Sam. 'Like I've never quite believed about Brit. I can't have a son who's a stunted cripple – '

'That will do, Sam,' said Sera, giving him the Hitler-eye.

'I can't quite believe Brit is the way he is. I keep thinking, I know it sounds stupid, but I keep thinking that one day the real Brit will jump out of his body; a Brit who's six feet tall with long legs that he swings in long strides.' Sam smiled a helpless smile.

'But,' I said, desperate to break the mood, 'that bit about getting things by chanting mantras is a bit thick. I mean, it's just false hope. Because it can't happen. And Jeroo never used to be so easily taken in.'

But there was Jeroo the next morning waving her brand-new TV licence over her head like an enemy's captured colours. 'It's very simple,' she said. 'My mantras worked on the minds of the judges.'

'What judges?' I said, my voice cracking as if I were thirteen again.

'The judges who judged this contest which I'd entered – write a slogan and win a television.'

'What was your slogan?' I demanded. I mean, here I was always writing these beautiful things in my head and now she had won a prize for writing on paper.

'Television every night, keeps your mornings gay and bright.'

I moaned. If she could win with a slogan like that, those mantras had to have something going for them. 'You didn't believe me, did you?' said Jeroo. 'Well, I'm flinging a challenge to all of you. Make a wish, however outrageous. Then repeat the mantra I give you one hundred and eight times – '

'Why a hundred and eight? Who not a hundred and seven?' I said.

'A hundred and eight completes one *mala*. You know what a *mala* is? It's a string of holy prayer beads.'

"Maybe I can get a shorter rosary.'

'You aren't taking this seriously, Brit, are you?' said Sera, her voice rising like a sports commentator's when the runners approach the finishing line.

'Of course not,' I sniggered.

'You complete one *mala* of this mantra,' said Jeroo, who had been scribbling for nine days. 'If it's a big wish, ninety days. Then tell me what happens. Now I must get home – haven't cooked a thing.'

'Hey!' I said. 'One more thing. Was that TV set Japanese?'

'Sony!' she said airily and was gone.

That settled it. I grabbed the little chit of paper and put it in my shirt pocket.

'Throw that into the wastepaper basket, Brit,' said Sera firmly.

'That's what I picked it up for.' I was going to use it to help me pass part one of the BA exams I'd taken a couple of months before, a year after I'd lost Tina and maybe a tanker-full of tears shed mostly in that wheelchair-sized bathroom. Well, I shouldn't have been surprised when I got my first exam-paper and thought it was someone else's, at least not when it went on happening right up to the fifth and last paper on the history of modern Europe. But I was shocked. Because it had never happened to me before. All those times I threw up and kept a gardenful of butterflies in my tummy, I knew I knew what I had to do.

Now with the results aiming at me like a rifle I knew I was headed for ATKT. Allowed to keep terms, while you mugged up all your last year's stuff and got a second chance in November. Saying you were an ATKT student was a bit like saying you were seeing a shrink – people stared while they waited to catch a glimpse of you pulling funny faces or walking on your hands down the street. What with the way I looked, I couldn't afford that.

Jeroo's mantra became for me what a marrow transplant is to a leukaemia patient. And I took it up as eagerly, rolling the eight magic words off my tongue one hundred and eight times. Of course, that took up quite a bit of my time, especially since I had to make sure no one, not even Dolly, knew what I was doing.

The exam results were no surprise. I didn't just squeeze through; I got a very respectable second. That made the mantra as precious a part of my life as jerking off. In fact they went together beautifully. When my jaws ached repeating the mantras, I turned to my cock; that made the pain disappear faster than aspirin.

I said mantras for a movie ticket when the board outside the theatre shouted 'House Full!'; when I wrote my first short story for the correspondence course magazine; when I desperately wanted David Reuben's *Everything You Wanted to Know About Sex* . . . but was afraid to ask for it.

Sometimes the mantra worked, sometimes it didn't. I couldn't ever admit it didn't, not if my head was being crushed under an elephant's foot. And I soon found out why it failed when it did. I didn't pronounce the words carefully enough sometimes and that's when I didn't get what I wanted. I began to mouth each word carefully, baring my teeth and stretching my lips. If I felt I'd gone wrong I said it again. Soon it began to cost me half an hour to complete a *mala* instead of the usual quarter.

And there were so many *malas* to finish before I could fall asleep having tied up all my fears securely for the night, One, so Sera wouldn't get breast cancer, another so Sam wouldn't drop dead of a heart attack, a third so Dolly would always remain a bachelor girl, yet another that someday I could make a living by writing, just one more to help me find True Love. This was apart from the urgent ones, like those movie tickets.

Poor Jeroo. She never knew her great triumph. 'Did it work?' she asked hopefully, nine days after she won that TV set.

'Of course not!' I said, shamelessly sitting on my happy results.

'And the sooner you give it up the better,' said Sera, wagging her finger at Jeroo.

'But at least you tried it, Brit,' said Jeroo, looking for a silver lining.

'Did you?' said Sera, her voice dangerous.

'No!' I said.

'Then why did you say it doesn't work?' said Jeroo indignantly. 'That's being unfair to Swamiji.'

'Tell your Swamiji to go suck an egg,' said Sera.

'Don't you dare say that!' gasped Jeroo. 'Swamiji is a pure vegetarian.' We roared; Jeroo looked surprised. That was when I knew she was really losing her marbles; when you stop finding yourself funny, you're finished.

One day, Sam caught me in the bedroom opening and shutting my mouth like a puppet. 'Tell me what's wrong, Brit,' he asked so gently I couldn't bear to disappoint him.

'It's just my jaw – it's hurting just here.' I chose a place.

'Maybe it's cracked,' he said. 'Let me get an appointment with the radiologist.'

'It *can't* have cracked,' I said quickly. 'My bones don't crack any more, remember?'

'That's what we say every time,' said Sam. 'Every time you are fine for more than six months. But it's never really over.' He kissed my head while his fingers tenderly moved over my 'fractured' jaw. He smiled a wan smile and said, 'Tell me if it's worse. Please. Will you?'

And I said, 'Promise.'

Another day, Jeroo came for our usual bridge evening looking distraught. 'Waste! Waste! Oh, the waste! I can't bear it,' she cried. 'Why couldn't he have told me earlier? Millions down the drain.'

'Your money?' asked Defarge, looking pleased. 'Have you lost it all?'

'So materialistic – this woman,' said Jeroo under her breath. Loudly she said, 'I'm talking about mantras. Swamiji told us today that all mantras said in the bathroom are as worthless as a botched up ballot paper. Those were his words. And,' her

100

voice broke, 'and I always said my mantras in the loo, most of them, I mean!'

You could've felled me with a house fly's wing. I was dismayed, devastated, destroyed and all the other words like that beginning with 'd'. If Jeroo had sent a million mantras down the drain, I had drowned a billion. I now knew what people felt when they said they'd lost everything in that fire or earthquake or whatever.

The bathroom became for me what Simla in summer was to the British. Sitting among the glazed tiles, watching the sunlight in the water pails rippling shadows on the white walls, I was a prince. My time was my own, and no mantra could claim me. I could shut my eyes and forget that such a thing as a mantra ever rolled on man's tongue, or that tonight I'd be awake long after the cats making noisy love in the street had fallen asleep, trying desperately to finish that last *mala*.

Part Two
Trying to Grow

12

'It was her eyes that did it,' said Defarge, twisting the end of her sari into little bandages around her fingers.

'I can't believe it,' whispered Sera, 'because I've always had such a strong mind, such *will*-power.'

'Yes, but we didn't know what she was trying. Otherwise,' said Defarge, lifting her head, 'even I wouldn't have been tricked. And this son of yours – what was he doing sitting like a statue?'

'Don't you blame him, Defarge. He warned us loud enough – my clever baby.'

God knows, I did. Of course, it was rationing that was the culprit. All of us got a ration of rice from the government shops, a quota of low-price, low-quality rice. 'Such as we wouldn't even feed our dogs,' Sera used to say. Everyone was on the look-out for the rice-ladies, tribals from Gujarat clad in blouseless saris, their heads crowned with sackfuls of long-grained rice that made every housewife reach for her purse.

That morning, one such raven-haired, green-eyed woman rang our doorbell. Defarge was at our place bursting with some news that she promptly forgot at the sight of the rice, white and thin like tiny needles. 'Look,' intoned the rice-woman, her voice deep as a man's, 'look at the rice in my hand and say how much you will buy.' They looked. Bending over her proffered hand they were bewitched by the rice-spell she had cast. 'How much will you take?' the woman purred.

'All, all,' they sighed languidly, 'every grain you have.'

'What about the price?' I shouted from my bedroom, interrupting a *mala* that I'd now have to start all over again. But

105

Defarge would normally ask for the price before she knew what was selling. This was very strange.

'What does it matter?' said Sera weakly. 'We want the rice.'

'At any cost,' giggled Defarge.

I wheeled myself to the drawing-room but I couldn't see the rice-lady; Sera and Defarge were in the way. They were counting the measures that she was pouring into Sera's giant rice-bin. 'Ten, eleven, twenty . . .'

'What are you doing?' I cried. 'What will we do with all that rice?'

'Eat it, silly boy!' giggled Defarge.

'That will be one hundred and fifty rupees,' throated the lady.

Sera got up to fetch the money. 'Don't worry,' said Defarge, tucking her hand inside her petticoat, producing two crisp notes from some concealed pocket. 'You can pay me back later.'

'OK!' said Sera cheerfully. 'And do give her a tip, dear Defarge.'

The moment the door shut on the rice-lady, the rice-spell cracked. And what a noise it made. 'Look at that,' said Defarge, going so pale you couldn't see where her face ended and her hair began.

'Come on!' said Sera indulgently. 'You've hidden it some-where.'

'Hidden rice? In my clothes?' said Defarge. 'Do you think I'm so dirty?'

'And anyway,' I said watching her big tummy, 'where's the room?'

'Where is the rice?' said Sera, ignoring me. 'I don't have it, you don't have it; the bin is almost empty.'

'Just a fistful of rice,' said Defarge, mournfully running it through her fingers.

'We've been cheated,' said Sera flatly. 'I'm phoning Sam at his office.'

'Is he going to chase the two-rupee harlot through the streets?'

'Don't use such language,' said Sera crossly. 'My child is here.'

'Child! Huh! Soon he'll be shaving and still you will call him baby, baby!'

'Do you think,' I said hastily, 'that the rice-lady was a hypnotist?'

'What's that?' said Defarge.

'Mesmeriser,' said Sera impatiently. 'That's right, Brit. It was the rice in her hand that did the trick.'

'Like Mandrake the Magician,' said Defarge, nodding.

'Not so benevolent,' said Sera.

'Oh, my!' Defarge began wailing. 'What will we do now? My hundred and fifty rupees.'

'Don't worry,' said Sera, putting an arm around her, which was easy since Defarge only came up to her shoulders. 'I'll pay you half like I was supposed to.'

Defarge threw her arm off. 'Why only half?' she said angrily. 'Have I got even a grain of rice that I should pay half? It was your house, your idea to buy the rice.'

'I like that!' said Sera. 'My house and my idea. Suppose the rice-bin were full of slender, fragrant grains, would it still be my house and my idea that counted? Would it? Answer me. Why are you silent, you sly cat?'

The doorbell rang. 'The rice-lady!' the quarrelling women gasped. 'I'll pay half,' said Defarge hastily.

I opened the door and smiled. Standing there was this six-feet-tall guy, about as young as I was, his sloping eyebrows knitted into the most comical, doleful look.

Defarge shrieked, 'Cyrus! I forgot! Forgive me! Sera, I came to tell you before that thief knocked at the door. Oh! I should've been home – you are early.' She embraced his waist with her fat brown arms. He patted the back of her white blouse abstractedly all the while staring at me over her head with a speculative eye. I turned my chair so he wouldn't be able to see my legs.

'Do I live here?' he asked gently.

'You live with me!' said Defarge proudly. 'Not here – there!' She pointed at her flat through our open door. 'This is Cyrus,' she said, 'my cousin-brother's son: he's come to stay with me. His father has been transferred to Delhi.'

'New Delhi,' I said.

'I say,' said Cyrus, suddenly crouching in front of me, 'could you lend me a large safety-pin?' His face was brown, not brown like Defarge who was born that way but the sort

107

of golden-brown that pale skins turn in the sun. 'It's my fly,' he said. His mouth drooped at the corners trying to resist a smile that would not quit.

'I think I can find one,' I said. 'You'll come in?'

He nodded and held the curtain open for me to wheel through. 'Phew!' he whistled. 'I'm glad Coomi didn't notice.' He pulled his thumb out of his waistband. It was red and creased.

'Who's Coomi?'

'My aunt.' He jerked his red thumb at the drawing-room.

'You mean Defarge's real name is Coomi?'

'You call her Defarge?'

'Everyone does.'

'Cy-coo,' cooed Defarge, 'have you brought an envelope from your pappa?'

'It's in my bag. I'll give you the money as soon as I unpack, Defarge.'

'Why're you calling me Defarge? Am I as beautiful as that French master-knitter?'

'Exactly the same,' said Cyrus, letting himself smile with every sturdy white tooth in his mouth. I saw my lantern-jawed grin in the mirror and turned it off.

'The pin,' he said, pleading with his eyebrows.

'Oh, yes! The pin.' I managed to drag out Dolly's massive dressing-table drawer. There was a twinkle of tiny pins but only one large one that Dolly used to keep her sari pleats in place. I picked it up and gave it to him.

'What are you two doing inside?' shouted Defarge. 'Come on, Cy-coo, I've made yum-yum *dhansak* and big-big kebabs for you.'

'Yuck-yuck,' said Cyrus through his teeth, forcing the pin through the thick blue denim of his jeans. He clicked it shut; we went out of the room. 'Thanks a lot,' he said. 'By the way, what's your name?'

'Uh-hm – Daryus.'

'We call him Brit,' said Defarge. 'Brit is short for his brittle bones. Poor, handicapped boy . . .'

'That's what you think, Defarge,' said Cyrus, smiling easily.

'At least,' Defarge went on, 'now he'll have a friend next door.'

That night I just didn't feel like making mantra *malas*. But I knew that would be like pulling out my finger from that hole in the dyke. So I broke out in a sweat though it was December and my room faced north. And like the hippie I'd once seen in a lane behind the Taj Mahal Hotel, injecting dope into his bloodless arm with a blood-encrusted needle, I began muttering.

The next morning I sort of hoped Cyrus would drop in. He didn't so I started a new *mala* to make him my friend.

That evening I was listening to *Saturday Date* on the radio when the doorbell clanged.

'Don't open it, pussy,' shouted Sera from her room down the passage. 'Must be a thief.'

'He wouldn't ring,' said Sam. 'It's probably Dolly.'

'Before midnight? Are you crazy?'

'Well, she's forgotten the latch-key; she's back early.'

'Don't be too sure. Brit! You wait near the phone to dial the police. I can't see you. Are you there?'

I unglued myself from the radio and took my post.

'I wish,' said Sera, 'I could come out and face him. But one of my nightie buttons is missing.'

'There's someone who says he knows you, Brit,' said Sam from the door.

I went out grinning. Then I thought of the crumpled cotton shirt and washed-out grey shorts I was wearing and I stopped grinning.

'Hi!' said Cyrus. 'We go for a walk?'

'Brit, it's late,' said Sam.

'Oh, that's my father,' I said, hoping he'd shut up. 'And this is Cyrus; he's staying with Defarge next door. I'll come,' I said.

'Brit, it's late,' said Sam. 'You've got to look after your health.'

'I'm fine,' I said. Sam nodded and left the room. I loved him. 'I'll – I'll just go and change,' I said.

'Change?' asked Cyrus, wrinkling his smooth straight nose. 'What for?'

'I can't go out like this – in shorts.' I had a thing about going out in shorts: people stared.

'What d'you think *I'm* wearing?'

'That's different,' I said, looking at his light-brown, muscled thighs.

'To hell with the difference,' he said. 'Why the fuck should you bother? Let's go.'

The fuck made up my mind for me. I snatched my latch-key; he took over my chair and began pushing. 'Where would you like to go?' he asked.

'Wherever,' I replied. I didn't know where you went for a walk around midnight.

'OK,' said Cyrus. 'We'll go to Apollo – have it all to ourselves, for once. Want a cigarette?'

'I wouldn't mind,' I said, sounding as casual as a chain-smoker.

'Light one for me,' I said, not too sure about which end I should set on fire.

How flimsy the little white stick felt in my fingers. I put it in my mouth and sucked like I imagined I would on Raquel Welch's nipple. Suddenly there was a gas chamber in my chest and the taste of burnt chicken in my mouth. For the first time in my life I saw stars.

'Breathe,' said Cyrus. 'Breathe deeply. Fucking shit! I didn't know this was your first time.'

I relaxed. My ribs were aching but not enough to go home. 'Now I know,' I said, 'why good Parsees don't smoke.'

Cyrus laughed, his teeth white in the night. 'Serves you right for fooling me,' he said. We raced through the shadowed streets. 'Whoo! this is like driving a Ferrari,' yelled Cyrus. 'Boy! Does your chair move!'

'It's Swiss,' I said. 'The one I use at home is Italian.'

'God! Don't tell me you're one of those – '

'What?'

'The kind who have Kraft cheese for breakfast, Plumrose sausages for lunch, whoop it up in their imitation Dior clothes, end the day on caviare and champagne – all imported, of course. They don't enjoy anything Indian.'

'I think that's the kind of life I'd like,' I said.

'You're a fool if you lean on that sort of thing to have fun. I'd choose a moonlit walk and good company over all the caviare in the world.'

'So would I!' I shouted.

'Good!' said Cyrus. 'How d'you like that whore?' I saw a small woman in a white dress: her face might have been Tina's.

'My cousin is one,' I said.

'Really? You mean for fun?'

'Not really,' I sighed.

'Tell me about her.'

I told him. It was the first time I'd told anyone.

'So that's that,' I said and turned to see if he was yawning. He was trying to erase a tear with the back of his hand. I didn't know what to do. 'It's not so bad for me any more,' I said.

He said, 'I suppose not. But it's worse than ever for her. You know what? My pals and I used to get this great kick, driving through the red light areas, laughing our heads off at the whores, and the men with their tongues hanging out. Can you imagine? I was laughing at someone like Tina . . . It embarrassed you that I cried, didn't it?'

'I shouldn't have seen you.'

'You mean grown men can cry as long as they aren't caught at it?'

'You've said it.'

'You're an ass. Grown men don't care who sees them cry. You ever cry at the movies?'

'No; I'm afraid I'll make too much noise.'

'So you blink and stretch your eyes wide open to make more room for the tears?'

'Ya,' I said. That's exactly what I did. 'But I cry,' I said, 'when I read poetry.'

'Poetry? What sort of a weirdo are you?'

'What!'

'Poetry is false, like a painted mouth.'

'False?' I squeaked. 'Are you crazy? It's like distilled water – the closest you ever come to purity.'

'You can't drink distilled water. You know what poets do? They drag their feelings up a hill and let go. What you read is the crash.'

'That's because they live on the mountain-tops. When you live at that altitude you're bound to have accidents.'

'You can't live on a peak; life is here on the plains.'

'So what are you studying?' I asked, feeling curious.

'Law; I'm going to be a solicitor.'

'And earn fat fees.'

'So what's wrong with earning?'

'I'm not going to earn much: I'm going to be a writer.'

'That's nothing to be proud of – not earning much, I mean. If you're going to write, you'd better plan to write well and become rich.'

'Struggling writer in a garret – it's an honourable life,' I said, as a sort of insurance, thinking of yellowed unpublished manuscripts.

'Nothing noble about being unsuccessful,' he said, shaking his head, and his silky hair went flip-flop. 'Just means you aren't good enough.'

'Mozart was poor; you can't say he wasn't good enough.'

'He lived in a world of feudal intrigues, not in Bombay today.'

'I guess it's no use arguing with you,' I said, thrilled with my defeat. I was tired of being the smartest kid around, especially when I knew I wasn't a genius. And Ruby and Tina and Dolly – I wouldn't have exchanged them for a new pair of legs, but I couldn't have talked to them like I'd talked to Cyrus who'd just out-talked me.

'What's the time?' he asked.

'A little past midnight,' I said, looking at the hands saying five to one.

'Shall we go home?'

'Whatever you like,' I said. 'Actually, you're the first person who's ever asked me. When I'm out with my parents or my sister or my friends they turn back when they want to.'

He chuckled. 'I might do that myself when our walks become a daily affair.' My heart jumped, as if I'd entered a bookshop.

'Why,' I said, breathing slowly, 'why did you stay on in Bombay? Didn't you want to go to New Delhi, be with your parents?'

'What sensible man would leave Bombay? You know what

New Delhi's like? It's monstrous. If you aren't a minister or a diplomat or a judge you're a ghost. Hell! You can be anyone in Bombay; as long as you've got brains and bluster, you've got it made. And then New Delhi's got the muddy Jamuna. Bombay's got the sea.'

'You like the sea?' I said, vaguely disappointed. 'I'm afraid of it; imagine getting lost in the endless grey.'

'Shall we try?' He laughed, swooping my chair through the break in the sea wall.

I screamed; I was sliding straight into the sea.

'Don't panic,' said Cyrus, his voice strong. 'There's a ramp here for people to walk on. It's cent per cent safe.'

'I don't believe in percentages; can we go back?'

'We're too far gone to turn,' he chuckled. 'Look! put on your brakes – we can sit here.'

'Here!' I squeaked. 'On the landing-stage for the boats?'

'Sure. And if we're lucky – '

A wave roared into my face, like a giant's sneeze. I howled, 'Save me – f-a-a-s-t!'

Cyrus sat cross-legged on the concrete, laughing, his shoulders moving up and down. 'You think you're going to drown? I said if we were lucky we'd get some sea-spray. That's what we're here for.'

'I haven't come here,' I said, trying to wipe my face with my handkerchief. A wave jumped and snatched it out of my hand. I had to laugh. 'D'you think it's OK to swallow this water?' I said, thinking of how Sera boiled and filtered our drinking supplies back home.

'Of course it's OK. It has all the shit and piss in Colaba pouring into it by the minute.'

I pretended to retch on him. 'I don't mind,' he said. 'Couldn't be much worse than this.' He got a smack from the sea in reply.

Riding my rocking-chair hard and crazy, I was thinking of all the things Cyrus and I would do. They included such improbables as comparing jerking-off techniques and taking a joint trip to the moon which I could see hard and bright as a gold sovereign above the sleeping Causeway.

For three hours that street where I lived was the Vatican and

113

I was the Pope. I surveyed it: Transport House from where the huge red buses lumbered out like blushing elephants every morning; Electric House where irate customers lined up to complain every time their electricity bills surprised them; and opposite me the giant cream archway to the Parsee Colony, whose red-tiled roofs shone in the moonlight – a whole town with its own fire-temple and shops and school and playing-fields where I would be living like most Parsees this end of town did, if my grandmother had not bought a love-nest for her British lover.

I scowled at the first milkman who stomped his heavy-footed way into my kingdom. If I had Swiss Guards I would've had him thrown out; but I didn't so I decided to go to bed. I discovered there was no way I could get into my wheelchair – it had rolled five feet away, further than my long arms could reach.

It didn't matter a blink. I rocked myself to sleep.

The next day, when Sam found me huddled in the rocking-chair, he carried me to my bed as fast as he could, before Sera had a scales-attack. I woke up grinning like Heathcliff. I'd missed a nightful of mantras and nothing had gone wrong.

13

I STOPPED READING poetry. There wasn't any point going crazy over beautiful stanzas if I couldn't share them with Cyrus. Five days later, I packed away my art books. I couldn't draw if you offered me a streak of grand slams at bridge but I loved pictures. And Sera and Sam had bought me shelves of books.

'After all,' Sam had once said, 'he never wears out his shoes.'

'Yes,' said Sera, 'he hardly ever outgrows his clothes. We might as well spend on dressing up his mind.'

So every time they saw a book on the Ajanta paintings or Raphael or Amrita Sher-Gil they plonked down the rupees and bought it for me; and I spent more hours with it than there were paise in the price. Cyrus couldn't tell Michelangelo from Modigliani, so I packed away all the artists who came before, in between and after into the top shelf of my book case in the drawing-room where they looked lovely and where I couldn't reach them.

Cyrus was mind-deep in politics and economics and, of all things, science. When he talked about swirling nebulae and black holes, cosmic rays and circuits complex as a man's brains, I listened like I used to listen to Dylan Thomas.

That was to come. That day I waited for the night. Defarge came to see us – she came for a cup of Nescafé every morning at eleven – and she couldn't talk of anything but Cyrus whose father paid her a thousand rupees every month to keep him in comfort. 'But I,' she cackled gleefully, 'can make three, four hundred profit from that.'

'That's what you think,' said Sera darkly. 'You don't know how much growing boys eat.'

'Neither do you,' said Defarge, looking meaningfully at me.

'I'm glad I don't,' said Sera. 'My Brit has never been a burden to me.'

'You are forgetting the doctor's bills,' said Defarge. 'It's a long time since your son has broken a leg.'

'Touch wood!' said Sera, hastily looking around for some, tapping her head as a last resort.

'The best thing is that Cyrus is out the whole day – I don't have to give him lunch or snacks in between. He comes home at nine o'clock, goes out all evening with his friends.'

That meant I had to wait till after dinner to see him. But after dinner I had a date with my mantras. The day before I'd forgotten to chant them. Today I had no excuse; and if I didn't say them today all the charms would break. Of that I was as certain as I was of being Sera's son. I didn't know what to do.

So I made two slips of paper, wrote 'C' on one and 'M' on the other, folded them identically and picked one. It said, 'M'. Whoever decides things this way is an ass, I decided. That was really the end for the mantra.

'I'm going next door,' I said, opening the door quietly. It was about ten at night.

'At this time?' shouted Sera. 'Nothing doing! Yesterday you managed to give me the slip but you're not going out tonight.'

'Dolly does – whenever she wants.'

'Dolly's different.'

'You don't have to remind me,' I said, hoping that would paralyse her.

'Oh, yes, I do,' said Sera. 'And don't you start pitying yourself. You're delicate, you've got to be careful.'

'I agree,' said Sam. 'You aren't as strong as Dolly is. You've got to try and understand. Remember I told you once life wasn't going to be easy?'

'You were talking about girls,' I wailed.

'Oh, God!' Sam whispered and I felt awful. He bent down and hugged me like a bandage to his wounds. 'Try to understand,' he said, stroking my hair.

'There's nothing wrong with me.' I was trying so hard not to cry I thought my teeth would break against each other. 'As long as I don't fall I'm safe. I'm not delicate at all, at at all.'

116

'I thought you were proud of your English,' smiled Sam.

'Let me go,' I whispered. 'I'll come back before midnight. I promise.'

'Let him go,' said Sam, looking at Sera.

'Just because . . .' she answered, her eyes angry.

'No,' said Sam. 'Not because — We live with that like we live with each other. It's something else.'

'What?' asked Sera slowly, worried I'd hear something I shouldn't.

'We must let him go, darling. We're so scared for him we're shutting out his air and light. School, college, friends, picnics. He's hardly had any of those. Think what we got out of it all when we were his age.'

'Nonsense!' said Sera loudly. 'He has so much we didn't. Books and music, and we didn't play bridge when we were teenagers.'

'It's not the same, darling. Books and bridge aren't people.'

'Why are you doing this,' she said, 'making him discontented? Teach him to be happy with what he's got.'

'That doesn't mean he doesn't want more. Let him go, and to hell with his legs.'

'And when he's laid up in plaster like a mummy, are you going to look after him?' she said, muffling the last words with a hand to her mouth.

'I know it's been tough for you, my love. More than for any of us. But d'you remember that morning he was born? How brave you were? You said he was going to grow up like any other boy.'

'I wonder what I'll cook tomorrow,' said Sera. 'I've told the butcher to get me some chops — maybe I'll roast them.' She walked away slowly to her bedroom, old as her fifty-nine years.

Sam smiled his rueful smile. 'Off with you,' he said. 'It's not much longer till midnight.'

I crossed the lobby and rang the bell, stretching my arm to reach it. Defarge opened the door. 'Cy-Cy-Cyrus? Is he there?'

'He's busy,' said Defarge, touching her scarf to say she was praying and wouldn't talk any more. Defarge at the end of the rainbow was too much to take. I wanted to scream so loud it would shatter the half-moon reading spectacles on her Parsee nose. Instead I gasped. Behind Defarge, Cyrus was making funny faces. He was naked as low as I could see. Defarge saw me grinning and turned her head. 'Oh, my!' she said, clutching the end of her sari to her face; I knew the georgetta was transparent. She stood there sucking in Cyrus's biceps, smooth like a statue's, his wide chest silky with hair and the nipples large and crimson. I followed her eyes through the makeshift veil as they made their way down Cyrus's tanned tummy, flat and sinewy, to his blue jockey-underpants, which seemed a size too small for his cock which curved between his thighs, shadowy with small dark curls.

'I'm glad you came,' said Cyrus. 'Mind if we sit and listen to music? I'm too pooped to walk.'

'Perfect,' I said sincerely.

Defarge tore her eyes away. 'Get dressed,' she said.

'I am dressed, Defarge. This is how I sleep every night.'

'I see,' she said, nodding understandingly and patting his head, letting a little finger wander to his neck.

'Hey! You're tickling me,' said Cyrus, ducking.

Defarge laughed flirtatiously, swishing her sari. 'Good night, boys!' she sang, and left.

'D'you think she has the hots for me?' whispered Cyrus, and I laughed so loud he had to jump up and shut the drawing-room door. He slipped a cassette into a gleaming tape machine and switched off the lights. His body vanished and a Chopin waltz took over.

'Gorgeous,' I breathed.

'Shsh! You don't talk when Chopin's talking.'

'Oh!' At home we talked through Chopin, Mozart and everyone else. Sera even sang along. I shut my eyes.

When the tape clicked he jumped up and slipped another one in. Sounds twanged out, groaning and creaking and wailing. 'My God!' I moaned. 'What's this rubbish?'

'Rubbish? You crazy or something? You know who's playing?'

'I don't care. I never listen to Indian classical stuff. Makes me want to puke.'

'Go ahead; you know where the bathroom is. By the way, that's Ravi Shankar.'

'Oh!' I paused, thinking of the blonde lovelies from London and Paris and Washington DC who screamed in ecstasy every time they heard Shankar's sitar. 'Giving it a fair chance,' I said, 'it does sound beautiful.'

'Really?' Cyrus's voice grinned in the dark.

'No, I said that because I felt like an ass wanting to puke at Shankar.'

'If nothing else,' he said, 'your books will be remembered for their startling honesty.'

'It's midnight,' I said. 'I've got to go.' He opened his mouth. 'No,' I said, 'don't say Cinderella.'

He came closer and stood next to me smelling of Pears soap. I looked at his dark thighs and thought of Wagh Baba. He sat down cross-legged on the floor in front me so, so close I could see a tiny pimple below his left nostril. 'Don't go now,' he said. 'We'll listen to Mozart.'

'I've promised,' I said. I told him why I'd promised.

'OK,' he said, pulling his lower lip into his mouth. 'I'll take you home.'

We crossed the lobby. The moon held him in a spotlight.

'You look like you're made of gold,' I said.

He struck a pose. 'There's a statue like that somewhere, isn't there?'

'Michelangelo's David,' I said.

He laughed and turned away, throwing a whistle over his shoulder.

I didn't reply; I was watching the muscled hollow of his spine.

A couple of nights later Cyrus had gone to a party and I was lying in bed with nothing to do but jerk-off. Minutes of heavy breathing later, I realised something funny. I wasn't watching Marilyn Monroe surge and shudder. I was staring at a man, his mouth hungry and gasping, nostrils dilated like a dancer's, a tiny pimple staring back at me. I'd never come with such a bang.

Then it all happened like Barbara Cartland says it does. I

woke up, saw a triangular cone of blue sky and watched it shimmer like the surface of an enamel vase. I took a bath and the water felt like satin on my skin. The toast I ate for breakfast melted in my mouth; the words of the newspaper sang to my eyes. I breathed mentholated oxygen.

I waited for Sera to go shopping, then I shouted, not squeaked or squawked, but roared from deep inside the cave my pigeon-chest made, 'This is love! The divine love!'

It might sound like lust, but lust is as much part of love as cream is of milk. A square inch of Cyrus was enough for me – an earlobe that curved towards his cheek, a finger of hair that tickled his neck, the white underside of his arm when he lifted it, chapped lips, the bend of his waist, the nostrils that flared when he laughed . . .

We became partners in what Cyrus called 'the serious business of living'. We took in every play that hit the boards, laughing our-selves breathless at the pseudo-Yankee accents of a misplanted Broadway comedy, sniffing and blinking when Anne Frank, writing her diary by lamplight, said, 'I want to live even after I'm dead.' We went to concerts and took bets on whether the audience would applaud between the movements.

We ate out; one evening at the Rooftop Rendezvous, the swankiest restaurant in the Taj. Walls of glass, the city and the harbour glistening at our feet like a movie-shot. 'So romantic,' said Cyrus. 'And here I am – '

'Stuck with me.'

He laughed. 'Oh, well, you're better company than a gaggle of girls.'

'And boys?'

'Oh! Definitely. Men . . .' He grimaced. 'Most men can't talk about anything but their last fuck or the next smoke. Girls, they're fine, but as soon as you're alone with them, they touch their hair and simper and say, "Tell me something nice."'

'And you do.'

'Sometimes,' he grinned. 'You're different, Brit. You can talk about more than Screwdrivers and who's an easy lay. Talking to you is like talking to a very intelligent woman.'

'Thanks very much.'

He brushed the hair out of his eyes with the back of his hand. 'I'm not the wordsmith, you know that.'

'Stop acting and say what you meant.'

'Come on! You know you don't think or talk like most men do.'

'Depends on the men you choose.'

'OK, but you've got your eyeballs trained on different things. You notice stuff I wouldn't.'

'Like?'

'Like I see a girl and think she's stacked, has the face of an angel. You see her and think she's lovely but cold, maybe because she's scared guys want her for her boobs – you understand?'

'What's that got to do with talking like a woman?'

'That's how women think. They never see an envelope without wondering what's inside. You do that too, right?'

I nodded stiffly.

'God! I don't mean you're a fairy or something.'

'I should think not.' I took a deep breath and rumbled out a manly laugh hoping that my blush, hotter than the Charlemagne Châteaubriand in my plate, was invisible by candlelight.

In May Cyrus took his first-year law exams, and I sat my last BA papers at the same time. We used to study together for a week or so, until I realised all I was learning was the shape of his head. (I sat behind him so we wouldn't be tempted to talk.) Now I finished my portion for the day earlier and spent the time till midnight with a book, thirstily watching the sweat-drops on Cyrus's tensed neck muscles.

'We'll go to the Cricket Club for a swim after the exams,' said Cyrus one evening.

'I won't swim,' I said.

'I'll teach you, Brit. You'll be able to. I'm sure.'

'That's not the point.' The blush was gone. 'I . . . I can't . . . I can't share a pool with so many people – it's filthy.'

'Fucking shit! The water's purified and everyone takes a shower before, even after.'

'I don't think that's enough. Now, if I had a pool to myself . . .'

121

'You're mad.'

I smiled. 'I think it's time you returned to the Indian Contract Act.'

'God! It's midnight. I'd better get going before Sera roars out.'

I nodded. 'See you tomorrow.' The door shut and I threw my arms over my head with relief. It was ridiculous, but it was the only thing I could think of. I was sure he didn't believe me: no one would.

I couldn't tell him the truth. I couldn't say, Look, Cyrus. Look at my body. Picture it in nothing but swimming trunks – osteo-warped.

I fought myself all night and the next evening I agreed to swim once the exams were over.

There, in the changing rooms, Cyrus took off his clothes with the speed of an anxious bather when the tap is running dry. I watched and smiled and smiled.

'What are you smiling at?'

'I was thinking.'

'Of?'

'Of how quickly it's grown.'

'Brit! Are you being funny?' Cyrus looked down at his big dark cock, swinging in a devilishly languid arc.

'I didn't,' I gasped, 'mean that. I was talking about our friendship.'

'Oh! That! God! I'm crazy to think what I did. I'm afraid I'm getting a bit of a complex about this.' He pointed downwards.

'You should be glad. It's a huge turn-on – for the ladies.'

'Which one are you, Masters or Johnson? I keep forgetting who's the man.'

'To complain about a thing like that!' I said, dying to continue the conversation.

'It's embarrassing,' he said, shaking his wet head. 'People think you've got a perpetual hard-on.'

'That would be gigantic,' I said.

'It isn't, I assure you,' he laughed.

'Don't pretend.'

'OK. See for yourself.' I didn't know what to do. Because watching him grow like the magic beanstalk was making me do the same. I turned my chair around, ever so slowly, until my back was turned to him. 'Saw that?' he said. 'If you call that gigantic, you've never seen a blue movie.'

'I haven't.' Was he tall enough to see me over the chair's back? I was shivering so much, I was terrified I'd dislocate a joint.

'Now to get it down,' he said, and I knew I was going to get a stroke. He turned around and I came in a mushroom cloud of semen. The first atomic orgasm in history, I thought, and no one to record it. That made me laugh so much. I went down quicker than ever before so that, when Cyrus turned with his black trunks on, I smiled, serene as a celibate.

When we went to the pool and he lifted me gently into the shock-cold water, I stifled a squeak and looked round. There were half a dozen people sitting under flowering yellow sun-umbrellas. But I couldn't see if they were watching me. I'd known I was short-sighted for a long time, because I could never read the Censor Board's certificate that flashed on the movie screen before every trailer and film – Dolly had to tell me what I was going to see next. I didn't want specs because they'd hide my eyelashes which were the better part of my face. I'd kept my secret and now it was paying off a bonus. I paddled in bliss and the whole of Bombay could have stared for all I cared.

My glee wasn't a day old when Sera smashed it. 'Brit,' she said, mopping the dining table after breakfast, 'last night I heard you and Cyrus talking about a telescope.'

'Ya. We're going to make one and share the cost.'

'What's the use, Brit? You won't be able to see anything through it.'

'Why ever not?'

'You squint at the calendar on the kitchen wall, you hold the book you're reading six inches away, you stare through people you meet in the Causeway and you're trying to fool me that you can see fine?'

'Well, maybe not so fine. But I bet I'll be able to see the moon through a telescope.' I laughed and wheeled off to my room.

'Not so fast, Brit,' said Sera, her voice glinty as the chromium on my wheelchair. 'You're going to see an oculist today. Did you hear me?'

'Yes, Sera. Fucking shit,' I added softly.

I went with Sam. The oculist was a funny, jerky little man with a grin full of plastic teeth. 'Oh, my!' he said, shining a light in my eye. 'Blue sclerae, how pretty! Now what do blue sclerae indicate?'

'*Osteogenesis imperfecta*,' I said helpfully.

'Oh! Yes, yes, yes!' He giggled. 'It's been forty years since medical college. I forget things. Well, do you want to hide that lovely blue and those long eyelashes with which you must be winking at all the girls under thick glasses?'

'No! Of course not.'

'Then contact lenses are the answer,' he said, sounding so much like the commercials on TV that Sam automatically replied, 'No, that's out of the question for him. Cleaning and all that wouldn't be easy.'

'Very well, then,' said the oculist, straightening up.

I read the chart, the few lines that I could. 'Minus six,' said the oculist, twitching out for a pen.

'Six!' said Sam. 'It can't be. This is his first pair.'

'But it is, it is,' said the oculist gleefully. 'A rather thick pair of glasses. Since contact lenses are out – '

'And so is blackmail,' I shouted.

The oculist glared at me, his mouth doing a jig. 'I know why you are this way,' he said, his eyes joining the dance. 'You are a wicked boy and God has punished you.'

'Balls!' I hit him in his blinking eye. 'God is dead, or haven't you heard?' Then I saw Sam's face, white as cottage cheese, and thought he'd have a heart attack; I'd be stuck with this puppet till Dolly or someone arrived. I shut up.

'You mustn't get so aggressive,' said Sam in the taxi home. 'I know it was awful of the doctor to talk like that but *you* were rude first.'

'I wanted to be.'

'Oh, dear. But that's never any use, is it?'

'It is. Makes me feel better.'

'You need to be rude to people to feel good about yourself?'

'Of course not,' I said impatiently. 'But when someone's trying to make you feel rotten and you give it back to him, you feel good.'

124

'You shouldn't care. It doesn't really matter what people say when they're cross.'

'It does to me.'

'I say,' said Sam, 'when are you going to start writing? I mean, really writing every day for six hours like a professional.'

'Writing? Who said I was going to write? It's a lousy profession – you don't make any money.'

'We don't expect you to.'

'That's terrible,' I shouted. The taxi-driver turned to smile indulgently. 'Why don't you expect me to earn? That's unfair!'

'Unfair?' said Sam. 'I thought it was rather fair not to make demands on you. Considering we didn't make you right.'

'I'm right to myself,' I shouted. 'And it's awful of you to go on thinking I'm not. How would you have felt if Sera had said to you when you got married, Darling, I don't expect you to earn a living? You would have felt terrible, as if you – you – you – '

'Yes?'

'As if you had no business being alive.'

Sam sat with his head thrown back against the seat. His eyebrows trudged into his forehead and his eyes tried to focus on something. 'I'm sorry,' he said. 'It's been so difficult. Trying to know what we should do. You don't know what it was like, Brit, when you were born.'

'Tough, very tough,' I said, wishing I hadn't started all this.

'Not tough. Just strange. So unimaginable – '

'You had to grope your way forward.'

'Yes. And every time we stumbled we kicked you.'

'You didn't. Or I wouldn't have turned out so well.' I winked.

Sam put his hand on my head. 'I love you,' he said, his throat hardly bobbing. I wanted to say, Same to you, but I thought he'd feel I was poking fun.

In the lift, he asked me, 'So what's going to take the place of writing?'

'Law,' I said. 'I'll probably be a solicitor, which means I can work from an office.'

'What made you choose law?'

'I don't know,' I said, so quickly he probably knew I didn't want to tell him.

'He says he wants to read law,' he yelled as soon as he heard Sera singing 'This is the Army, Mr Jones' in the kitchen.

'Who says?'

'Brit, darling; who else?'

'Brit wants to study law?' Sera came out, her hands dripping from the tap. 'You mean you want to become a lawyer?'

'A solicitor, he says!' Sam was trying to divert the oncoming storm away from his head.

Suddenly my face and neck and hair were wet, though not with water, as Sera hugged me, crying, 'Oh, Brit, lovey, darling, sweetie – '

I put my arms around her neck and squeezed as tight as I could. For once, I knew she was glad to have me.

'Let's celebrate,' said Sera, her face glistening.

'Oh, yes!' said Sam, 'and we can call over the boy next door. He's been taking Brit out almost every day.'

'So what? He's my friend.'

'His name is Cyrus. You aren't going to call him the boy next door, Sam – Cyrus. Remember, Cyrus.'

'Don't worry,' said Sam, chucking my chin. 'I won't embarrass you. Don't you think we should call Ruby, too?'

'No,' I said. I knew what a pretty girl would do to Cyrus – take his mind right off me.

'Of course we should,' said Sera. 'Supose she comes over and finds out we haven't asked her, how bad it will look!'

'How awful she'll feel,' said Sam.

14

Ruby came first. 'You devil, you serpent, Brit. It's taken you six months to introduce me to your dishy friend. I could kill you – '

'He wants to keep him for himself,' said Dolly, who was home early for once. 'Don't you know he's gay?' I felt my ears redden though I knew she was joking.

'I've always suspected that,' laughed Ruby, looking so sensual in the sheer pink dress that licked her body, I felt a huge thrust of lust.

Cyrus came, looking sleek as a fox, his eyes long-lashed. He was laughing. 'To my colleague at the bar,' he said, giving me a box of chocolates, so heavy my hands fell to my lap.

'Swiss!' said Dolly, relieving me of the chocolates. 'Where did you get these?'

'I made them,' said Cyrus with a grin, 'and put them in the box.'

'You mean you can cook?' said Ruby, looking at him as if he were the Prophet Zoroaster himself.

'Oh! Just a little – chocolates, cakes, stuff like that.'

'You must teach me,' said Dolly. 'My cooking's hopeless. Sera says my husband will starve to death.'

Cyrus cocked his head. 'That would be a bit hard, wouldn't it? With someone who looks like you.'

I hooted. Dolly smoothed her black velvet dress over her knees and smiled. She was almost thirty but she didn't look any less lovely than Ruby.

Sera and Sam made their grand entrance, arm in arm. 'So glad you could come,' they said, ending in perfect unison.

'So glad to be here,' said Ruby and Cyrus together.

'Make a wish,' said Ruby, 'quick! Or the magic goes. You did? OK.' She stood up and kissed Cyrus on his left cheek. 'Do the same to me – Oh, quickly!' Cyrus rubbed his nose and kissed her behind her right ear, making her glow like an apple.

'Ruby, you're marvellously inventive,' I said. She put a hand on my neck, smiled sweetly and pinched me hard.

'Aren't you going to offer us those chocolates, Brit?' said Sera.

'Have one, do.'

'Like a dream,' breathed Ruby.

'Cyrus or the chocolates?' I asked.

'Shut up,' said Cyrus. Which was about the last thing he said to me for the rest of the evening. He was too busy with the three ladies. Reminded me of those Russian chess players who play any number of games simultaneously.

Sera almost beat Ruby in her enthusiasm. 'Cyrus, have some more *patrani machchi*. You said you liked it.'

'I think I will, thank you.'

'Wait a moment!' Sera unrolled the steaming fish from the plantain leaf in which it was cooked. 'There! Whenever Defarge starves you, come straight over. The way Brit eats, there's always enough for a guest.'

'You too, Ruby,' said Sam. 'You're always welcome.'

'And have been for the last twenty years,' giggled Ruby.

Dolly was strangely quiet. I made a face at her, rolling my eyes in Cyrus's direction, but she smiled and shook her head.

'There's one last bit of chocolate mousse,' said Sera, 'and it's for our chocolate prince.' She plopped it into Cyrus's plate.

'You know what, Sera?' said Cyrus. 'If I were you, I'd stop cooking for them and join the Taj as chief chef.'

Sera tucked her hair behind her ears, tilted her head and smiled wistfully at Cyrus. I wondered if she was thinking how grand it would be if he were her son.

Cyrus was looking around a bit desperately. He caught my eye and held a cigarette made of air between his fingers. I nodded. 'D'you think I might have a smoke?' he said, looking so lost I wanted to lunge over the forks, glasses, spoons and napkins and slip a cigarette between his drooping lips.

128

'You don't have to ask,' said Sera gaily. 'In fact, I think I'll have one too.'

'Darling!'

'Sam, you don't know this but I used to smoke when I was at college. Don't look so shocked. That was thirty – '

'Forty,' said Dolly cruelly.

'Years ago,' finished Sera.

'The things you discover,' said Sam to Cyrus, who nodded, smiling distractedly, puffing at his Triple Five. Poor Sam, I thought, bumped into the same boat as me.

'But I warn you,' said Sera, 'if you make my Brit a smoker, I'll never make *patrani machchi* for you again. Keep Brit away from cigarettes.'

'And girls,' said Dolly, perking up.

'You don't have to bother about that,' said Ruby, 'he prefers boys.'

'Oh, my God!' said Cyrus, rolling his eyes into his brows. 'Why didn't you tell me earlier? Sorry, Brit, I'm just not inclined.'

Sam coughed. I wanted to wax Ruby's silky brown waves off her scalp. The embarrassment was OK: what I couldn't take was the way Cyrus had buried my hopes, without a moment's thought. 'I'm just not inclined!' What sort of funeral oration was that? Now, if he'd said I'd love to, but –

'I think,' said Sam, 'Brit has had a tiring day.'

'Hint! Hint!' cried Ruby.

Sam smiled and stood up. 'Actually, I'm the one who's tired. You youngsters can carry on. Good night!'

'Good night!' said Sera, ever loyal. She went to the window where Cyrus was sending smoke rings into the Causeway. 'Thank you, Cyrus,' she said.

'Oh! That's nothing. I'll make you another batch – with brandy.'

'Thank you,' said Sera. 'But I wasn't talking about the chocolates. It's nice of you to be Brit's friend.'

'The pleasure's mine,' said Cyrus, bowing over her extended hand.

'Yes,' said Sam, 'till you came along Brit didn't have a single friend.'

'I like that!' said Ruby.

'I was talking about boys. Before you all his friends were girls – '

'Lucky guy,' said Cyrus, sucking in his cheeks.

'I'd better be going,' said Ruby. 'My parents are home tonight – for once.'

'You mean you normally have your place to yourself?' asked Cyrus.

'Ya,' said Ruby sadly. 'It gets awfully lonely. I mean, how many mags can you read? How many tapes can you hear? How many day-dreams can you dream?' Which was about as big a lie as Santa Claus because Ruby was hardly ever home. 'I say,' she went on, 'why don't you come down and see me some time?'

I roared. 'Mae West redux!'

'He's crazy,' said Ruby, drawing circles at her curl-obscured temple.

'I absolutely agree,' said Cyrus, trying not to smile.

'Tell Brit to bring you over some time,' said Ruby, shutting the door.

'Who needs Brit?' said Cyrus through the closing door.

Ruby tossed her most ravishing smile, white and pink, over her shoulder and left.

'Good night,' said Dolly. 'If I weren't dead beat – '

'Dead beat?' I said, wrinkling my nose. 'Where did you pick that up?' I was surprised to see her blush for the first time in her life – or at least in mine.

'He's such a – ' Cyrus shook his head. 'Embarrassing you like that.' Dolly smiled like a beauty and walked away.

'I wonder why she blushed,' I murmured.

'What a stupid question; obviously it's familial. And by the way, I'm sorry.'

'What for?'

'For ignoring you all evening. But you know – you're like – like a brother, I suppose, and when there are people around you don't spend all your time with your brother.'

'I know.' I felt as gracious as the Nizam with a courtier. 'And you don't ever have to be sorry with me. Because I – '
The breath went out of me.

'Yes?'

'I guess I love you.'

'You know, one of the best things about you – or at least what I like best – is that you always say what you feel. Even when it's not easy. That's something I can never do. Never.'

'But, why?'

'Perhaps it's got something to do with the kind of families we've got. You know how envious I felt – '

'Of whom?'

'You, dummy. Oh! I know you consider yourself quite unenviable – '

'I don't, other people do.'

'I don't. You know why? Because you've got Sera and Sam and such a lot of noise and giggles and fights.'

'That's how it always is at home.'

'Not at mine. You must remember I come from an aristo family – at least my mother does. When we want to say something to each other we make an appointment in the morning. Will you be free for a little while after dinner?'

I laughed and braked. 'You're serious?'

'Yes!'

'But that's abnormal.'

'Not for my family.'

'But why? Can't you change things?'

'I'm not sure I want to – any more. Brit, why the sudden taste for law?'

I had rehearsed this exactly sixteen times. 'Law's going to let me roll in rupees.'

'If you wanted to write, you must have had something to say. What happens to all that?'

'I leave it unsaid.'

'What if you choke on unsaid words?'

'You sound like a play.'

'But it might be true.'

'I don't care. Because I'm happy. Sam's delighted. Sera's delirious.'

'That's something else I envy you for. When I told my parents I wanted to read law – '

'What happened?'

'My mother fell ill. She missed three mah-jong evenings in a

131

row, not to mention a charity première – I even remember the film, *Chariots of Fire*.'

'But I thought law was a good solid profession.'

'Are you mad? When her son could've been a concert violinist?'

'What!'

'My *dark secret*.'

Cyrus grinned but his eyes didn't join in. 'Why am I talking like this? God – it's all dead.'

'Never mind. I'd like to know.'

'I was pretty good at the violin. I used to spend every moment I could snatch from homework and school practising. And I was taking exams – you know, the usual Royal Academy ones. And in my last year I won a gold medal.'

'You were the best student.'

He sighed. 'Explicit language! Anyway, I won a scholarship to the Menuhin School in London.'

'My God! And you threw that over? If I were your mother I would never have played mah-jong again in my life.'

'I didn't throw it over; I thought fighting cases would satisfy my brain more than making music. It sounds insensitive but that's how I felt.'

'Didn't you adore your music?'

'I did. But it wasn't enough. It was an unhealthy kind of passion.'

'Music? Unhealthy?'

'Sure. I was using it to push away everyone, to drown the anger, you know – that's no good. It's like building up your body at the cost of your brain.'

'What?'

'I don't mean that, but something similar – I might have been a fantastic violinist on stage and a crackpot off it. That wasn't the kind of person I wanted to be.'

'You mean you had to put away your violin if you were going to grow.'

'That's about the closest anyone has come to understanding what I felt.'

So this, I thought, sitting in the centre of my mind's polished stage, is what a writer means when he writes, '. . . and I thought my heart was going to burst'. But I said, 'Did you explain things so clearly to your mother?'

'What did she care? She lost the best piece in her show-case.'

'Don't sound so bitter, Cy,' I said, manoeuvring my chair next to the end of the sofa where he was sitting, patting the back of his head, trying to keep things as brotherly as I could. His hair was like soft warm air in my fingers.

'Don't call me Cy,' he said. 'That's what my mother calls me in front of other people – she thinks it sounds English or American or whatever. "Cy, why don't you play something for Lady Manekbai?" Can you believe there are still people who call themselves Lady or Sir?'

'Well, they can't help it if they're titled,' I said, trying to concentrate on his words instead of the tensed muscle and smooth skin under my fingers.

'Fucking shit! They can fling back their titles from where they came – Rabindranath Tagore did it. And the worst thing was I knew what they liked so I'd play a Kreisler trifle and Lady Manekbai would say, "How pretty! But far too short, Cy. Give us something long and brilliant." So I'd start on something like Bach's E major *Partita*. Soon as the first few bars were over they'd settle down to a disgusting conversation about whether you got a better steak at the Taj or the Oberoi, and how their hairstylist was getting quite unreasonable – what if she'd worked with Sassoon – sixty rupees for a cut was daylight robbery.' He relaxed; the muscle under my hand disappeared. He smiled ruefully. 'What a long story.'

'Thank you for telling me.'

He shrugged and swallowed. Then he said, 'It's so crazy Sera and your father and you all thanking me like this. And all along, I've been so glad you became my friend.' He put his hand on my shoulder, almost touching my right cheek. I could see the fine hair on his wrist swaying under my breath like wheat in a field. He stood up. 'See you tomorrow. Will you come over? We'll make the telescope.'

'Oh, yes! That would be great.'

'Bye – and thanks for the neck massage.' He shut the door and I didn't know what to do. I wheeled over to the door and kissed the grainy, polished board. I heard his door shut behind him. Just a gender away.

I wanted Cyrus: his mocking mouth, his quiet eyes, his thighs and hair and cock. Now, if he were someone else, someone who thought life was the food you ate and the movies you saw and not the winds that blew inside your head; or someone who got out of a taxi without thanking the driver; or someone who blew his nose into his hand instead of his hanky, then I wouldn't have given a damn if he looked like Shashi Kapoor or Sean Connery or whoever; not if he had a cock that would've made him a blue movie star.

What if it were the other way around? If he were as perfect as he seemed to me but he looked like Walter Matthau? I wanted to believe it wouldn't matter a thought. But that wasn't true. Because I thought about it for a million minutes and this was what I was sure of – I just didn't know.

15

'TELL HER,' HISSED Sera, 'not to phone before eight. I'm crying with the onions, Dolly's in the shower, Sam's out walking God knows where, and you're still snoozing.'

I put a finger on my lips, took the receiver from her and said, 'Hi!'

'It's eight o'clock,' said Ruby, 'and you still haven't brushed your teeth?'

'How d'you know?'

'I can hear your sleepy tongue. Listen, is it OK if I come over tonight, after dinner?'

'No, it isn't – because Cyrus and I are making a telescope.'

'I'll help.'

'You can't.'

'Don't be mean. I'm crazy about that guy. You know how it feels to be crazy about him?'

'No.'

'Say yes, Brit. Can I come?'

'Look,' I said, turning round to see if Sera was about, 'if you play with Cyrus, you're going to be a fallen woman.'

'If he does the pushing, I'd like nothing better.'

'Don't be a fool. Sex is just a game to him,' I said, feeling like Mrs Danvers in *Rebecca*.

'I don't care. I want that man. Oooh! Brit!'

'Go ahead and see him. But not in my time; not after dinner.'

'OK, you gay rascal.' And she was off hooting like she was on laughing-gas. I put the receiver down and waited for the red tide to recede from my cheeks.

Making the telescope was great fun, though we had different ideas about how to use it. 'Let's get it to the window!' I squawked, as soon as the cardboard tubes and lenses were fitted together. 'There's a full moon tonight.'

'So?' said Cyrus. 'You want to watch the man in the moon?'

'Don't be silly – the craters, of course.'

'My dear boy! How much you have to learn.' Cyrus smiled, half shutting his eyes.

'Come on.' He carried off the telescope and I went chasing after him right into the bathroom.

'What are you doing?'

'Shush! You'll wake Defarge.' He trained the telescope at the building opposite. 'See that flat there, on the third floor?'

I stood up with my hands on my chair. 'That's someone's kitchen,' I said with disgust. 'You want to see pots and pans?'

'I guess you could say that,' he chuckled. 'Look! Wait, I'll bring it down. Now shut one eye and look.'

I looked. The square of light was as close as the room I was sitting in. Through the windows I saw a young girl with long black hair unwind her orange sari. She wore nothing underneath. Her breasts, brown and large as coconuts, jiggled as she bent down to undo the sari from between her legs which were as long as Betty Grable's in Sera's scrapbooks. She began to pour water over herself, making her skin glisten.

'My turn now,' said Cyrus. 'I've waited six months for this.'

'You mean you used to watch every day?'

'Hardly, considering I was with you most nights. And anyway it wasn't much fun without the tel.'

'D'you think we should?'

'She obviously doesn't mind.'

'She's the *bai*. She can't demand curtains from her mistress.'

'Shush. You're spoiling the erotic ambience.' Cyrus laughed from somewhere between his legs. As usual, he wasn't wearing much. Just a pair of red jockey underpants. I could see the back of his thighs, black curls on cream skin like barbed wire on snow. His hips were small, tightly held in the scarlet nylon. I stared, feeling quite safe; Cyrus wasn't going to turn around till that girl had had her bath.

'Want to look?' he asked.

'No; I wouldn't dream of spoiling your fun.'

'OK. Tomorrow you can have her all to yourself.'

136

'Yes,' I said faintly. I had just spotted the tip of his cock like an arrowhead between his thighs. My hand reached out like a mechanical arm to make its way through his legs. Cyrus stepped back, caught his foot in the front wheel of my chair and staggered so I knew he was going to crash down on me smashing every bone to talcum texture. I screamed, Cyrus let go of the telescope which smashed with a thud in the courtyard below while he landed on my chest, barely managing to avoid my legs. There I was, my mouth on his bare shoulder, his whole warm weight against me, and for all I cared he could have been a sack of onions. He got off my chair; I stayed still as a statue.

'Brit. What's wrong? Can't you move?' I didn't reply. 'My God! Are you paralysed or something? Move. *Move.*' I breathed and lifted my head.

'Why are you crying? God, is something broken? Can't you talk?'

'Maybe,' said Defarge from behind me, 'his voice box is broken.'

'Oh! please, Defarge . . . Brit! Brit! Please don't sob like this.' Cyrus put one arm around me; I could see a silky tuft of hair in his armpit.

'Don't touch him!' screamed Defarge. 'When his bones break no one must touch him.'

Cyrus took away his arm and I wailed, 'Nothing's broken; nothing at all.'

'Then,' said Cyrus, standing up, 'Why are you crying – '

'Like a girl?' finished Defarge.

I shook my head. 'It isn't pain,' I said again and again. 'It isn't pain, it isn't – '

'Then what is it, Brit?' He knelt and put his arm around me again.

I whispered right into his ear, so Defarge wouldn't hear, 'It . . . it's the terror. Of hurting again. It's like someone – jumping on you in the dark. And for me – it's always dark and osteo is waiting.' I began to sob.

'Don't talk like that, Brit. Everyone has accidents, everyone feels relieved when they escape unhurt.'

'And you know what, I lose everything. Law and astronomy

and Bach. Even sex. I just become the kid I was. The one with a leg stiff in a cast.'

'What,' said Defarge, outraged at being cut off, 'were you two doing in the bathroom?'

Cyrus grinned. 'You have a dirty mind, Defarge. I was just showing Brit how the flush works.'

'I'm sure it's going to be very useful to him,' she said, 'since he is so short he can't ever look inside.'

'Don't be mean, Defarge.'

'She's a bitch,' I said softly.

'Oh, yes! Heard that,' said Defarge. 'Just you wait. I'll tell your mummy-pappi first thing in the morning. With the milkman.'

Cyrus saw me redden and winked. 'I've got something to do before I sleep tonight,' he said quickly. 'I have to write to my father.'

'Why?' demanded Defarge suspiciously.

'Why?' said Cyrus, widening his long eyes. 'Because he's my father. And he likes to know how I am, how I eat.'

Defarge tightened the faded green-and-white-patterned dressing-gown to her throat.

'I'm so sleepy,' she yawned. 'I won't be able to wake up with the milkman tomorrow. Anyway, I was only joking, as if I would ever complain about you boys. And you.' She wagged a finger at Cyrus. 'Go to bed early. It's past midnight. My cousin-brother can wait for his letter.'

'OK,' said Cyrus, skipping with his hands behind his back. 'Off to bed! C'mon, Brit.'

I let myself in with the latch-key. 'Sleep well,' said Cyrus.

'Huh-uh!' I said, surprised to see the light on in my bedroom. Dolly was already home and it was Sunday night. Cyrus shut the door behind him and I felt a guilt-cramp. I hadn't thanked him for stopping Defarge in her dirty tracks.

'Hi!' I said. 'Home early?'

'Ya. We didn't go disco dancing.'

'Oh!' This wasn't working very well. It was really my fault. Dolly and I hardly talked any more. With Cyrus around I didn't need to. And she was always there when I needed her to take me for a haircut or to get movie tickets for Cyrus and me. I didn't love her less; it was just that we were less of a brother and sister. 'Dolly,' I said, trying to sound twelve again, 'something awful happened today.'

'Did you get hurt?'

'Sort of.'

She jumped off her bed. 'Where? Tell me where. I knew something like this would happen, the way you've been gallivanting with Cyrus.'

'You sound like Sera.'

'Never mind. I know all the things he does. Like whirl you around on your back wheels, and letting go of the chair at the top of the ramp, giving you a heave to see how far you'll go before the chair runs out of push – '

'How – how do you know all this?'

'I used to watch when you started going out alone with him. I was terrified, Brit. But I knew you hated that, so I'd turn off the lights and watch you go. And then he'd do all these tricks on the Causeway and you'd laugh. Big show-off!'

'I wasn't showing-off. I was having fun - for the first time in my life.'

Dolly's big black eyes were brimming. I felt like a swine.

'Brit, there are other ways you can have fun. Less dangerous ways – movies and plays. Oh! I can take you wherever you want to go.'

'Thanks,' I said, hugging her neck. 'Dolly, why did you blush yesterday?'

There under the crook of my elbow she started again – red as Kashmir cherries. 'It's a long story,' she said. 'I'm not sure I should tell you.' I looked at her and nodded sympathetically. 'I'm in love. With this guy. He's a Muslim. Don't look so stunned. It's worse. He lives in New York. He's a doctor. In a hospital. I told him I couldn't . . .' I breathed again, but she went on before I could let my breath go. 'He said he won't give up. He'd write every day. I love Salim. I don't know what to do.'

'Marry him,' I said jumping off the bridge just like that.

'Brit, you mean it?'

'Of course! How could you refuse someone you love?'

'But Brit, what about you? You haven't thought of that.'

'What *about* me? You think I can't get on without you?'

'What about concerts and stuff? Cyrus isn't always going to be there, you know.'

'There's such a thing as a video.'

'Ya. I could send you one from New York.'

'And I'm going to have a slave – '

'Your old dream; the big man who'll reach the tops of the cupboards. But Brit, you weren't my only problem. Salim's a Muslim – '

'So how does that make him different from anyone else. Oh, yes! he'll be circumcised – '

'Shut up!' said Dolly, biting her lip with pleasure at the picture. 'What'll Sam say?'

'Here's Sam. Let's ask him.'

'No, Brit, not at night.'

'It's one in the morning. Saam!'

'You'd like some water, son?'

'No, come out of the kitchen.'

'Yes?' said Sam, looking elegant in his rumpled blue pyjamas.

'I love you,' said Dolly, hugging him. They made a beautiful pair, his silver locks and her brown curls tumbling over a baby-pink nightie.

'She wants to get married,' I said, 'to Salim who's a Muslim doctor in New York.'

'Oh, dear!' said Sam from the corner of his mouth that was not kissing Dolly's hair, and we both knew he was thinking of Sera's reaction.

'Now, we know, Sam,' said Dolly, 'that people are just the same – '

'No matter where they worship,' finished Sam. 'Yes, darling, we hear it on the telly every day! "A man's a man for a' that." Oh, dear! Are you engaged?'

Dolly shot me a look of alarm from Sam's arms. 'Yes,' I said, 'she's agreed to marry him. But he's in New York at the moment, so we have plenty of time to get used to the idea.'

'He's awfully modern,' said Dolly. 'The whole family's been living there for ages.'

'Will he have four wives?'

'Oh, Daddy! Don't be silly. Salim loves me.'

'But he can have four wives if he loves them all – '

'We'll have a civil marriage – then I'll be safe. OK?'

Sam freed himself from his daughter. He held her by the shoulders and looked at her with regret, his eyes slanting downwards.

'Darling,' he said mournfully, 'there is an insurmountable problem.' His head was shaking uncontrollably and he was saying no with his hands. 'How will you live without pork curry and smoked ham for the rest of your life?' Dolly whooped and Sam hurriedly shut the bedroom door while I looked at them feeling proud.

'Let me show you his picture,' said Dolly. She slipped a hand inside her pillowcase and took out a huge photograph which she gave me. Salim was eating an ice-cream cone, which reminded me of Tina and our obscene sign language. I swallowed and looked. He had a high forehead or he was balding, his eyes were gentle, brown under heavy sloping brows, he had large pink lips and tongue and a shaggy brown beard. His nose was – 'My God! He looks just like a Parsee!' I said.

'Really? Jolly good. Show that to me. Hmm; you're right. Brit might've looked like that if he were – '

'Brit's just as handsome,' said Dolly, loyally blind.

'Yes, yes,' said Sam, still looking at the snap. 'Still – oh, well, I'd better go to bed. Golden slumbers, darling.'

'You mean erotic dreams, Sam,' I said. Dolly flung a pillow at me taking care to choose the softest; Sam beat a hasty retreat. We laughed our heads off and went to sleep. My last thought was that if I'd still had the mantra-madness there would have been one *mala* less to make tonight.

'The Muslims are the traditional, nay, the historical enemies of the Parsees. And to give yourself to one of them is a shameful act of betrayal, nay, High Treason.' Sera took a deep breath.

'It's morning,' said Sam.

'The British conquered India and you worship them, Sera darling.'

'They didn't push us out of our homes.'

'By our homes you mean the Iran of the seventh century – '

'AD,' I said.

'Whatever; the Muslims made us pitiful refugees.'

'Oh, cut it out!' said Dolly, leaping out of bed, her hair like the mad wife's in *Jane Eyre*. 'You know you're talking shit, the height of stinking shit. What the hell does Salim have to do with the Arab tribesmen who beat the hell out of the milksop Persians more than a thousand years ago?'

'I am talking shit, am I? *Sam*!' Sera bawled, her eyes like tiny sprinklers.

'Go on, cry and get Daddy's sympathy,' taunted Dolly.

'Darling, please,' said Sam, not knowing who he was addressing.

'She,' sobbed Sera, 'wants to marry a filthy Mussalman – '

Dolly screamed. 'Don't you call Salim filthy, he bathes twice a day.'

'They stink,' howled Sera, 'all of them. You saw what happened to Tina. You'll end up in a bawdy house in Brooklyn, just like her.'

'How dare you call my husband a pimp; I'll – I'll wash the dye right out of your hair.'

'Your husband! Did you hear her, Sam? She's already married and all this is a charade, a party game for her. Oh, God! Why have I been so unfortunate in my children?'

'Keep Brit out of this,' said Sam quietly.

'I bet,' said Sera through her dentures, 'I bet my father's furniture she's preggers.'

'Sera! You don't know what you're saying, darling. Accusing your own daughter of – ' Sam shrugged.

'Of pre-marital sex. Say it, Sam. Say what you feel and put her right. And, by the way, I never went to bed with Salim. I wish I had. I would have had something of him inside me at least!' Dolly began to cry. Sam put his arm around her.

'I will never consent,' said Sera, sounding like the Ranee of Jhansi refusing to surrender her state to the British.

'Then I,' said Dolly deliberately, 'will go on a fast unto death.'

'Blackmail,' said Sera grimly, 'won't work on me.'

'It worked on the British Empire, Sera,' said Dolly sweetly. 'Remember Mahatma Gandhi?'

'Huh!' Sera snorted. 'I'm no gentle, fair-minded Britisher; I am Persian, pure Persian as – '

'A rug,' Dolly said.

A deathly silence thudded down on our heads. No one talked. Dolly sulked, Sam went for day-long walks, I had said what I had to. Two nights later Sera started little conversations that flickered and died. Dolly was none the worse for her fast – she was surviving on warm water and honey.

Sera had never had the three of us sending her to Coventry. So now she smiled at Dolly: Dolly turned on her stomach and went to sleep. She kissed Sam's head: he didn't kiss her back. She winked at me: I pretended I didn't have my specs on.

On the third day the doorbell shook the silence. 'Come in, Defarge,' we heard Sera say from the drawing-room.

'All quiet on the western front?' said Defarge. It was one of her favourite phrases; she used it to draw out info.

'Yes,' said Sera, making for this one exit to escape the fire she'd started, 'we've been so busy. My Dolly's getting married to a young Muslim doctor from New York, I've had no time to come and tell you. Come in; congratulate her.'

'Congratulate her for what? You should be in mourning,' said Defarge, dismayed.

'Don't you dare say such things to me on this auspicious day, Defarge, or I'll – I'll never take your *dhobi's* clothes when you are out, nor will I lend you my *bai* when yours pretends to be sick every second day nor – '

'But – but,' said Defarge, quite broken, 'I only thought – '

'What have you done for my Dolly all these years? Brought along that deranged Dinsu? Compared to him, my Salim is a gem, nay, the gem of gems! He comes from a fine aristocratic family. So westernised you would think they were from *there*, and he looks like a Parsee!'

'Look, Dolly: she's insulting Salim – '

'Oh, shut up,' wept Dolly, 'you know she thinks Parsee guys are the cat's whiskers.'

'She married one,' said Sam.

'I think it's time you broke your fast,' I said fetching the Toblerone I'd stashed away since Dolly's last trip to Singapore.

143

It was half eaten. Dolly had been supplementing her honey and water diet.

'Where's my share?' called Sera from the drawing-room, sounding as triumphant as Margaret Thatcher at the fall of Port Stanley.

16

Cyrus came around lunchtime, kissed Dolly, said, 'I knew I didn't stand a chance,' mumbled at me, 'I've got to rush, have a lunch date,' and was gone.

I was sure he was meeting Ruby. When he didn't come that night I was certain. Then I wondered if I'd hurt him last night by not saying thank you. I was terrified I'd never see him again.

Cyrus didn't turn up the next evening or the next or . . . I woke about sixty-five times every night, opened my book on the Indian Contract Act and sobbed into the passages Cyrus had marked. Or I sat at the window and watched the stars because they reminded me of the telescope. The day I spent in a night-black fog, looking at plastic bags and Sam's razor with a speculative eye. I cursed Ruby, because I bet if she hadn't been around to entice him, Cyrus would have got over his hurt if only because he'd have wanted someone to talk to. I could see his firm hands in her hair and his arcing mouth mocking kisses into her neck and I had to pull down the shutters on my mind. And think of other things.

Like Dolly was going away really soon, as soon as Sam got his visa and stuff. Because there was no way Salim could come to Bombay for the next two years and even Sera thought thirty wasn't exactly young to get married. So the plan was for Dolly to fly out to New York with Sam, on her last free tickets, and get married there.

We thought it was absolutely right for Dolly to take Sam along instead of her mother because she was always his daughter like I was Sera's son. That's how it is with almost every family I know. Both parents are crazy about both kids but in some

145

tiny way each adopts one – a kind of division of labour. I don't know how it works for people who have more than two kids because Parsees almost never do. They feel it's some sort of extravagance, like having a television in the bedroom.

At last Cyrus came over. 'Hello!' he said with his killing smile. 'Sorry I've been neglecting you.'

'You shouldn't be,' I said, taking deep, slow breaths. 'You come because you like being with me, not to give me company. At least, I hope it's that way.'

'Brit,' he said, falling into his familiar cross-legged seat in front of me, 'have I . . . hurt you?'

'No.' I thought how easy it would be to fall off my chair, right into his arms.

'I know it's been – how many, ten, eleven days?' Twelve, I thought, and you didn't even keep count. 'But I've been busy; really, I have.'

'Of course; you don't have to give me an account.'

'Fucking shit! Stop that!'

'Don't shout at me, Cyrus.'

'OK, so I didn't meet you, so you feel awful. I'd have felt miserable if you'd stopped meeting me suddenly. Why can't you say so? What's happened to your famous frankness?' His face turned a darker brown and, if his skin was finding trouble holding in that blood, his eyes were thrown open to make more room.

'Cyrus?' I whispered. Then I was lifted off my chair and he was saying into my hair, 'Brit, I'm sorry, but will you promise never, never to stop – '

'Stop what, Cyrus?' My hand was on his neck and I was rubbing his earlobe with my thumb.

'Being my friend. Because I never will, not even if you never will, I mean, never do, I mean never – ' We started laughing louder and louder as if someone were turning a knob in our chests.

Then I realised I had a huge hard-on pushing into his tummy, and the way he was holding me around my back, there was no way I could move away without falling out of his arms. And there was no way I could turn soft as long as I could smell his clean hard smell and see his small nostrils flare with the effect of carrying me. I kissed his eyelids and he smiled, so I kissed the drooping corners of his mouth. Then I shut my eyes and held him for every moment that had passed since he asked for that safety-pin.

I could've stayed that way till Sera crew the morning open but Cyrus had shifted his mouth to mine and begun sucking with small milky sounds. I opened my mouth to the bristle of his stubble and the gush of hot breath from his nose while I felt his big man's hands grasping my bottom.

My hard-on was melting away and I didn't know what to do. I mean here I was on the brink of passion and all I could think of was that I didn't want Cyrus's toothpaste-tasting tongue in my mouth where it was slowly pushing its way past my transparent teeth. Somehow it felt all wrong as if I had clasped the wrong partner in the dark.

I gagged and Cyrus drew his head back and said, 'Sorry, this isn't working.'

'Not for me either,' I said, feeling my sovereign mouth with my tongue. I shook my head and felt his warm face with my fingertips. A huge tenderness was lapping against my insides, a sea of semen and tears.

'Are you gay?' he said, at last.

'I don't know, I don't know,' I said. 'I look at you now and I want you, and I'm angry with myself for feeling what I did when you were holding me. As if I was one of a pair of Siamese twins – '

'Um, I know; we're much too alike, aren't we, stubble and muscles.' He put me down on the large carved sofa and sat on the floor in front of me.

'Don't do that,' I said wearily. 'Oh, what I thought it would be – '

'Well, at least I didn't have any expectations,' he said, grinning.

'Then why did you?' I said. I knew why I did. But my reasons couldn't have been his; as clear as I could see he had no reason to want me.

'I knew you wanted me.'

'You tried to make love to me out of charity?' I shouted.

147

'Shsh! You want to wake them up? It wasn't charity, you ass. I wanted to because I knew you wanted me like crazy.'

'You knew? All along?'

'Sure. The way you'd stare and stare at my crotch.' He began to laugh, watching me all the time.

'D'you really mean that?' I was feeling what I later found out was drunk.

'Of course. How do you think I knew? And that neck massage you gave me? Oh, boy! I'll never – '

'OK, so what if I wanted you?'

'You know what it's like to be wanted that much?'

'Of course not, you idiot.'

'There's no need to get angry when you're sad.'

'You know, I really love you.'

'Why did *you* want me, Brit?'

I'd rehearsed this about sixty-seven times. 'You're tall, I'm four feet nothing, you've got muscles in your thighs when I've got matchsticks, you have a voice like hot chocolate – '

'Stop being funny.'

'I'm not. You *have* got a voice like hot chocolate and osteo makes me squawk. You've got a swimmer's chest; I've got a pigeon-chest. Girls love your body; they don't look at mine except to shudder – '

'That's not true. No one thinks about that, once they know you.'

'You look good and not all the cosmetic surgeons in America can make me like looking at myself.'

'Is any of that important?'

'Don't tell me beauty is bone deep and all that crap because it isn't true. I want to be straight and tall because I've got just one life and I'll go through it without anyone ever wanting me like I wanted you. It's like – '

'A sweeper watching a Brahmin?'

'Yes, you either hate that something you can never have, or you adore it.'

'Tell me more.'

'The desire of the moth for the star.'

'That doesn't explain lust.'

148

'It does. If I could have you, which meant you wanted me, that meant my body was as good as yours.'

'Whoo!' he gasped, spreading his palm on his chest, letting his tongue hang out. That tongue.

'Wait,' I said, 'you haven't heard everything.' My passion had escaped solitary confinement and it couldn't stop talking. 'I was opting out of the race – '

'For girls?'

'Yes.' I made a face like that chap in *MAD* magazine.

'But you were entering another race, weren't you?'

'You were out of reach. So where was the race?'

'. . . but I wasn't out of reach, was I?'

'As soon as you weren't I got out of your arms. Don't look like that, I'm not crazy. It's just that wanting you was a faking, wasn't it?'

'That hard-on was no fake; everything you wanted to do with me wasn't. What the hell, Brit – this fucking frigidity, where's it going to get you?'

'But don't you see! I couldn't do things with you because it would have been like a poor girl marrying a millionaire for his money. You'd say that was sick wouldn't you?'

'That girl never felt for him what you felt for me.'

'Feeling, feeling, tell me, what's the use of feeling?' Do all men sound like their mothers when things get tough? 'I've felt sorry for myself, and frightened for myself, and what good has that done me? You've got to know what makes you feel something.'

'By which time love is desiccated – '

'It was never love.'

'Are you sure, Brit?'

I looked at his solemn face, his mouth turned down at the corners, eyes large with what I was feeling, and I knew I wasn't sure. I didn't answer him.

He smiled and put his warm hand on my knee. 'You are looking for something Brit. Will you be brave enough to grab it when you find it?'

'I don't know, I don't know, I don't know,' I said, answering that other question.

'Stop it,' he barked in George Patton style. 'Stop looking

like Osteo Brit. Think of the problems you'll never have – '

'Waiting in a bus queue with smelly fishmongers – '

'Squelching your way through monsoon slush on your way to work – '

'Getting pick-pocketed in a crowd – '

'Being knocked over by a speeding taxi – '

'Wearing out my shoes – '

'Helping with the housework when the servants are on strike – '

'You never did that, I bet. Your mother wouldn't let you, and Defarge wouldn't dare.'

'I have problems you never will,' he said, trying to look like Saint Joan and ending up like the Dauphin.

'Like?' I said sceptically.

'Wanting someone because they want you. That's one of the reasons why I sleep around. If a girl wants me really badly. God! It's so exciting I can't resist.'

'What about what you want?'

'Sometimes I wonder.'

'But you were ready to go gay.'

'I wanted to know what it would be like – you've got to try everything once.'

'That's cheap.'

'That's brave.'

'Wanting a girl just because she wants you – that's not brave. Just shows you're terrified of never being wanted again. Like I felt with Ruby after I missed that kiss.'

'Ruby! God! She's something!'

'Take care you don't get her preggers,' I said.

'Preggers? Ha, he! Where did you get that forties phrase from?'

'Sera – she thought Dolly was preggers.'

'Dolly's going away *soon*, isn't she?'

'Will you take me around and things?'

Cyrus bit his lip. 'I'll try my best but I'm going to be a bit busy – '

'I understand,' I said, swinging away on a trapeze and my brave act. 'I'll only ask when it's absolutely necessary.'

'Very funny. Brit, look! Just because I can't spend so much

time with you doesn't mean I don't want to. I just want to do something else too.'

'Sure, you don't have to worry about me.' A cock crew from the servant's quarters of the building behind us, where we'd seen the bathing *bai*.

'Four o'clock! Sera's going to slaughter me if she wakes. I'm going. Put me in my chair.' I was thinking of the time when Sam had found me Cyrus-drunk in the rocking chair.

'OK, here goes!' He swung me into his arms. 'Take care you don't get another hard-on. You know what that does to me.'

'What!' screamed Sera. 'Am I going mad? Or did I hear right?'

'Fucking shit!'

'What!'

'Put me down,' I said through my teeth, realising my hands were clasping Cyrus's bottom because his arms had sagged with shock.

'Sure,' he said, letting me down gently.

'Are the two of you perverted?' said Sera.

'It was all a joke,' said Cyrus, flashing his Sera-stumping smile.

'I don't think so,' said Sera, trying to keep her voice from flying out of the window. 'Defarge told me how she found you in the bathroom one night, some time back. I didn't pay any attention because I know her imagination is as dirty as those books they sell at Flora Fountain. But I was wrong.'

'Look,' I said, 'do you really think we're lovers? Do you think a guy like Cyrus would want a guy like me? We're not even the same size.'

'Aaahah!' said Sera, clapping a hand to her mouth. 'How d'you know what size he is? You've seen him, haven't you?'

'Not that size, Sera,' said Cyrus. 'This size – look.' He stretched an imaginary tape-measure from my hair to my slippers.

'Then what were you doing in each other's arms?'

'I was lifting him into his chair.'

'Brit doesn't need to be lifted into his chair. All you have to do is move the chair over to him and he shifts into it by himself. You've known him long enough to know that. You *are* perverted – both of you.'

'Well,' said Cyrus, the smartass, 'you need two hands to clap.'

'Saaaam,' howled Sera.

'Yes, darling,' Sam stepped out from behind the door, where he was awaiting his cue.

'Our son is a pervert.' She dropped her words with the dull thud of paperweights.

'Homosexual, you mean,' said Sam. 'No one is a pervert any more. You can slice up half a dozen women and you're only socially maladjusted.'

'I'm not gay!' I shouted in panic. 'At least, I don't think so,' I added, not as loudly.

'Nor am I, if you want the truth,' said Cyrus.

'Of course they aren't,' shouted Dolly from her bed. 'They drool over *Playboy* magazine and that has pictures of naked girls.'

Sera looked at Sam doubtfully. Sam nodded and smiled back. I blessed their innocence.

'Why were they in each other's arms?' said Sera, shaking her white head.

'OK, I'll tell you why,' I said, smiling like Hercule Poirot in the last chapter of an Agatha Christie. 'I'm giving up law.'

'But you've hardly started, lad.'

'Isn't that good? I haven't wasted too much time.'

'No!' cried Sera. 'Please, Brit – no – it's bad enough Dolly leaving us and now you – '

'What's the connection?'

'What are you going to do?'

'Write.'

'Hooray!' said Cyrus, raising me in his arms like a glass of champagne. I'd never, in my life, been so high. That should've told me where I was headed next.

17

'ARE YOU SURE you don't want to come along, Brit?'

'Quite sure,' I said for the two hundredth time. I knew what it would be like at the airport, especially if I were there. Puddles of tears and a crushful of hugs while I fought my blush like a soldier without a rifle, doomed to failure. I would've had to ask Cyrus to come along to haul me into the taxi on the way back – I was too heavy for Sera to manage. And I wasn't going to ask Cyrus for a thing if I could help it.

'Take care of him,' said Sam, kissing Sera's cheek.

'You should be asking him to look after me,' she said gaily. 'After all, he's the man in the house when you're away.'

Sam smiled ruefully. 'I keep forgetting,' he said. 'Well, Brit, look after my wife. See she doesn't shop too much.' He ruffled my hair. 'Are you too old to be hugged?'

'I think so,' I said, adding, 'I'll be twenty-one next week.' I had to keep reminding them, because they were always doing things like offering me their laps to sit on at the movies.

'Twenty-one,' said Sam, putting on his midnight-blue jacket. 'You know, Brit, it hasn't been half as tough as we thought it would be the night you were born.'

'The virtues of fear,' I said, making a face.

'I'm ready,' shouted Dolly from our room.

'Have you talked to her, darling?' asked Sam.

'Oh, don't be silly! She knows.'

'Yes, yes, darling, of course she does; here she is.'

'See you, Brit,' said Dolly.

'Write that bestseller quickly.'

'What's that, Brit? You haven't told me about it.'

'Just an idea I have.'

'He's going to write about us; an exposé called *The Cruel Kotwals*.'

Sera gasped. 'Don't you dare, Brit Kotwal!'

'She's joking, darling; come on, we're late. It's already seven and the flight's at ten.'

'OK. Brit, will you manage dinner? The chicken's in the fridge – you just have to heat it.'

'I will.'

'Will you be careful with the gas?'

'Sure.'

'Turn it to the right and listen for the click.'

'Ya, I will.'

'Don't worry; we have the latch-key.'

'I never worry.'

'He won't have the time, Sera. He's got an orgy slated for eight o'clock,' shrieked Dolly.

The cab coughed and crept through the Causeway traffic. I watched till it disappeared behind a red double-decker bus. Dolly was gone. It didn't feel any different. Then I realised Sam was gone for now. So was Cyrus. And Ruby. I didn't have anyone left. Except Jeroo and Defarge, and they didn't add up to much. Sera – but she was just my mother. There was nothing to do. But jerk off. Even that was tough without thinking of Cyrus. I didn't want to think of Cyrus because I now knew how queer it felt in his arms.

I smiled at my pun and tugged at the drawer in my desk where Dolly and I kept our erotica. There was a brand new *Penthouse*. Covering the cover-girl's surely-gorgeous body was a long white envelope, with the words 'Brit-Owl' printed on them. I wrenched it open. Inside, Dolly had written:

Dearest Brit,

I wanted to talk but I didn't want my last picture of your face in menstrual red. Well, I've told Sam to let you have my nest-egg, the one I was going to use in my old spinsterhood. You and I have always had a joint account at the bank down the road so there should be no problem. Maybe you should get yourself that slave right away.

Brit, I've hated you sometimes. When I've had to do

things for you I didn't want to. Also, when I missed parties and movies because Sera and Sam were out and I couldn't leave you alone.

But all along I've tried to remember how hard it's been for you. And I know if the Old Man in the Sky offered to exchange you for that strapping elder brother who'd bring dishy guys over – the one I've always dreamt about – I'd say, No thank you very much.

Your sis,
Daulatbanu

P.S. Hey! I don't write badly for a writer's sister, do I?

How I cursed her when I finished reading. For writing in ink. As if she didn't know that it dissolves in brine.

Of course, after that I was in no mood to jerk off so I heated my dinner and had it, taking care to listen for the click when I shut the gas.

Tap-tap-tap. I froze. No one ever tapped our door. Except Defarge who felt it was rude to ring bells after sunset. And it couldn't be her dropping in to check on me because she'd fallen out with Sera.

The insistent tapping at the door went on. I felt sick with terror and the chicken stayed undigested inside me. Then, one of the mirrors flashed. I wheeled into my bedroom – how silently I could move – and I switched on the radio. I started a conversation with the man reading the news. The thief would know I wasn't alone and he wouldn't dare.

'I'll get the door and come back,' I shouted to the transistor even while I turned the latch.

It *was* a thief. The Cyrus-thief.

'What's wrong with you, Brit?' she said, smiling in shocking-pink flounces. 'Talking to yourself. And switching on the radio when you knew I was waiting.'

'It's you,' I said, cold as tap water in winter.

'Yes, I thought you'd be alone, so I'd give you company.'

'You don't have to.'

'Oh! Stop being an ass. Cyrus told me you've got this funny idea everyone's trying to be kind to you. What's the matter, Brit? You've never thought that before.'

'I have – only I pretended I hadn't.'

'OK, cheer up. You've got some dinner for me? There was cabbage at home today – yuck.'

'I'm sorry; I've just finished.'

'What's the matter, Brit?' she yelled, standing up while her dress swung about her, 'You want me to go? Are you expecting Cyrus?'

'Well, since he isn't seeing you tonight, he might have the time to see me.'

'How dare you – '

'How dare I?' I squawked. 'You dare say that to me, when you took my pal, gave your word, broke it like a broomstick – You! My oldest friend sold me out for a fuck.'

'I know I'm not supposed to do this,' screamed Ruby, 'but I will!' She hit my cheek, knocking my glasses to the floor. 'I don't care if your bones break like those glasses but you aren't going to speak to me like that.'

I reached down for them. I couldn't be dignified while Ruby was a blur of colour. 'Well,' I said, 'you haven't succeeded in breaking my bones *or* my glasses.'

'What a bloody pity!'

'But the fact remains,' I said slowly, 'that you sold me off for a fuck.' Ruby began to cry, the tears making dark spots on her shocking-pink breasts. 'Cry a little louder,' I said softly. 'It still won't be half as loud as the sound inside me. You know I last saw Cyrus ten days ago? D'you know how I wait? Listening for the lift door, his footsteps? He's the only friend I've ever made – the rest of you are just there. I've been living the whole day for the night. Now what have I got?' I knew I was going to join Ruby crying very soon.

Then she said, 'Brit, I swear I haven't spent a single evening with Cyrus, not to speak of nights.'

'Really?'

'The only time we meet is when I bunk college – we go for lunch or a morning show or for a cuddle.' She was dry-eyed now. 'Isn't he beautiful, Brit? God! When he takes me in his arms – '

'You don't have to be graphic.'

'What's there to be graphic about? We haven't done much more than smooching and stuff. I want to go all the way!'

'Why don't you?'

'Because he says he doesn't love me.'

'Then leave him.'

'Open and shut – that's what you think life is.'

'Naturally; I've know so little of it, haven't I? Did Cyrus tell you that? After all, how many people have I met? How many places have I seen? I never leave this tiny tip of Bombay. So what do I know – right?'

'Come on, Brit,' said Ruby, looking as embarrassed as I was beginning to feel. 'Cyrus and I hardly ever talk about you. And who says you don't know anything? I've always thought of you as the little wise man.'

'Thanks a lot. I don't want to be the little wise man, OK? I'm just a man like Cyrus is a man. Only I don't look like him.'

'So who says no?'

'Oh, go away!' Ruby moved towards the door. 'Is that true, what you said about never seing Cyrus at night?'

'I swore, didn't I?'

So Cyrus was just tired of me. 'You'll come again, Ruby?'

'Of course I will.'

'I'm sorry I made you cry.'

'Ass! Now I'll have to apologise for that slap.' We grinned at each other. She shut the door.

I knew what I wanted to do. I pulled out the sheaf of papers and Dolly's gold Parker pen. I wrote a story about a man who discovers he's the last leaf on the tree. And he's only twenty-one.

It got published and I got my first cheque. But I got something bigger from that story. I didn't feel alone any more. How could I? I had just talked to fifty thousand people. Unless, of course, that magazine had cooked its circulation figures.

Well, into those Dark Ages after Dolly left came Zarthost. He entered my life and hovered on the periphery like a spot of light that I could see from the corner of my eye and always be glad of.

His name was Zarthost but everyone called him Jerry (*'nice*

English name, no?' said his mother who had the misfortune to be called Rati, a name that could only turn mousey when shortened. I think I liked him so much, that first time I met him, because he was as ugly as sin. I told him so when I got to know him. 'Then you,' he said in his strong, flat Parsee accent, 'can only be compared to Original Sin.'

So I liked him because he was ugly and that was such a relief after going gaga over every little bit of Cyrus. He was dark in a way only the poor are dark – not suntanned, not the velvety night-black of South India – dark as outworn black leather shoes. This was strange because Jerry had enough money to buy out the bookshop at the Taj which was what he seemed to be doing when I first saw him. He was carrying a pile of books that hid his torso up to the chin; I could only see a nose that made mine look like Julie Andrews's. And thin slit eyes which hardly managed to stay open under the weight of fierce black brows that crossed his forehead like Hadrian's Wall.

I counted twenty-two books in his arms before I realised that the man behind him was *his* man, his personal servant, who was hefting a rustle of magazines ranging from *Life* to *India Today*. 'Excuse me,' I said, trying to edge my chair past him (I was enjoying a long browse while Ruby had her hair done at the hotel's beauty salon).

'Sure,' he answered and the next minute I was feeling like a potentate to whom some tributary had brought an offering of books: there they lay, free of Jerry's loving arms, at my feet. 'Hell, I'm sorry,' he said, 'but the way you look I got such a shock, an electric shock.'

'Are you mad?' I said, not to hit back but because I knew he couldn't be anything else to talk like that to me who had 'Made Of Glass – Handle With Care' stamped all over.

'Of course not; I'm just buying books because I have to spend a month in Davier – '

'That is?'

'What are you, a Parsee or a prince?'

'A Parsee Indian prince, maybe,' I said, wondering if I'd discovered the equivalent of the fabulous Jewish-American princess.

'Actually, that's what I am,' he said simply.

He was sitting on a pile of books between the shelves selling dictionaries and spiritual enlightenment. 'Davier is a little seaport,' he said, 'where the richest Parsees – the real rich, I mean, the old, old rich – have their ancestral mansions. We are getting ours renovated, fixing electricity and running water – '

'You live without?'

'Of course; what's there to do after dark – eat and make love.'

'Are you married?'

'No, but my mother is showing me girls – I'll choose one soon. Oi! We are making a terrific jam. Let's get out – I'll pay for my books, then you'll come with me for a hot dog at the coffee shop?'

'Oh, yes; thank you,' I said, feeling as brave as an explorer. I watched his books as he dumped them at the pay-in desk with dismay. James Hadley Chase, Harold Robbins, Danielle Steel, Jacqueline Susann, (unredeemed by *Every Night, Josephine*) – it was as if someone had asked me for the names I'd never read and gone and got them all.

'Tell me about the girls your mother is showing you,' I said, watching his face in the laminated orange table-top at the coffee shop.

'First you tell me; do you just go for a snack with any man you meet?'

I began to blush; did he know? Then I saw his stubby hand, brown as earthenware, on the table and I lifted my head. 'No; only, you make me curious.'

He rubbed his nose with the heel of his palm. 'I like you, *yaar*.' *Yaar* was an awful word that only Hindi film types used; it meant a cross between a lover and a pal.

'I like you too, much to my astonishment.'

We laughed. He told me about the girls. No, they didn't meet at Apollo; instead he was invited by hopeful parents for tea. He was a BIG catch, big as the lobsters he ate in Davier. His family owned a *vaadi*, orchards stretching over acres. 'Mangoes,' he said, 'big as a nursing mother's breasts.' I thought of Wagh Baba. 'And just as suck-able.'

What am I doing with this vulgar man? I wondered.

'And we have a bakery, three shops selling grain and sugar – '

'All in Davier?' I asked sympathetically.

'Where else? In this stinking city?'

Our hot dogs arrived; Jerry bent over the plate and sniffed his – luckily, the waiter wasn't watching him. No one who goes out with me ever gets a second glance; I am more than two eyes can take in at once.

'Tell me more about the girls.'

'You must have eaten *Khariya* for lunch.'

'Trotters? I hate them; they used to feed me jelly made from them.'

'*Khariya* makes you want it,' he said, raising an obscene eyebrow, 'makes you want it so much you stick it into – '

'Brit, are you crazy?' said Ruby, walking in, her hair a mass of crafted curls, a mad mix of gold, auburn and ebony.

'Who's that?' said Jerry, his mouth open, revealing a brown hash of half-chewed sausage.

'Hi! I'm Ruby – and Brit, what d'you mean by wandering off without telling me?'

'Oh, oh! I'm sorry, it's just that Jerry here – '

'Never apologise to women,' said Jerry through the sausage.

'Bullshit!' said Ruby.

'Talk like that and you won't stand a chance in the market.'

'What market?' squealed Ruby, as if she'd been squeezed hard.

'The marriage market, girl. Boys want good girls – '

'Girls don't want boys like you,' shouted Ruby, and I knew if I didn't stop this it would end with Jerry finding his face in the bowl of tomato ketchup.

'Girls want boys who've eaten *Khariya* for lunch.'

'We must go, Ruby; it isn't very safe – the lanes behind the Taj – let's go; thank you, Jerry.'

'Give me your phone number, *yaar*, you owe me a treat.' He grinned, I grinned back, flashing my lantern-jaw.

'Oh yes, give me yours,' I said, hoping to control the speed of this relationship.

'Two,' he said.

'Yes?'

'Your turn.'

So it was going to be dual-control. I rattled off my number feeling like a train that was chugging into a strange station.

'See you soon,' he said, 'then I'll be gone for a long time.'

'Such mercy,' said Ruby, crossing the white lobby as fast as she could teeter on her tall red heels.

We had reached the glass wall of the exit and the doorman they'd dressed up like an Indian maharaja was about to show us the way through when I heard Jerry shout in a voice that was obviously used to his acres of orchard. 'Oi!' he bellowed, 'Oi! I forget to ask.' The waiting Americans, French and British looked up expectantly. 'Have you always been this way or did you get polio or something?'

Before I could answer, and I would have answered because I was too embarrassed to feel offended, Ruby had thudded me down the steps and crossed the street to the sea.

'Why?' she asked again and again. 'Why, Brit? Couldn't you see he was a slob, a country bumpkin, a yob? Why did you have to go with him to that café?'

'Because,' I said, 'because I want to step out – '

'But you do every day. We've been going everywhere.'

'The same where. I want to go somewhere i have never travelled,' I said, remembering to keep the 'i' small. 'I am tired of my beautiful – '

'Glass world,' said Ruby, as usual trying to get me back from wherever I had blown away.

'Yes, I've lived inside a crystal paperweight and now I want to know the real world, other people, people who are not like me.'

'No one is like you, remember?' said Ruby, and I threw my arm back to tickle her tummy that was as ticklish as the soles of my size-four feet.

18

THE FIRST OF Dolly's many letters arrived. I tore them up as soon as I got them – but I remembered every word:

Salim's father has two wives. Poor Sam turned pale as an egg. The first one was an arranged marriage when he was a teenager in India. She is a Boo! – you know what I mean, veiled in black from head to foot. D'you remember that rhyme I taught you when you were tiny:

Trip a Boo!
Strip a Boo!
When she's down say
Peek-a-Boo!

And you said it to the first Boo! we met on the Causeway. Only you spoke as distinctly as poor Tina when you were a baby, so we were lucky. The second wife, Salim's mum, is a research assistant in a lab – she is from Pakistan – très chic.

The wedding's on your birthday – but I'm not a bit nervous. The worst (best?) part is over – I didn't see the point of waiting. Are you shocked? Not more than I was when I knew you liked boys. Now you are red as a bangle; don't be. I think it's pretty natural, the way you've grown up with girls. Boys are to you what girls are to boys who've grown up with boys. (Can you repeat that without looking?) Of course, there's another explanation: you knew you were going to be considered different as long as you lived; so you thought better to be stared at as homosexual rather than handicapped!

My charming sister – didn't she realise it wasn't an either-or situation? That I was now at risk of having a double 'h' after my name?

★

162

'Hi!' said Cyrus, that same night. 'You coming?'

'Where to?'

'Hanging Gardens.'

'Just now? They're shut.'

'Doesn't matter. We'll have a ball. Come on.'

'Oh! OK.'

'Brit!' cried Sera from her room, 'you aren't going anywhere. It's almost midnight – '

'It isn't, Sera dear,' said Cyrus. 'It's exactly 10 p.m.'

'But you aren't taking him anywhere. I'm all alone here and if anything happens to him – '

'Nothing has happened to him for years, Sera. And remember, it's his birthday today.'

'You remembered,' I said.

'You are responsible,' shouted Sera, 'if anything goes wrong.'

As soon as Cyrus pushed me out of the lift I saw the cab waiting with Ruby in the back seat. I should've known. 'Wait a minute,' I said, putting on my brakes at the top of the ramp. 'Did you come just because it was my birthday?'

'Fucking shit, Brit. Why are you bugging the life out of me? And will you please release your brakes? I'm sorry. Look, I'm sorry,' and he was balancing on my ramp. 'I should've called and fixed this; I sort of took it for granted you'd come. But I so wanted to celebrate with you and I wasn't sure I'd be able to.'

'I'm not sure I want to come.'

'Well, I'm sure I want you to come.' He bent over and snapped the brakes loose.

'Sorry, darling, for making you wait.' Darling, and he doesn't even love her. He opened the door in the back and lifted me in.

'Happy birthday,' she said, and I whirled so fast I got a catch in my ribs. There was no light in the cab but the orange street lamp was bright and the girl sitting next to me wasn't Ruby. Unless Ruby was wearing a wig of thick, straight nylon hair and she had had cosmetic surgery that had turned her face oval, her nose into a convex cashew nut, her mouth into a pout and her brown eyes black as the night outside.

'Thank you,' I said, remembering Sera and my manners.

'I don't believe you've met,' said Cyrus, getting in from the other door with a delighted grin on his innocent face. 'Amy, this is my old pal, Brit. Brit, that's Amy who's been keeping me busy all these nights. Hanging Gardens, driver.'

Ruby would've been bad enough but at least she was my friend, I'd given her to Cyrus. As for this creature who was sitting between us, to her I wanted to be nasty as a Nazi. 'I say, is your name really Amy? Or is it short for Aimai?' which is one of the stupidest Parsee names and went out with Queen Victoria.

'It really is Amy,' she said. She had this funny way of speaking as if she were on stage – saying each word clearly with the right emphasis and expression. 'My parents were the Raj kind, you know.'

'Hmm.'

'Anglophilia, the Parsee disease,' said Cyrus.

'What about you?' said Amy. 'Is your name really Brit – after Britain?'

'Glass houses,' murmured Cyrus.

'No,' I said, 'my name is Daryus. I'm called Brit because I have brittle bones and I hope you are embarrassed.'

'How lovely! Imagine celebrating your problem. Needs guts.' I didn't know what to say.

'I didn't shave today,' said Cyrus.

'Oh! Thank you, sweetheart! You're going to look so distinguished with a beard.'

'I think you'll look awful.'

'Oh no, he won't. Trust my eye, Brit.'

'I'd rather believe mine.'

'Don't pay any attention to him,' said Cyrus. 'Thinks he's having a conversation from one of those ancient novels, *Pride and Prejudice* or whatever.'

'*Pride and Prejudice* isn't ancient,' we said together. Amy laughed, I didn't.

'So that makes him quite different from you, doesn't it?' she said. 'You hate speechifying.'

'I'm no good at it.'

'I don't care. Makes me feel grand. "Words cannot pay you what I owe."'

'John Wain,' I murmured, looking out of the window.

'Don't be ridiculous,' said Cyrus, 'I bet the Duke never said that in any of his movies.'

'Oh darling,' said Amy, laughing and laying her head on his shoulder. 'Brit was talking about a poet, John Wain – W–a–i–n. Are you a Wain fan?'

'I like his poetry.'

'So do I. But I can't find any of his stuff here. I managed to get some from London. The British Council has his novels; it's the poetry I want. One is not enough.'

I wondered if I could ask to borrow that one. Maybe it was worth swallowing my pride – for Art's sake.

'Why don't you borrow it from Amy?' said Cyrus.

'I don't have the time.'

'I'll give it to you and you can keep it till you do.' She kissed Cyrus's cheek.

'Here we are,' said Cyrus to the driver. 'Please wait; we'd like you to take us back.' He got out of the cab to haul my chair from the boot.

'I read your story,' she said, turning to me. 'It made me cry.'

'It wasn't meant to.'

She smiled and I saw with delight that her teeth were crooked.

'Do you write much?' she said.

'No, this was my first story.'

'That's wonderful. If your first attempt was so good – '

'You *flatter* me,' I said.

'I don't. I'm a pretty good judge of these things.'

'Sez who?'

'I do. And I'd better know how to judge books because I'm going to be a librarian.'

'Really! That's what I've always wanted to be.' But there was no way I could carry a pile of books and steer my chair round at the same time. I didn't want her to ask why I didn't so I asked Cyrus, 'What's the matter?'

'He's refusing to wait.'

'So tell him to go,' said Amy, flinging back her wig.

'And who's going to get us a cab at midnight?'

'We'll walk till we find one.'

'It isn't safe for a girl.'

'I've got Brit and you to protect me.'

'OK, come on.' Cyrus plonked me into the chair. Bombay

shimmered below us, slung like a heavy gold necklace on the dark throat of the bay.

'What does this remind you of?' asked Amy because she wanted to be asked.

'A city,' said Cyrus. 'A proud city with so much life it burns into the night. What does it remind *you* of?' he asked, turning.

'Naples,' said Amy and, unfortunately, I together.

Cyrus sniggered, 'Look what all those books have done to you. You've never seen Naples and yet you can think of nothing but that when you see your own city lying at your feet.'

'Our imprisoned imagination,' laughed Amy.

'That's not true,' I said. 'All those books have let our minds fly to Naples and connect two sights halfway across the world.'

Cyrus lifted his eyebrows at me as if to say, You're so clever. 'Never mind,' said Amy. 'I loved your strong, simple image.' And then they smooched right there in front of me as if I were a statue in the park.

I remembered another kiss I'd seen – Tina and Rohit's. Nothing good had come out of that. I hoped nothing would come out of this, either; I wondered what would happen if I mentioned Ruby's name and a wicked giggle escaped me. It was OK; they weren't listening. It was incredible; they were still locked together like one of Rodin's sculptures. That reminded me – a Rodin exhibition was coming to Bombay soon and I was terrified of missing it. I couldn't think of anyone who'd want to see it with me.

'Why,' said Amy, 'do they have statues of old, ugly men? Why can't they have someone like you? Young, tall, with lips that curve down in a smile?'

'I agree,' I said in spite of myself.

'Shut up, Brit.'

'Don't be rude,' said Amy, 'just because you're embarrassed. Brit, one day when we are rich we'll put up that statue. Right here – where he's standing.'

'I think it's time to sing "Happy Birthday" to Brit.'

'You dare not!'

'Oh, yes I do!' said Amy. Which in my head earned her a

slap. They sang, Cyrus with his arms behind his back, Amy, swinging her ridiculous nylon hair from side to side.

'Shall I kiss you?' said Cyrus.

'Of course, darling!' I twittered. He bent down and kissed my cheek with a loud squelch. I recoiled at more than the bristle and for a second I wondered if this was all for the best.

Amy shook my hand. 'I hope we become friends,' she said. 'We have such a lot in common.' She looked at Cyrus who was watching us sardonically. I could've killed him; he had obviously told her my whole gay past. Yes, past. I didn't reply.

'Let's go,' said Cyrus. 'Or we'll never get a cab.'

We trotted down the speed-breaker-breasted hill. 'Ooh! I'm cold,' said Amy and Cyrus freed one arm from my chair to hold her close. I didn't fancy tumbling downhill. Of course, Cyrus hadn't thought of that. I'd probably end up as pile of powdered bone.

'Just let go of that chair, Amy.' So now he was making jokes about my helplessness. How my hero had fallen! Taking me with him. I had my faults but being declamatory as a bad politician was not one of them. Till now. I wondered if they'd hear if I started howling. The chair had stopped. I twisted round to see what the matter was. They were smooching again, his hands on her round bottom, moving in circles. Well, I guess I should have been grateful we had reached the bottom of the hill.

'Pussy, wake up,' said Sera gently. I opened my eyes like a shot. I didn't want her to know I'd gone to bed at three in the morning. Cyrus had dropped me off without even waiting to see if I managed the latch-key, because Amy was waiting in the taxi and, who knows, the driver might have taken off with her. If only.

So anyway, I got back, changed into shorts and got into bed, but I couldn't sleep. I looked around for something to read – there was a new book by V.S. Naipaul and a couple of romance comics that Dolly had left behind which had to be returned to the mobile library on the pavement across the Causeway. I wanted poetry. I went to the shelf and remembered where I'd buried Shelley and Swinburne and Oscar Wilde and all the rest that night the stars shone for Cyrus. I pushed my arm up to my elbow into a pile of books, snatched at whatever there was and an avalanche swooshed down on me. Books hit my head, arms, chest, knees before they hit the floor. All the poetry I had loved and locked away was at my feet. But I was too tired to pick it up. I left it there and went to bed.

'Brush your teeth and wash your face,' said Sera.

I looked at the sky. It was grey – I knew the sun couldn't have come up at Apollo yet. 'What's the matter, Sera? Why did you wake me so early?'

'I'm sorry,' she said.

'What?' This was the first time in my whole life that my mother had apologised to me; something was seriously wrong.

'Yes, Brit, I'm sorry because I know how late you went to sleep; I heard those books fall. But I had to tell someone. Sam is dead. Don't worry. We'll manage. I'm here to take care of you. And as usual,' she smiled bravely, 'I'm prepared.'

'Yes,' I said, feeling numb as my nose in winter, but I knew that wasn't right. She needed me to feel all broken up. You can't have a brave act without an audience.

'How – how did he die?' I asked, my voice beginning to shiver.

'I'm not sure,' she said, smoothing my bedsheet with her palm as if she were trying to iron it. 'It was an accident, Dolly said. On Fifth Avenue – he was trying to cross. They said he must have misread the traffic signals – '

'How could he? He was Mr Walker,' I said, thinking I was making him sound like the Phantom.

'Yes, I thought of that too. And there was – '

'It was the wedding yesterday, wasn't it?' I said, feeling a sob for my Dolly.

'Yes, but this was after. But listen! they found a large scarf tied around his forehead.'

'It must be cold; it's almost cool here.'

'Brit, think. Was Sam the kind of man to tie a scarf round his forehead? My husband had style, Brit, he'd wear a hat.'

'What does it matter?' He wouldn't ever wear his blue suit again.

'Do you think, Brit?' And Sera's voice was trembling like it never did when I was born.

'What, Mum, what?' Like a doorbell through ear-plugs, I heard myself calling her something I never had.

'Do you think, the scarf might have been – '

I shut my eyes. The blindfold. Fifth Avenue instead of the Causeway; no Sera to stop him. No proof for me to be thinking this but his sense of style. I was thinking, deciding what would make it easier for Sera – an accident, senseless, meaningless, or this, Sam's way, his last classy act.

'How could he? How could he? How could he?' I couldn't say anything else and all the time I was thinking: Of course he could. He had been on his own almost all his life. He'd been through school and climbed up the bank ladder, met Sera and had me, which was harder than climbing. And he'd fought, sure as Sera had fought but without her brave act to keep him safe. Because he never stopped feeling; he couldn't pretend to himself that everything was all right. Maybe he looked at life too straight. I knew how he must have felt. Being able to shut his eyes and move, for once. Without worrying whether Sera would go off balance or Brit would break a leg or he'd lose that new job which paid him half of what he used to get at the bank. Such fun, such bliss. I mean, there's only so much you can go through. After that you've got to take a break. I remember that *Kusti* he kept tucked away between his shirts and socks.

But Sam didn't want a break this long. He loved us too much and he hoped too much. Or he wouldn't have fed me powdered pearls. But I couldn't tell Sera all this. She didn't want me to be wise. It was so easy to cry. All I had to do was think: He wanted to hug me before he left and I didn't let him. Because I was trying to grow. Trying – not grown enough.

'Pull yourself together, Brit,' said Sera. 'We have to if we are going to get through this. There's no time to sit and cry. There's so much to do – no funeral, thank God. I told Dolly to – '

'Don't get the ashes here,' I sobbed. 'That's ghoulish.'

'I won't, Brit.' She hugged me tight. 'I told Dolly she can keep them. It made her feel better. She was crying like a . . . like a . . . widow.'

169

So was I and my ribs were starting to hurt ominously.

'No funeral; but we'll have some prayers. I'll tell Defarge; she's good at arranging all that. The fire-temple and the priests and the notices in the papers. Jeroo's no use – all she'll do is give me a mantra to mutter. I'm not like her. I don't lose my head. Oh, please stop crying, Brit, or you'll crack something.'

The next day, we had the *uthamna* in the hall of the squat-domed fire-temple that guarded the Parsee colony across the street like a fat white Buddha. Which was sad because most of Sam's colleagues from the bank had to stand outside. They weren't Parsee. Their presence would have defiled the fire-temple. So they came and waited; listening to the prayers that wafted through the arched doors together with wisps of smoke from the burning sandalwood and incense. When we came out – Sera dressed in an unadorned white sari, the end covering her white head like a veil, and I pushed along by Cyrus, wearing white pants and the long muslin *dagli* with bows all the way from my collar to my knees – they shook hands with us.

'Such a gentleman. So kind, so good.'

'He is surely in heaven.'

'He will be great man in his next birth.'

Sera nodded gravely like the heroine of a Greek tragedy, not that I'd ever seen one. Nor had I seen the mourners before. Sam had had no time for friends, what with me around.

Ruby came up to me. 'He always asked me to stay for dinner,' she said. Her eyes looked as if she had conjunctivitis. I nodded, and smiled.

Some distance away, on the same pavement as us, Defarge, dressed in black, surrounded by some relatives we didn't quite recognise, was making a *festaa*, crying loudly, beating her breast. Sera and I watched with horror while she groaned, 'What ill-luck is hers! A widow with a crippled son. Helpless. You, You . . .' she thrust a palm into the sky, 'Why did You have to take him away and leave them behind?'

Suddenly Amy was next to me, kneeling in a grey chiffon sari. 'You blush too?' she said. 'I'm glad; I always thought it was some sort of leftover from the nineteenth century when ladies swooned.'

'I do that too when I feel like it,' I said, letting the words fall like acid. She had no business coming here. Cyrus wanted to see her whitewashed face while he sat through the endless *uthamna*, I thought.

She smiled. She smiled again. 'I know it's bad form and all that,' she said. 'But I've brought the John Wain. It's for you. I'll get another copy for myself.'

'I'll return it,' I said grimly. 'I don't like taking other people's books.' I shifted in my chair to signal Cyrus to move. He paid no attention. Jeroo floated up to me; she was wearing a most inappropriate pink nylon sari. 'Isn't it fitting,' she said, a smile walking in and out of her mouth, 'that Sera should bid him farewell here where he saw her for the first time.'

'I know, Jeroo.'

'Do you think,' she said vaguely, 'that he'll meet Tina up there? Won't be much use, though; Sam never learnt sign language. You look as if you've been crying too,' she said, turning to Amy. 'Anyway, who are you?'

Amy blinked and shook her head. 'I was thinking of someone,' she said.

'Someone you loved and lost?' asked Jeroo eagerly.

'Yes – I mean no, not loved and lost like . . . I was thinking of my father. He died four months ago.'

'Don't say died. His soul shifted to another plane.'

Amy cocked her head and nodded. I wished Jeroo would shut up. Defarge was still at it, pouring imprecations at the fire-temple, which she obviously thought was God's address.

'This is intolerable,' said Sera, marching across to her. 'If you don't stop this *festaa* right now, this moment – ' Defarge wailed like a dog in a hit and run accident and entwined herself around Sera who dusted her off, flicking her sari impatiently. 'All these people are watching you, Defarge. And for your own sake, to save you from shame, I am warning you that I will no longer buy your bread from the *powwallah* when you go to the pictures on Saturday evening if you don't stop now.' Defarge stopped.

'Remarkable use of psychology,' said Amy, smiling and tossing her head to push back the hair which was throwing a curtain across her face. I deposited one more slap into her account. I mean, she had no business laughing at a freshly-minted widow.

'Let's go,' said Cyrus. 'Amy, see you later.'

'Can't I walk with you?' she asked as if she were sure he wanted her to.

'I'm afraid not,' said Cyrus, smiling shyly. 'Brit and I have to talk.'

'Oh! Sure. See you, then. See you, Brit. Let's meet more often.'

'I don't think I'll have time.' I subtracted a slap from that account. We walked away along a long green lawn that would take us to the gates of the Parsee Colony and the Causeway. 'So,' I said, 'what did you want to talk about?'

'Nothing,' laughed Cyrus. 'I just wanted to get away from her. Didn't want Ruby asking funny questions.'

'Do you realise what you are doing?'

'Yes.'

'And you don't care?'

'Look, I've told Ruby I don't love her. I've told Amy I believe sex doesn't always go with love. I'm not being dishonest – '

'You're just taking care of their feelings.'

'Oh, shut up, Brit. You make it impossible for me to confide in you. I didn't tell you about Amy. I knew how you'd react – all horror, no understanding. You've got your values, I've got mine, OK?'

'What you mean is you can't stand it when I make you feel guilty about betraying both Amy and Ruby.'

'You left yourself out. I've betrayed you too, haven't I? By falling in love. We're almost home, thank God.'

'Cyrus,' I said, twisting around in my chair so I could see his face, 'is it really so awful for you to talk to me?'

'Are you crazy?' He smiled his dark-eyed smile. 'We're friends – we've got to quarrel sometimes.'

'I thought friends never needed to quarrel.'

'Come down from the clouds, Brit!' said Ruby from behind. 'Tell me, who was that beautiful chick you were talking to?'

'One of his new journalist friends,' said Cyrus. 'You getting jealous?'

'Why should I? I've got you,' she said, undoing the top bow of his *dagli*.

'Just a slice,' I said, but they weren't listening. Cyrus was pushing me up the ramp Sam had had made for me. I shivered. I felt as if all my life I'd been bundled up against the wind, and now one by one my woollies were being taken from me.

19

THEY HAD A swing instead of a sofa in their drawing-room. When Jerry wheeled me in, his mother jumped off the swing in such a hurry the little servant girl who had been pushing her to and fro was knocked to the floor. 'Don't show off in front of the sahib,' said Rati Davierwalla. 'So pleased to meet a famous writer.'

Jerry had phoned more often than I had feared in the weeks after that evening at the Taj. Each time Sera had fielded his calls and ferociously flung them back. 'His father is dead; he is not seeing anyone.'

One morning, while I was still talc-white after my bath, Jerry walked into my flat. (It was mine now Sam was dead; leaving it to Sera would've meant another dose of estate duty when she died.) 'You're mad or what? My father died too, last year; as if you have to stay in purdah for ever after.'

'How did you know where I lived?'

'Bombay Telephone Reverse Directory.'

'Oh.'

'Come, we'll go.' I smiled in terror. 'I'll show you my house now I have seen yours.'

He lived in Princess Street and I couldn't help being disappointed. 'Why,' I asked, forgetting everything gentle Sam had ever taught me, 'why do you live in this noisy smelly street when you can afford to live at the Hanging Gardens?'

'Lucky house,' he said with a shrug, 'and lucky you I only live on the first floor.'

He hollered up the stair-well and an obedience of servants came thudding down on their bare feet. 'Lift!' he commanded with one finger and I was hoisted up in my chair to their shoulders.

I looked down and Jerry was grinning, his big ugly face bright with delight. 'I love this!' I yelled. 'It's the only time they'll chair me shoulder high.'

'Most welcome,' Raty said, 'to our humble dwelling.' No truer word was ever spoken. The swing was upholstered in tomato ketchup-velvet, the chandelier was pink crystal with little emerald prisms hanging from the centre, the five chairs strewn over the orange lino floor were easy chairs, the kind you find in colonial clubs, and the walls were shiny grey emulsion, three of them, the one facing the window being red. It reminded me of Sam with that plastic bucket. And I was as homesick as the Duke of Windsor on 11 December 1936.

'Cheer up,' said Jerry. 'It's not *so* bad. Is it?' He looked as if he'd lost those orchards in Davier.

'I'm sorry, it's just so . . . new.'

'Anything you want, you say,' said Rati kindly. 'Rose, Mangola, Vimto, Limca, Thumbs Up, Sprint, Tango.' With each offer her oiled black plait swung over her shoulder and back, over and back. She was wearing the kind of sari Sera wouldn't wear to a wedding – peacock-blue with gold peacocks emblazoned all over.

'Brit won't have any of those,' said Jerry. 'I know what he likes.' He disappeared into the flat.

'I dressed up to honour you,' said Rati, feeling the weight of the thick gold chain like a manacle round her big brown neck.

'Thank you, Mrs Davierwalla.'

'Silly boy! Call me Rati Auntie.'

'Yes, Auntie Rati.'

'My Jerry, you know, he likes you *so* much; all the time he is talking-talking of you. I said what is so special about this boy? Bring him here; I will see and say. I have seen, now I will say – '

My ears perked up; until now I had been listening to her very carefully, paying no attention to what she said. Because I wanted to catch the particular rhythm of her speech, record her strange idiom in my brain to use some day in a story I would write.

175

'How strange you are looking,' she said, her eyes amused but kindly so, 'like you are big in brain – '

'But small in body,' I said helpfully.

'Brittle bones but . . .' She actually paused for me to finish; I stayed silent. 'Brittle bones but English heart.'

I began to wonder if she was all right.

'Stout English heart,' she said. 'Your accent, your name, your profession – all are English. I attended English-medium school in Davier, only four girls like me in the town. I can appreciate English culture, John Geel-Good, Windsor Castle, Lord By Ron and Hussy Caroline, White Cliffs, Dover sole, cucumber sandwich, Elizabeth and Essex, Sixty Glorious Years, Father Christmas, *not* Santa Claus,' she finished triumphantly.

'What an interesting education you must have had,' I said.

'And I married a palestine,' she said mournfully. I wondered if that accounted for Jerry's weird looks. But the surname was vintage Parsee; maybe she had kept her own.

'How did you meet him?' I asked.

'In Davier. He would come and go. You understand?'

'Oh, yes.' She meant he was one of those Arab smugglers who were always landing on that coast near Davier (with their contraband Sony tape-recorders, Sanyo transistors, JVC videos) in their sophisticated little ships, still called *dhows*.

'He was a palestine but my father gave me to him – '

'For?'

'For? For what does man give woman to man?'

'I don't know – business?'

'Funny boy. Security, children, sickness, food.'

'And after you were given . . . you went to . . .?' I didn't dare name the country her Palestine had become.

'Where?' she asked ominously.

'You know what I mean . . . Haifa, Nablus, Jerusalem.'

She sprang out of the swing and swooshed across the lino to where I was. I knew I'd done something awful, offended her in a fierce way. I screamed like only Osteo Man can.

'Are you OK? Are you fine? Are you getting a fit?' she asked, holding my head back like a dentist.

'Yes, I'm sorry I talked of those places.'

'What places?'

'You know, 'P'.''

'I can't understand you. My poor Daryus used to say, the more brains a man has the less sense he makes.'

'Who was your poor Daryus? – that is my real name too.'

'Daryus was my mister.'

'Your?' Mister could only mean the male counterpart of mistress.

'My mister – late Daryus Davierwala of lamentable memory.'

Spouse-shocked as I was I couldn't even smile at that. 'But you said . . .' My voice was as petulant as a spoilt child's. 'You said he was a Palestinian.'

'Yes,' she said, 'he was.'

'But his name is as Parsee as mine.'

'Yes, he was a Parsee palestine. You know what a palestine is, don't you?' I shook my head in surrender. 'A palestine,' she said patiently, 'is a man who does not appreciate English culture.'

'Oh, of course,' I breathed, 'a philistine.'

'My Jerry is also a palestine.'

'What did you say I was? Look what I got! My last one saved up all this time.' I looked at the bottle of Coca-Cola as if it were that last phial of smallpox stored up in some lab. Coca-Cola was banished from India in 1977 like its predecessors Kraft cheese and Nestlé chocolate before I was born. Most people I knew managed to get a can from their local smuggler when the urge hit them badly. But to have stashed away a bottle for Job's years. What wicked alterations might have worked themselves into that secret formula, I shuddered to think.

'How sweet!' exclaimed Rati. 'He is shivering with pleasure.' After that, there was no escape. I downed the drink, feeling it buzz on my tongue as if I had slugged a mouthful of insects.

'Who knows!' said Jerry. 'It might work magic on you – turn you from Brit into Hard.' He slapped his stomach and fell about laughing. How easily he saw it – my small strange body, and with him I felt the gap between myself and what I happened to be almost closing.

'What shall we play?' asked Jerry.

'Play?' I nearly suggested the Ice Game, then I said, 'Bridge?'

'Golden Gate or Sydney Harbour?' He saw my face. 'I'm only joking, *yaar*. No bridge for me. I like games like Flush, make money, lose money.'

'Oh no! I couldn't. My parents, my mother, I mean, doesn't like me gambling.'

'You never have to ever tell her. Shyamoo! Get the cards, chips, table!'

'I really don't think I can – besides, I haven't brought any money along.'

'Never mind, I'll take your watch if you lose.' I looked at it, my Citizen quartz, my first and only electronic tick-tock, Dolly's last real gift.

'And if I win?'

'I have something good, you will like it for sure.'

'What, Jerry? That one?' said Rati, rolling her eyes like an Indian dancer. He nodded.

'Ten minutes,' I said. 'Only ten minutes of Flush.'

Jerry leaned across the card table and whispered into my ear, 'When you do *that*, do you also say only ten minutes?'

I went as red as the wall opposite but I said, 'Your deal, Zarthost.' I picked up my three cards – a deuce, a deuce, a deuce. A trio, I couldn't believe my luck. We had gambled half the pile of chips before Jerry asked for a show. I put my cards down and smiled like Defarge does when she's heard of some young girl's engagement. He had a knave and a knave and knave and he'd won.

'My deal,' I said, dry-mouthed. The cards felt warm to my fingers – I had a fairly decent run. Three minutes later I found Jerry had an indecently good run. I looked at his heap of chips and felt as deprived as a peasant in the Grand Moghal's court.

'Third and last deal,' cawed Jerry. 'I'll have to get a new strap for that watch – my wrist is twice as big as yours.'

Oh, never mind, I thought, it's going to look like a tiny hat on an elephant's head when he wears it. I was breathing like an asthmatic by the time I saw my cards – a king, a roi, a rex. The only combination that could beat me was a triplet of aces. But I knew all about the law of averages from those medical books that told me how I was the one with osteo and Dolly wasn't. I played my little molehill of chips with the confidence and ease of someone who knows he's going to make a mountain of it. When the cards were down, I was loosening my watchstrap.

'Thanks,' he said, as if I'd handed him a glass of water. I would have to tell Sera I'd lost the watch.

'Now for something with less tension – '

'Stomach worship,' said Rati from behind me where she'd been watching her son gyp me out of my sister's parting present.

I smiled sweetly. 'Oh! I didn't know I was having lunch with you; that's very kind.'

'Mention not,' she said, but I shall. I shall sing of hot chapatis silky with butter, pungent pickle of dark dates and golden almonds, tiger prawns fierce in their chilli-red sauce, tender kid gentle in creamed cashew nut, an emperor's pilaff with more raisins than rice and crowned with chicken breasts, a millionaire's custard crammed with plump apricots soaked in tongue-burning rum. When I'd finished, my tummy felt as taut as my poor cock used to be through those long nights with Cyrus.

'Now for another game!' said Jerry gaily and I searched myself up and down for something more to lose. Maybe I could gamble my eyelashes away. But Jerry had something else in mind. 'Perfect after a heavy lunch,' he said, as we went huffing up the ladders and slithering down the snakes I hadn't played since I could read a book.

'Evening-time, video-time,' announced Rati and, against my will, my eyebrows flickered up and down. 'Let Brit choose,' she said graciously. 'We have three films, all English, all top class: *Mad Monkey Kung Fu*, *Conan the Barbarian*, *Nightmare on Elm Street*.'

Groan, yawn or scream. 'Scream,' I said.

'You want some? Vanilla, chocolate – '

'No!' I shouted, stopping her ersatz Goon Show. 'I'll see the nightmare.'

I saw it, and saw it again that night in my sleep, and for four days after.

'I think I must go,' I said, looking at the sky instead of my wrist. The first star was glowing like a kiss in the dark; I wanted to be home.

'The driver will drop you,' said Jerry. 'But first – '

'But first . . .' said Rati, swtiching on the shocking-pink and parrot-green chandelier. Jerry put a hard square package into my hand.

'Keep it well,' said Rati. 'It is so valuable to people like us – '

I undid the white string and unwrapped the brown paper. Then I tore the tissue that bandaged the gift. I was prepared to gasp and squawk and let my eyelashes hit my lids but all I did was breathe deep and slow, again and again till I could speak at all. 'But this is a first edition,' was all I managed to say as I felt the precious weight of Housman's heartbreaking *Last Poems* in my hand.

'Read,' said Rati, 'what I have prescribed on the flyleaf.'

I knew what Cyrus would have to say when he read what she'd written and he did. 'Sounds like you bloody deflowered her,' he chuckled, his knees leaping with delight as he sang in a falsetto: 'To my first English Man, Brit, from your compatriot, Rati D. Davierwala.'

'How can I ever thank you?'

'Mention not,' she said, while Jerry looked like Father Christmas. 'We have to thank you for coming to our humble' – she looked at the chandelier in unconscious irony – 'abode, a fine gentleman like you.'

'Don't throw that tissue away,' said Jerry. I frowned and crumpled it suspiciously.

I suppose I knew what I expected to find. 'That's not fair,' I said, holding my grin on a leash.

'It is,' said Jerry, 'when you know how to stack the cards like I do.'

I gasped and squawked and let my lashes hit those lids. 'Be careful,' said Jerry softly, kneeling next to me. 'In life you'll have to know more than the books you read – '

'Or write . . . Hey' – I had plenty of practice breaking moods with Sera and Sam – 'the big fire-temple is bang opposite your house. Auntie Rati, do you go and pray every day?'

She recoiled. 'Oh, no,' she said, 'certainly not. Only on good days – my Jerry's birthday and such like. But I'm glad it's there opposite blessing us. Therefore, this is a lucky house.'

'It certainly is,' I said, watching my watch tell me the time.

20

THE NEXT THING we did was get that slave for me who turned out to be a guy called Esmero from old Portuguese Goa. Cyrus and Sera taught him how to lift me in and out of taxis carefully, how to tip my chair and pull it up a flight of steps or roll it down. He nodded his grey head and slapped his pockets confidently.

The first time I went out with him alone was to the British Council Library. I told him he could do whatever he wanted for two hours, as long as he came back for me at noon. At one-thirty I started feeling hungry. At two-thirty I started feeling giddy looking at books. At three-thirty I wanted to cry but the thought of being twenty-one stopped me. At four-thirty I wanted to die because closing time was just half an hour away. I knew Sera was out for the day, having lunch with Jeroo and seeing her first movie since Sam died. I also knew Cyrus was never home before eight in the evening.

'Hi!' said Amy. 'When did you come in?'

'This morning,' I said with difficulty; my tongue felt like it was supposed to when we played Lost in the Desert.

'Wow! Marathon read?'

'Not really; my man has forgotten to fetch me.'

'You mean you are stuck here?' she said in a horrified stagy manner, wide eyes and all.

'Sort of,' I laughed casually. 'I don't mind. There's more to read here that I can manage in a day.'

'But what about lunch and stuff? Oh, Brit, you must be dying.'

'Don't worry, I'm fine.'

'Look. I get off in half an hour – I'm training here. But I'll ask them to let me go straight away.'

'Please don't do that. You can't take me home.'

'Of course I can. I've seen Cyrus do it. You tell me how.'

'You can't lift me,' I said wearily. I realised I wanted to pee. But the toilet here would be useless. I never sat on a seat because I was too small, too terrified of falling in. At home, I had a special ring that fitted on. I wondered what would happen if my bladder went bust. There would be a noise, like the water-filled balloons Ruby and I used to toss into the Causeway. The librarian would come runing. 'Silence, please!' she'd say, then scream and hitch her skirts up when she found her ankles wet.

And now Amy was going to help me. I'd rather have died than accept, but this was turning out harder than dying. I knew I'd let her take me home. I couldn't even hate the people I wanted to.

'I've done it!' said Amy. 'Let's go.'

'You didn't have to.'

'Of course not. I wanted to.' She smiled.

I looked at her crooked canine and her nylon hair tied up; at last I knew why they called them pony-tails. What a bastard I was thinking that even while she was pushing me through the doors.

'You wait here,' she said. 'I'll fetch the lift. It won't come up on its own.'

'Thanks, thanks a lot.'

'My pleasure,' she said, patting my head. We drifted down and reached the steps. She rolled my chair down on its back wheels without any accidents. 'That was easy,' she said.

'Thanks; thanks a lot.'

We didn't have to wait long for a cab. 'OK,' she said. 'Now you tell me how to lift you.'

'Like this; around the chest.' I wondered if my armpits were sweaty. She bent her knees to get a lift. I didn't rise an inch. I exhaled to make myself lighter.

'I can't do it,' she said, turning up her white palms, her eyes wide with astonishment.

'I told you you wouldn't be able to.' I wasn't sure if I believed she couldn't. Maybe she was just getting her own back for all the times I'd been nasty to her.

The taxi-driver came to my rescue. 'Let me try, sahib,' he grinned. I knew he might crush my ribs, but what the heck, I was desperate.

'I should've known,' said Amy with a smile, sitting next to me in the back seat. 'It needs a man to lift a man.'

A man? Who was she talking about? I was Brit Boy. But I had to admit she was right. Even if I didn't look much of a man. I had started shaving last month. I couldn't decide if I should be good and grateful, talk nicely to her, sort of keep her happy because she was doing this for me. Or should I be what I wanted to be – cool and nasty?

'Do you feel obliged,' she asked, looking out of the window, 'when something like this happens?' I shifted to make more room for the pee in me. 'You don't have to answer,' she said, 'if you don't want to.'

'I felt horribly obliged.' Especially when I don't like the kind helper.

'I thought as much the way you've been shifting in your seat as if you were dying of embarrassment.'

'How perceptive,' I said.

'You shouldn't, you know.'

'Shouldn't what?'

'Feel bad about this. It's nothing.'

'Thanks for nothing.'

'No, really. Look, if you saw a blind man trying to cross a street, wouldn't you help him across?'

'I can't. So it makes no sense.'

'Well, it does to me. You see an old lady struggling with heavy parcels, you rush to help her. No one thinks they're doing anyone a favour.'

'I do.'

'But when you see someone – someone with a problem?'

'My problem is that I forget. I forget I have a problem. Then when I have to ask someone for help, I feel as awful as you'd feel if you had to be lifted into this cab.'

'But how?'

'Funny, isn't it? When someone is the way I am, you'd think he'd *never* forget it. But I do. For hours, days. Till I pass a mirror or am ditched at the library.'

'Oh, Brit.' She swallowed and smiled and shook her head. Thank God her eyes were dry.

Why did I have to tell her all this? Because, hell, it was ages since I had really talked to anyone, and I didn't admit it to myself, but I was as lonely as Robinson Crusoe before he found his Man Friday.

'Here we are,' said Amy. 'This time I'd better let him do it.' I didn't answer. She waited while I paid the cabbie. At least she didn't offer to pay.

'Will you come in?' I said, while I prayed that the latch-key would fit. It didn't. I took it out, put it in again. Three times. Amy was watching the Causeway from the lobby windows. 'Will you come in?' I repeated.

'No, I won't,' she said. The door clicked open. 'Because I've got to get home and have a bath and dress. Cyrus is coming for dinner.'

'OK,' I said, quite relieved. Now I could pee as soon and as long as I liked. 'Thanks; thanks a lot.'

'Thank you, Brit. For talking. Even if you regret it now.' She sent me a wink and a smile over her shoulder and disappeared into the lift. It was too dark for me to see that crooked canine.

Luckily, Esmero came to see me before Sera returned from the movies.

When I opened the door to him I wheeled back until I bumped into the wall. He smelled like an unwashed goat. 'Ten ruppish,' he slobbered. 'Ten ruppish for doctor injection.'

I had to smile at that, lovely word, though I was terrified. I'd seen drunks reeling in the road but never one in my house. Esmero was towering over me while I sat with my back to the wall. 'Please move,' I said as firmly as Sera.

'Not moving. Twenty ruppish for hot medicine.' Again I smiled. His smell was turning my stomach like exams had never done. 'Don't shmile,' he threatened, 'give me thirty ruppish now or I throw you from that window.'

He bent down shakily and thrust his face into mine. I saw little bits of dirt in the ridges of his sunken cheeks and his lips sticky with some grey juice. He came closer. I thought he was going to kiss me. I thought of Cyrus and his laughing mouth which I'd refused. I remembered the impotent hours I'd spent at the library. Rage pumped through me till I felt it surge in my fingertips. I lifted a big book from the shelf on my left with one hand and smashed it on Esmero's head. He groaned and fell back. I lifted the book from the floor and poised it over his bloated belly which dared to stare at me through his unbuttoned shirt. He opened his eyes and drew his legs in for protection. I let the book fall on his knee. He whined shrilly and began rolling towards the door. I pushed him, shoving my front wheels into his back, his torso, his shanks, till he was at the top of the staircase. I rolled the wheels into him and he tumbled down shrieking impotently seven times, till he thudded on the landing like a dead thing.

Wheeling into the flat, I slammed the door. I was shivering like Sam had once shivered when he had malaria; little jerks in the muscles and teeth hitting each other in a crazy tap-dance. I breathed deeply, held my breath, counted ten, let go. The counting helped; I stopped twitching.

Then I saw the book I had crashed on Esmero's head lying on the floor. It was so huge, I wondered how I'd ever managed to lift it with one arm, and that my left. I bent down and peered at the book's spine: *The Complete Works of Shakespeare*. Seeing it lying there on the speckled tiled floor, a strand of Esmero's hair clinging to its shiny red cover, made me sad in a frightening sort of way. Not for the book I'd never use again, not for Esmero lying broken at the bottom of the stairs. For myself, and what I'd done. Like Hitler or someone who felt so awful about themselves, so weak, so powerless, the only way they could feel all right was by making someone else feel that way. Even while I shut my eyes and insisted over and over again: This is what osteo has done to me. I knew it was as foolish as saying osteo was making me write all those stories I was selling. I knew I couldn't hide behind my bones much longer.

Dolly was cured. After Sam went away, her letters had been so weepy you felt like drying your hands when you finished them. Now, she wrote:

I know you can't see it like this but I think Cyrus falling in love is fantastic. That means there's hope for you. You

185

know, normal – I'm sorry – straight sex is enormous fun. All the *Playgirls* and *Penthouses* are to the Real Thing what zircons are to diamonds.

Sera writes me these horribly cheerful letters – is she trying to make me feel better or is she working on herself? The last one about this 'perverse picture' she had seen about a man who leaves his wife for another man who leaves him – she thought it was hilarious. Have you seen it? Seems to be just up your street.

Esmero must have been a filthy experience. Knowing you, you've turned it into a story. What about *The Cruel Kotwals* – are you shaping it in your head? What am I going to be like? Crazy? Kind? Kinky? Or just me – super sister?

She'd said it.

Cyrus became very attentive to me. Maybe, I thought, he feels sorry for my slaveless state. It was like old times – we went to concerts and carnivals and to the Cricket Club for a swim.

I did see that Rodin exhibition I was worried about. It was great. Actually, Cyrus took me only because Amy wanted to see it.

The Kiss was not quite at my eye-level and I was dying to touch it, so I thought of asking Cyrus to lift me high enough. I didn't care that the crowd would stare. I mean, Rodin wasn't going to be in Bombay again in my lifetime. But I couldn't take the idea of Amy watching me being hoisted up, my legs dangling useless as a rag doll's. I wanted to kill her, because a minute later she stood on tiptoe, her white shift dress climbing above her knee, and kissed *The Kiss*. 'For God's sake, stop that!' said Cyrus, frowning with embarrassment. 'They'll chuck us out of here.'

'People probably think you're cuckoo,' I chimed in.

'You didn't mean that, did you?' she said. 'Because it's exactly what you would've liked to do.' She had this way of ambushing me with the truth; she'd done it in the cab about the obligation, and now this.

Cyrus walked away to show he wasn't with us.

'How did you know?' I said.

'Remember the Bay of Naples?'

I smiled, trying to keep my lips straight. Cyrus came up close and without looking at us said, 'How about dinner at the Trattoria?'

The Hotel President had this terrific Italian restaurant with waiters in red-and-white-checked aprons that matched the table-cloths and glazed pottery in blue and beige and brown studding the cream walls.

'Table for two?' said the maître d'hôtel (who was distinguished by the apron he didn't wear) when he saw Cyrus wheeling me in.

'See, Brit,' said Amy, shrugging her shoulders, '*I'm* the odd one out.'

If only she were. 'I'm going to wash my hands,' said Cyrus. 'They're filthy from hauling your chair in and out of the boot.' He made a face at me.

'Were the two of you . . .?' Amy shrugged her shoulders.

'Two of us, what?' I said.

'In love?'

'You mean gay?' I asked.

'Well, yes?'

'No, we weren't.'

'But you adore him, don't you?'

'That's one way of saying it.'

'You don't want to talk about it?'

'I don't mind.' I was dying to – I mean, I liked talking about Cyrus more than a Marxist likes talking about Marx.

'You hate me for taking him away?'

'There was nothing to take away. We didn't *do* anything – smooch or hold hands or Princeton fuck.'

'Whatever is that?'

'You rub rods,' I muttered.

'Really? Oh, Brit! God! That's hilarious. And don't keep blushing like that. I'm sure it isn't good for your health.'

'You keep your nylon hair off your face.'

'Nylon! Is that how it looks?'

'Like a brown shower curtain.'

She went hysterical, holding her forehead, shaking, stuffing the checked red and white napkin into her mouth. She grabbed

Cyrus's glossy new packet of Dunhills and flung it into the potted plant behind her.

'What's that for?'

'Stop him smoking – I'm scared he'll die on me.'

'So am I.'

'Then you won't tell him? Promise?' She held out a hand. I hit it hard. She didn't flinch and her black eyes smiled. Like coals in a snowman's face, I thought. Not that I'd seen a snowman outside a picture book.

'Hands off!' said Cyrus from behind me. I lifted mine away in a hurry, leaving her red palm spread out like a croton.

'Call the singer to our table,' she wheedled. 'Ask him to sing something romantic.' Cyrus crooked a finger at the singer who was a dark Goan trying to look like Paul Robeson. He came to us twanging a Spanish guitar. ' "Fascination",' whispered Amy.

' "Fascination",' cried Cyrus. The man began singing, so softly he really was singing just for us. Cyrus was making priest's eyes at Amy; she was making priestess's eyes right back. No wonder they were in love – people who look alike often are. (Does love turn them into twins?)

I didn't know where to look. It's hard being the bone in the kebab. I tried reading the menu but that seemed awfully rude to the singer, so I looked at him but he was looking tenderly at Cyrus who was looking greedily at the red cigarette box peeping out of the green leaves like some exotic fruit.

The singer finished and Cyrus said, 'Now something for Brit.' I looked at him, surprised. ' "Outsider",' he said, with his lip-dipping grin. 'Pass me my box of cigarettes from that plant behind you.'

'What box?'

'The one that's as red as your face.'

The singer grinned and began, 'Someone else is in your arms tonight . . .' I looked at Cyrus to get the true feeling. I strained my ears like mad but I couldn't catch the sound of my heart sighing. What a letdown. I turned away my face from his and saw Amy caressing the hair at his wrist; then the lights went out in a splash of dark.

'Are you feeling sick?' Cyrus was saying. 'Are you going

to be sick? My God! why did you go dumb like that? What – have you broken something?'

That pricked. 'Of course not!' I said. 'I don't break any more.'

'Then why did you slump in your chair like that? Gluing your eyes like – like some doll gone bad.'

'I felt dizzy.'

'Maybe you really aren't well. Would you like to go home, Brit?' asked Amy, her voice ringing like a temple chime in the breeze.

I looked at her and grinned like an idiot. Her hair wasn't a shower curtain; it was a veil woven from the softest silk in China. And her eyes – God! Did I really say they were like coals in a snowman's face? When they resembled nothing more than the sea at midnight flecked with fluorescence? And her mouth – did Sophia Loren ever pout?

'OK, so what will you eat?' said Cyrus.

'Nothing,' I said gaily. 'Absolutely nothing.'

'You OK?'

'Perfect; I couldn't feel better. I wouldn't want to.'

'Rodin has gone to his head,' said Amy.

'That's beautiful,' I said, taking care not to grin like an idiot.

'You mean,' said Cyrus, 'you actually liked something about Amy?'

'Darling,' said Amy, ignoring him, 'have you heard of the Princeton Fuck?'

'No; can't say I have. What is it?'

'It's how they fuck at Princeton!' I joined her harp-music laughter.

'I have a real stock of those,' said Cyrus, 'so don't provoke me.'

'I won't,' said Amy, her eyes wide with mock-awe. She stretched out an arm and touched his shoulder, letting her arm drop till her index finger was on his nipple. I groaned.

'Something is wrong,' said Cyrus. Amy's finger fell into her lap.

'No, it isn't.'

'What's hurting, Brit? Is it your ribs – did I lift you wrong?'

'Why d'you go on? I told you my bones are fine now; nothing happens to me. Ever. I'm absolutely healthy.'

'I'm sorry,' he said quietly.

'Don't be an ass.'

In the cab after dinner Amy sat between us as usual and I could smell her hair sweet-scented as a monsoon breeze. The driver was rushing past the slums and the sea of Cuffe Parade as if there were a cop on his tail. I've never had a very strong base and I can't balance myself with my feet so I was swaying like a compass in a magnetic field. 'Hey!' said Amy. 'Hold on to me – tight.'

'Cyrus wouldn't like that,' I chuckled, my head somewhere near the moon that was racing us.

'But I would,' said Amy breathlessly. And I left the moon behind.

She hit me again when I got home and saw the John Wain she had given me. I spent about two hours hugging it, rushing to the window to grin at the moon, smelling rain-washed hair and generally doing things that could've earned me a free stay at the Poona Mental Hospital.

That wore me out, but trying to sleep was as impossible as keeping awake after swallowing a Valium. I fell to thinking. This was infatuation; that was as certain as osteo. There were causes enough. I was proving I wasn't gay. On the other hand, I'd never really wanted Amy, not the way I wanted Cyrus. And on the third hand, I didn't want Cyrus any more, so where was the question of proving anything? But I'd just set what was probably the world record for a hard-on. I'd stayed stiff ever since I'd been in that cab. Maybe my passion was just that – sexual frustration. I mean, in every book you read the hero loses his virginity when he's sixteen, unless he is the noble sort – then it usually happens on his twenty-first birthday. Which I had celebrated months ago. It just wasn't normal. So this girl comes along and zing! off I go.

Maybe it had something to do with the way Amy flirted with me. I knew she wasn't really flirting, because even when I couldn't stick her I knew everything was in tip-top shape in her cranium. Which meant she couldn't be stupid enough to flirt with someone who looked like me. But she thought I was a man and she liked my smile and we had clasped hands in a promise and in the car she had wanted me to hang on to her – so I could let myself believe she wanted me.

I didn't care why I had this passing passion. As long as it wasn't the real thing. Amy was going to be my neighbour's wife soon. That was as certain as the scorching summer ahead of us and as painful. A good reason to fall asleep.

21

THE NEXT DAY they came over just as I'd finished lunch. 'Let's go and see *The French Lieutenant's Woman* this evening,' said Amy who was always brimming with good ideas.

'We've seen it, sweetheart, and frankly I wasn't impressed. The book was three thousand times better.'

'Naturally. The book was a gorgeous cake; the deeper you cut the richer it became. You can't make a movie that way. You don't want to see it again, Brit?'

'I'd love to.' I would have gone even if it were *Mad Monkey Kung Fu*.

'Then why don't we go – the two of us?'

'Let's.'

'You won't be able to manage him, sweetheart.'

'Don't worry – we'll ask someone for help.'

'I'll come and drop you at the theatre; at nine I'll come and fetch you.'

'No, you won't,' I said so loudly, Cyrus put a finger in his ear.

'Why not? I don't mind.'

'That's not the point.' It was bad enough being crazy about his girl without taking his help to spend an evening with her.

'But Amy wants me to come – she needs help.' I shut up.

By the time we went into the dark theatre the movie had begun. 'You'll be OK, darling? If there are problems, just stay here. I'll come on the dot of five to nine – I've asked the usher, that's when it finishes,' whispered Cyrus.

'We'll be fine,' said Amy with a crooked smile that was so gorgeous I wanted to kiss it right off her mouth.

'Don't give her any trouble, Brit.'

'D'you realise you sound just like Sera did when you first started taking me out?'

'Come to think of it, yes. Maybe that's what happens when you grow precious to someone.' That invalid woman I met at Madame Manekshaw's funeral was right – most things come too late in life when you've learned to do without them. If Cyrus had said I was precious to him a year ago I would've felt like a millionaire; now his words were about as valuable to me as a breeze in winter.

'See you, then,' said Amy. 'And don't worry, darling.'

'Take care.'

'What will you do while we're here?'

'Go home, plug in to some music.'

'And plug out on Defarge,' I said.

Amy shook her head. 'God! That Defarge is some woman. I don't know how I'm going to live with her.'

Would you prefer it next door? I asked with my eyes, but she wasn't looking. So I said, 'I think the movie has begun,' and sure enough we missed that shot of Meryl Streep standing on the breakwater, her black cloak floating behind her in the wind, suddenly turning and showing you the trembling, self-aware face of the scarlet woman of Lyme. Not that I minded, with Amy next to me, only I was sitting in the gangway seat so it looked a bit strange when I kept watching the left half of the screen so I could see her profile from the corner of my eye. That's when that oculist had his revenge; with glasses you can't see anything from the sides. But she had this lovely way of flicking her hair away from her face that I could watch till the lights came on.

'Can I get you something?' she asked in the interval. 'An ice-cream or popcorn?'

'I should be asking you that,' I said, with visions of gliding up to her with a two-headed cone.

'What difference does it make if I do the fetching?'

'It does, when you're a guy – '

'Out with a gal?' she laughed. 'Hi!' she greeted a tiny bald kid who had stopped in the gangway and was staring at me with surprised egg-eyes.

I knew what was coming. I turned my back on him and

said, 'Are you enjoying the movie as much as you did the first time?'

The little boy said loudly, 'Papa, why is this uncle so small?'

'And what are you doing in a movie for adults only?' I growled.

'Oh!' said the papa who was a gloomy moustached man with a protruding belly which shifted his balance backwards. 'The manager is our friend so he allows us to bring the baby. See, the uncle is handicapped. He cannot do anything; he can only sit. So his kind sister has brought him to the cinema. What is your problem, sir?'

'You,' I said, smiling politely.

He looked as if he would topple over backwards into a graceful back bend. Then he turned down the corners of his mouth and said, 'You have learned no lessons from your birth.'

Amy jumped up from her seat like an advocate in court taking objection. 'You are a very foolish man,' she said, 'and your manners are rotten. As for *karma*, if it existed, it would take you a hundred more births to become what this man is.' The man watched her, his moustache in his mouth; then he turned and waddled away, fast. Amy sat down, grinning. 'I never thought I had it in me,' she said. 'Normally I get pinched in a bus and I don't say a word.'

'Well, thanks. Now you know what it feels like being a knight on a white charger.'

'I'm sorry,' she said slowly from deep inside her black eyes. 'I made you feel like a damsel in distress and you don't like it one bit.'

'I'm grateful. I don't enjoy being defended, as if I'm not big enough, you know? But really, that was lovely of you.'

She shook her head and her hair lapped her face. 'You're wrong, Brit. I didn't feel you weren't big enough. You are. A lot bigger than many people, maybe even Cyrus. And I'd have fought for him just as passionately.'

'I guess a lot of my problems come from the way I think people look at me – '

'Which is so different from the way they really do. You know, the other evening, on our way home from the library, you told me how you forget you're different.'

'Yes.'

'Well, I've forgotten too.'

The lights went down. 'Are you enjoying the movie as much as you did the first time?' I asked.

'More,' she breathed. 'But I wish the interval could have lasted longer.'

'Granted!' I laughed. The screen began to flash a long short film on family planning.

'Oh, good! OK, tell me, Brit – are you in love?'

'What makes you think so?' I said, nervous as a murderer in the dock.

'Cyrus. He said you and that girl Ruby – I saw her at your father's *uthamna* – were childhood sweethearts.'

'He told you that?'

'Yes. And that she was away on holiday in Kashmir and that she's coming back today and you're terribly excited.'

If I told her that Ruby was Cyrus's girl she'd leave him this very evening – then I'd never know if she really cared for me. To really care for me she had to love me more than the mind-picture of Cyrus she had; not prefer me to a Casanova. But if I didn't tell her the truth she'd think I didn't care for her. Whatever she felt for me would dissolve into friendship. 'That was a joke,' I said. 'Cyrus likes teasing me about Ruby because I was once in lust with her – and I told him about that. But I swear to you –'

'By what?'

'By Rodin,' I said, astonished to see where hope had dragged me, 'that there's nothing between Ruby and me.'

'Not even a sheet?' She laughed.

'Will you keep quiet, please!' said an irate woman's voice from behind.

Amy giggled and slid lower into her seat till her head was level with mine. 'Sorry,' she whispered, and her breath licked my ear so I had to pull my shirt down to hide my hard-on, 'for being horribly inquisitive.' I turned and we were nose to nose – all I had to do was pout and we'd be kissing. Instead I grinned like a genius and patted her hair.

'Your sister must be missing you like crazy,' she whispered. I let go of my shirt.

After that we sat silent till Jeremy Irons cried, 'Sarah!' as his true-life love drove away and the movie ended. 'Poor Cyrus,' said Amy. 'He must be waiting.'

'Well, he wants to,' I said, still smarting from her sibling fantasy. But Cyrus wasn't to be seen. We sat in silence for ten minutes, then Amy said in a shaky voice. 'This is my nightmare come true.'

'You think Cyrus has ditched us?'

'No; sitting like this in an empty cinema house with the blank screen looming in front of me. I'm terrified.'

'What? Is that a phobia?'

'And what a phobia. It's happening, just now, in real life.'

I turned my head. Her face looked as if she'd had a wash and forgotten to dry herself. 'Oh, my God!' I said. 'I'm awfully sorry. Look – just walk out of here and wait in the foyer. I don't mind sitting alone.'

The usher switched off the lights and Amy started crying. Then I knew I had to do something so I put an arm around her. With my height I knew it would end up on her left breast, but she understood and slid down. Now my hand was in her hair and I said, 'You aren't alone, you know,' and your damp hair tastes so good.

She smiled a trembling sort of smile and let her head rest on my shoulder which went down with the weight. 'Your shoulders are OK, aren't they?' she said.

'I'm OK.'

That's how Cyrus found us. He looked like a ballet dancer in his black sweatshirt and pale grey pants. 'I'm sorry,' he said, 'but I just couldn't find a cab.'

'That's all right,' said Amy, jumping from my arm and brushing past my knee so she could be close to him. 'You didn't know about my phobia, did you?'

'What phobia? And anyway, what were you doing in my best friend's arms?'

'Wouldn't you love to know?' she smiled. Her face was now dry and glowing.

'I was trying to calm her,' I said carelessly. 'She was scared out of her lips by the blank screen.'

'Lips? That was a Freudian slip, wasn't it? Oh, Amy! Be careful of him!'

'You be careful of him!' she said gaily, walking ahead of us up the gangway.

'Now, whatever could that mean?' said Cyrus.

'How was Ruby?' I mouthed, more to change the topic than to put him in trouble.

'Shut up,' he mouthed back. 'She's looking more gorgeous than ever.'

'More than Amy?'

'Oh! definitely. Amy's no competition for her. Sex appeal-wise.'

'Which only means Ruby has a lien on your cock.'

He roared, his nostrils flaring. 'Spoken like an ex-law student,' he said.

'What? What's spoken?'

'Nothing, darling. A little joke betwen us boys.'

'You've got filthy manners,' she said, smiling, waiting for us to catch up. 'But I'm crazy about you.' They kissed under the red-lit EXIT sign, and I thought what a guy Cyrus was. If I were him, just a little like him.

'Why did you change your clothes, darling?' she asked him in the cab. I waited for his answer while I rolled down the windows to see her hair flying in the hot breeze.

'Spilled some brandy on my shirt,' he said, lighting a cigarette.

'You would make a highly successful writer,' I said.

Amy wrinkled her high fair forehead. 'Why do you say that? I think he looks like a musician. One of those soulful violinists in a tailcoat we see at the Tata Theatre.'

'Don't remind him.'

'Of what?'

Cyrus lifted his arm from Amy's shoulder and gave my cowlick a tug. 'Of his looks,' I said. 'He gets very self-conscious.'

'There's no reason for lighting up your second cigarette in five minutes.'

'Being in love is an exhausting business,' he said, puffing away.

'A smokescreen,' I murmured.

'Smoking doesn't relieve exhaustion, darling.'

'Oh, stop nagging me, please. Love me as I am.'

'I do, darling, I do.' She hid her head in his chest; her hands went to his neck and stayed there caressing it like some marble statue. I wanted to puke. It was a long time since I had; would serve them right too.

'We'll drop Brit off, then go to your place. Your parents are away aren't they?' I wondered if Amy would slake the thirst Ruby had whetted and I wondered at the kind of things I was beginning to wonder.

'Lovely!' she said.

'Stop here,' said Cyrus to the driver. He leapt out of the cab, threw open the boot and pulled my chair out with a thud. Was he in such a hurry to get into bed? He swung me into the chair and Amy followed me out. 'What are you getting off for?' asked Cyrus, his arms akimbo.

'Do you mind?' she said, smiling. 'Brit, may I kiss you?'

'Sure.' I gulped. She bent down; her mouth was a flower against my cheek. I held her head against mine.

'Oh, boy!' said Cyrus. 'Perfect end to a perfect evening.' He rushed me up the ramp, into the lift, up and out of it. 'You'll be fine, won't you?' he called over his shoulder, taking the stairs three at a time.

The flat was empty. Sera was staying the night with Jeroo. I knew she was preparing me for the time she wouldn't be around any more. Because Sera had taken Sam's loss quite differently from the way Jeroo had taken Tina's. Jeroo had sunk into quicksand up to her armpits but then she'd stayed there, never drowning, half-sane. And certainly half-mad. We'd be playing bridge and she'd suddenly say, 'Look at the King of Spades watching me with his roving eye. Those awful sideburns – ugh!' She'd lift the card from the table, turn it over and put it down. And Sera, Defarge and I would have to remember what it was.

Sera had a hole somewhere inside her into which she was slowly disappearing. Physically, too. Nothing was wrong with her – I pushed her through a thousand rupees of medical tests. But her face turned gaunt and bony like some high-class fashion model's. And her clothes outgrew her so that she had to buy a whole wardrobe from the shops that lined Causeway like tanks in an aquarium. Fortunately, she bought a lot of clothes one size smaller than she needed just in case she shrank further, which she did in the next six months. This wasn't surprising, the way she was dropping things from her diet. 'Pupsie, I just can't stand meat any more – makes me sick.' Then it was milk, then chocolate.

'Sera is becoming an advanced soul,' said Jeroo. 'Soon she won't eat anything!'

'You mean she wants to die.'

'Oh, Brit. When will you learn?' She gave me a beautiful, pitying smile. 'She doesn't want to die. She wants to go to Him.'

I wasn't sure if she was talking about God or Sam when Sera came in and shouted, 'Don't frighten him like that, Jeroo. Brit, I don't want to go anywhere; I'm here in good old Colaba with you, for years and years as long as you need me.'

'Which is for ever,' I said untruthfully.

'Goody!' she said, kissing me on the head. 'Let's go, Jeroo – there's a lot to buy!'

It was her shopping that gave her away. She bought yards of muslin to swaddle her corpse because we'd all heard of people rushing out to get some while the poor Parsee lay there in his dying-in clothes. And she got a brand new *kusti*, woven from the finest, whitest lamb's wool, which would be wound round her waist when she was dead. Inflation was dying but she began stocking everything from Complan to toilet-paper. 'So that Brit won't have any problems for at least a year.'

'A year after what?' asked Defarge slyly.

'A year after today,' said Sera firmly. And just to prove she wasn't about to die she added, 'I am going to the movies for the third time this week!' Which was remarkable because Bombay was going through an English movie famine.

So the brave act went on. Or maybe she was trying to grow. Without Sam.

I thought of all that and anything else that would fill my head so I wouldn't think of Amy and Cyrus together in her bed, happy with sweaty love – it had got to be sweaty the way the temperature was soaring and staying up all through the night.

199

I was feeling disgustingly sticky; the sides of my arms were clinging to my shirt, and my feet felt like they were in a steamy pressure cooker. My face was greasy. I'd need to wash it three times to get it clean. I decided to have a bath. Also because it was great fun using the electric heater that Sera had just got installed in my tiny bathroom after years of 'No short circuits for my baby' every time I suggested it.

Trying to grow meant leaving behind a lot of old habits like lying on my bed and getting powdered but I never could get myself dressed in the bathroom. It was warm and steamy and cramped and when you can't stand up it's not easy (though I once won a race with a three-minute egg that Cyrus had put on just to see how quickly I could manage). So as usual, I came out, this time not bothering to wrap myself in the huge towel Sera had bought a dozen of especially for me.

My aversion to mirrors meant that the only time I looked at myself was when I was brushing my hair, and then I took care not to look below my eyelashes. But I was passing the mirror and I looked because I wasn't wearing my specs, and then I went closer and looked at myself with nothing on and then I knew. Clearly and definitely. Like finding some fact you've been looking for: one day you open a book and there it is in confident black print. I looked long and hard so that I would never forget. I saw my neck squat as a toad's and my hollow shoulders, one higher than the other like Richard the Third's, my rib cage thrust forward so that it bulged in the centre and sloped down at the sides, and below that my legs thin as a famine-child's, the shins bowed as if some kid had plastered on some clay as a joke, or an afterthought.

How stupid I'd been; I wouldn't have believed it of me. It was so fat a self-delusion that everything else had been squeezed out. To have thought, for even one moment, that Amy was charmed by this. The kiss this evening – if she really had fallen for me she wouldn't have done it with Cyrus looking on. And the other stuff about holding on tight and things; why, that's how all young people talked. ('There's nowhere to sit . . . My lap's vacant.')

I didn't know I was crying till I felt the tears, cold as caterpillars, crawling down my chest. I watched my eyes and they were surprised. I normally cried like a kid, huge breaths, sobs and sniffles. But this was something else, as if my veins had opened and I was bleeding brine.

22

I WAS THINKING of Jeroo's love-birds as the train puffed and sighed its way to Davier. 'Just listen to her,' said Jerry, 'the sounds she's making; exactly like a woman approaching . . .'

I ignored him; I was thinking of Jeroo's love-birds. She had kept a pair – in Tina's time. They were called Connie and Mellors because Tina insisted. Jeroo thought they ought to have English names and nobody except us would have recognised the real Connie and Mellors if they had walked hand in hand (though knowing them I doubt they would have been satisfied with so simple a pleasure) down the Causeway.

The feathered Connie and Mellors had a cage big enough for a tiger cub, placed in the centre of the shrubbery that grew in Jeroo's little garden. They had a bath big as a washing-sink and Jeroo got them the choicest worms and such from a luxury pet store. It was a good life. I could tell they liked it because they were always singing, not a very tuneful song, but then not many of us can.

They had a good life, yet, when Jeroo left their cage-door open – there was someone at her door that Tina couldn't answer – they flew out and sat on the ledge below her balcony, shaking in the wind. Of course, they didn't know a thing about earning their living or other bird-people and before night fell on Jeroo's garden they were warming two ravens' bellies.

When Sera said yes, I could go away and stay with Jerry at his Davier mansion, I didn't want to go but the door was open. And I went. To a house that I knew had neither light nor fans (if you live without a fan in India you are a candidate for canonisation, at least, beatification) nor a toilet that flushed but a hole in the ground with a wooden seat on top and a wicker basket below. I went because Sera let me go.

Jerry's mansion was not what I had expected it to be, a mini-Buckingham Palace. It was a biggish bungalow bang on the beach. It had that most palestine of names, Mon Repos. 'First,' said Rati, 'when I got married it was called Davierwala House. I made it this because Duke of Edinburgh was born in a house of the same name. You knew where? Say!'

'Corfu.' She was always playing this kind of Trivial Pursuit with me. 'Where did Lord By Ron expire?' she quizzed through the lav door. 'Can you say Victoria's nine offsprings' names?' she asked, a kind of historical alarm to get me out of bed, and I rolled them off backwards: Beatrice, Leopold, Arthur, Louise, Helena, Alfred, Alice, Edward, Victoria, sending her reeling with delight.

Then there was Fill In the Blanks: 'Peter Pan and?'

'Wendy.'

'Sarah?'

'Churchill.'

'Mistake! Bernhardt. Never mind. Mrs?'

'Miniver,' I said perversely.

'Simpson, silly boy. Lawrence?'

'Of Arabia.'

'Olivier. What has happened to you? Davier does not suit your head.'

'Suits the rest of me,' I said complacently.

Indeed, it did. The meals were gorgeous and gargantuan, punctuated with my favourite lobsters (in curry, alas! not Thermidor or Newburg), the sea breezes cool, the nights honey-gold with lamps that burned clarified butter.

And the days leaped with fun. Jerry and I would talk as he wheeled me backwards up and down the beach, for my chair wouldn't push through the sand, white as my untanned feet. Like wine-tasters taking a swill and spitting it out before moving to another bottle, we tried a dozen topics of conversation.

I tried authors. Now, we had this silly bit of snobbery, Amy and I, and sometimes Cyrus, about calling writers by their first names, because we liked to think we knew them. But for him, I used the full names.

'What d'you think of Iris Murdoch?'

'She's married to that chap who owns the tabloids, the boobs and bottoms man, is she?'

Alas! poor Rupert. I tried someone else. 'What about Anita Brookner?'

'Aaah! They've named a prize after her, haven't they?'

'No, but she won it. The prize they didn't name after her. Paul Bailey?' I said, one last hope.

'Any relation of Beetle Bailey?' he sniggered.

I should've stopped then, but I didn't. We are all of us thornbirds, aren't we? So I asked him about those two at whose page I worshipped – Philip Roth: 'Is he an angry man? Ha! ha! ha!' and John Irving: 'You've got the name wrong – it's Irving Wallace, you ass.' Then I shut the door on my book-brain.

Finally, we just talked – jabbered, whispered, shouted – whatever swooshed its way down our heads to our tongues, and we learned to know each other.

The days in Davier were magical days. One morning Rati insisted Jerry take me to see The Stone of the Saint. So we went in his Fiat, through the toddy trees, bumping over the baby coconuts strewn across the dirt road by the child-hating wind. Until we came to a clearing surrounded by a black stone wall about my height.

Jerry took me out of my car, lifted me from my chair and perched me on the six-inch-wide wall. I was shaking in the wind, like those baby coconuts must have done before they gave up, partly because I was so light – at sixteen kilos I was a dieter's delight – partly because I was trembling at the thought of falling off (was there an X-ray machine in Davier?).

Jerry was hollering into the wind and half a dozen men in red loin-clothes answered his call. 'They are the Keepers of the Stone,' he said, pointing at a huge flat grey stone a little smaller than the one Tess was lying on when they found her. It sort of grew out of the ground in the centre of the walled field. 'You watch,' said Jerry, scissoring over the wall.

The Keepers of the Stone were playing Ring-a-ring of Roses around their charge, chanting a frog-like hymn, full of croaks and grunts. They made room for Jerry in their circle and stopped. Then all of them stretched out their arms, with a fist at the end. They bent low, shot a little finger out of their fists and put it below the stone. They took a breath as loud as the wind and howled, 'Deeevjeee,' and lo and behold! The stone rose on their little fingers till it was shoulder-high and their breath gave out. Then it crashed back into its earth-home with a tired thud.

'Impressed?' said Jerry, arms akimbo.

I nodded silently; I had been holding my breath with them. 'How does it work?'

He shrugged. 'Holy powers,' he said.

'Come on!'

'Well, I'll tell you a secret. You won't tell Rati? God swear?'

'Man swear,' I mumbled.

'I came here one night with my gang from Bombay – you haven't met them, yet. About eight of us. We crept over the wall and got to the stone. We didn't know that song so we omitted it. We stuck our fingers out, took a big breath and yelled 'Coconu-u-u-ut' and it went up as high as our heads. What d'you think?'

Well, I liked Jerry much better after I heard that.

But I didn't like him one bit that morning he buried me on the beach. 'Don't take it ill,' said Rati. 'It is an age-old cure for limpy legs.'

'You mean polio; I don't have that. Anyway, it wouldn't work on polio either.'

'We'll see,' said Jerry, enthusiastically digging a hole in the sand with a gravedigger's shovel. He lowered me in up to my armpits then packed the sand in. I didn't resist; I pretended I was humouring them.

When they went into the house I pretended I was David Bowie in *Merry Christmas, Mr Lawrence* – soon Cyrus would come along to take a lock of my hair; then I pretended Amy was in the hole with me; it was dark in the hole, there was nothing she could see of me, there was nothing in the way of our love.

I left Davier the next day. Since Jerry was staying on, he sent three burly men to escort me to Bombay; that was a bit like using a shovel to serve a soufflé. When I was back home Sera looked at me and said, 'So you made it.'

'Was it some kind of test?' I asked crossly.

'Yes,' she said, smiling. I wondered who she meant had passed.

Back in my room with the Causeway hum for background music I felt my heart beat erratically as if I was afraid. Here I'd been thinking I was brave, charting new seas, Davier, Jerry and the flushless loo. When all the while I was running away as fast as my legs wouldn't take me from the stormy world. I guess Connie and Mellors wouldn't have agreed but the big, tough life is life in your cage.

It was past midnight when I finished giving Sera a lobster by lobster account of what I'd done in Davier. 'Don't go too much with these people,' she snorted. 'They don't seem very civilized. You have such lovely friends here, Cyrus and his fiancée – they are going to get married, aren't they?'

'I'm tired,' I said. 'Very tired and I don't want to be awake.'

It was morning. Sera was ringing the doorbell military fashion in rhythmic commands and the phone was calling. Sera could wait.

'Hello?' I said in my woozy voice.

'Did I wake you, Brit?' said Amy cheerfully.

I looked at my watch – it was eleven-thirty. The doorbell had taken a breath that wasn't about to give out. 'Wait a sec,' I said, 'there's someone at the door.'

'I'll wait; take your time,' said Amy.

I opened the door to Sera, Defarge without her dentures, Cyrus rubbing his eyes with nothing on but his sleeping jocks, Ruby with a white moustache of bleaching cream.

'What's the matter?' I said, wheeling backwards to the phone.

'I was prepared for the worst,' said Sera stoically.

'Cheeky bugger!' muttered Cyrus.

'Who were you talking to?' asked Ruby.

'Offspring of a swine,' said Defarge, and Sera pounced on her.

'Take care of your tongue, Defarge,' she shouted, her voice hoarse with relief.

'What were you saying?' I asked Amy.

'We were saying,' said Defarge, 'that this time every bone of his must be broken – that's why he is not opening the door.'

I cupped my hand on the mouthpiece and said coldly, 'I don't break bones any more.'

'So will you, Brit? Please?' pleaded Amy.

'I told Sera, at last God has lifted this problem child from your head.'

'One day I'll stitch your lips together on the sewing machine and you'll learn your lesson,' screamed Sera.

'What d'you want me to do, Amy?'

'I didn't know you looked this good,' said Ruby, watching Cyrus's cock as if it were a hot cheese roll.

Cyrus gave an embarrassed grin and looked down bashfully where she was looking.

'Brit,' said Amy, 'I'm calling off.'

'No, don't, wait a minute. What d'you want me to do?'

'Come over for dinner – I'm having a party. I'm saying this for the eighth time.'

'I'm sorry, there's a lot of noise here.'

'You look cute with that moustache,' said Cyrus to Ruby who rushed to the bathroom to wash it off.

I looked at him with envious disgust, mimicking his voice. 'You look cute with that moustache.' He grinned.

Amy yowled, 'What do you mean? How dare you?'

'I'm sorry; I wasn't talking to you.'

'Who were you talking to?'

'No one, no one.'

'Really?' The phone cord shivered.

'I was trying out a sentence for a story.'

'In the middle of a conversation with me – how charming!'

'Look, I'm honest,' I shouted.

'What do I care. Come tonight, if you like – Cyrus can get you.'

'Do you want me to come?'

'I wouldn't have asked, would I?'

'OK; I'll come. Just this once. Just this once, Amy.'

'Are you mad?'

I hung up.

'Who was it?' said Sera and Defarge, clinking their teacups in the saucers.

'Who was that?' said Ruby from the bathroom where she was still trying to wash off the bleach.

'I know who that was,' said Cyrus, looking at me so strangely I went pale instead of red.

'Look!' I said, entering the drawing-room. 'I was sleeping when you rang the bell; then I heard the phone and the bell together and I didn't know what to do. That's why you had to wait.'

'And summon the whole building,' said Defarge sweetly. Sera glared at her and moved away the plate of crisp Davier biscuits beyond her reach.

Cyrus came to me and said softly, 'Are you going tonight?'

'What're you whispering about?' said Ruby.

I grinned and nodded, looking at Cyrus. Defarge was also looking at him, her eyes screwed up the better to see his cock. 'Your poor wife!' she sighed and Cyrus stiffened. 'How will she accommodate you inside her?'

Ruby yelped. Cyrus stalked out. Sera snatched the unfinished teacup from Defarge's hand. And I blinked like mad to keep the pictures from my mind.

Amy's flat was a bit like Madame Manekshaw's bungalow – low carved tables, Chinese vases, copper bowls, a garden of potted plants on the verandah into which you stepped when you came in through the front door.

'I'm so glad you've come,' said Amy's mother, who had the face of a concerned Pekinese – tiny eyes, swirls of fluffy white hair, a mouth that had once been a pout but now looked as if it was full of hairpins. Amy was going to look like that when she was old; I was glad she wasn't going to be mine.

'My pleasure,' I said.

'Hi, Dina!' said Cyrus.

'Oh, hello! Thank you for bringing Brit.'

'His pleasure, I'm sure. I'll just go and look for Amy.'

He vanished into the party proper which was going on in one of the bedrooms. 'What a gorgeous house you keep,' I said to the Pekinese, throwing open my arms. 'Are antiques your passion?'

'Yes, dear; a passion I can't afford. What with wealth tax and estate duties. You know, Amy has told me so much about you, Brit.'

'Then you must detest me,' I said. Where was she?

'You know, Brit, it's lovely how you are able to laugh.' I laughed, and wondered how the Pekinese would look if it were bald.

'Can I get you a drink?' it asked. 'Scotch? Cognac?'

'A brandy will be fine, thank you.' I needed Dutch courage though I wasn't sure I'd be able to keep down the brandy. I never could stand liqueur chocolates.

The brandy looked jolly in its goblet. 'Brit, you must have a lot of handicapped friends?' asked the Peke.

'No, none at all,' I said, taking a gulp without letting my face show it; Glycodin, that I took for my cough, tasted better.

'Then why do you gesticulate and open your mouth so wide when you talk?'

'Do I?' I waited to blush and didn't. I looked gratefully at the brandy. But it was making me want to pee. I made faces at Cyrus who grinned and turned away.

'Shall I fetch Cyrus?' she said.

'Yes, thank you.'

Cyrus came, smiling down at the Peke who was blinking at him lovingly. 'C'mon in,' he said sardonically. 'You haven't said hello to Amy yet.'

'I want to pee,' I said.

He wheeled me through a maze of corridors, pointed to a curtained doorway and said, 'That's it. You'll manage?'

'Ya.' After all, I thought, no one ever falls into the toilet bowl. I wheeled myself to the door, shifted the curtain and saw the cement barrier about four inches high on the ground, meant to keep the house safe if the bathroom flooded. I kicked it.

'Hi! Need any help?' said Amy behind me. I turned. She was dressed in pearl-grey baggy pants with a matching blouse cut away at the throat in a thin long slit. Her hair was maddening, every strand of silk or nylon shimmering singly against her shoulders. 'Why didn't you greet me when you came in?' she said, smiling angrily.

'I was talking to your mother.'

'Did she remind you of a Peke?'

'Don't.'

'Don't what? Let me help you in.' She tilted the chair and took it over the barrier. The bathroom was huge with a bathtub on legs tucked away in a corner. There was a chest of drawers, intricately carved, two clothes racks without any clothes on them and a long mirror set in a polished black frame.

'Don't what, Brit?'

I gulped and said, 'Don't be so lovely, because I'm not going to see you again.'

She left my chair and sat down on the toilet seat. 'Why not, Brit?'

'Because we're good friends – '

'And that's not what you want to be?'

'No.'

'That's not what I want to be either.'

'I'm pinching myself.' I really was – hard and just above the wrist.

'You don't have to.'

I looked at her perched on that black seat, her face innocent and so perfect to me I wanted to cry. Then she was kneeling on the terracotta tiles in front of me, her arms hanging at her side. I reached out and pressed the flat of my palm to her head. 'Silk was never so soft,' I whispered.

'You'll make your fortune writing pulp romances – don't look so stricken! Oh! I love you – '

'Lots and lots and lots.'

'You have a nasty habit of finishing my sentences.'

'I didn't think a woman's body would feel so good.'

'You kiss by the book,' she said.

'Listen,' I said, my lips on her neck, thinking how glad I was not to have had anything before this. 'I know you won't want to – be with me always, but this is enough.'

She drew her head back and said, 'Is that how you feel?'

'That's what *you* feel.'

'I don't, so kiss me again. Ummm – your bones have given you a tough time, haven't they?'

'They've taught me things.'

'You mean you wouldn't have been the same person if – '

'Something like that.'

'Then I'm glad you have osteo.'

'I'd rather be standing beside you.'

'This is fine – if only you'd share your chair with me.'

'Welcome aboard!' I shifted. This was one lap I didn't mind sitting on. 'To think I hated you once.'

'To think I fell for you the moment I saw you.'

'Who're you fooling? Love at first sight – of this?'

'Do you always see bodies instead of people? I'm in *your* arms right now.'

'Correction – I'm in yours.'

'I hate your wisecracks. I'm in *your* arms right now not in your *arms* – got the difference?'

'Ya, but I still can't believe it.'

'If you use one more cliché I'll scream into that ear.'

'Nothing's as true as a cliché if you're hearing it for the first time.'

Brit? said Cyrus through the curtain. 'Don't you want to c me out?' He poked his head in and lifted his eyebrows. 'What a st pid question,' he said, managing to lift the corners of his mouth even though they were the heaviest things in the world.

I loved him for that. 'What about him?' I asked. 'Is your lap tired?'

'I could spend the night like this. I've thought about him, Brit; I love you more.'

'Is it so simple?'

'You mean I should stick with him because I met him first?'

'No – '

'You feel awful because you love him and now he'll hurt?'

'I guess so.'

'You were gay, weren't you?'

I nodded into her throat. 'How did you know?'

'Because straights haven't heard of the Princeton fuck.'

'We didn't do anything – I wanted to.'

'And now? Do you want to? With someone else?'

'Oh, Amy – no. But I do love watching beautiful men – '

'And you always will, till you realise how beautiful you are.'

'I'll never be beautiful.'

'You are – more sensual and adorable than Cyrus.'

'I know you mean it but I can't feel – '

'Give it time.'

'You know, you smile like an angel.'

'And I thought writers were original.'

'Amy, I still dream of men sometimes.'

'Day-dream?'

'Yes, but it means nothing. It's like going through a *Playboy* – I wouldn't sleep with any of those girls.'

'It's not the same.'

'Can you stand the idea?'

'As long as you are honest about it.'

'Isn't it too much to bear?'

'Isn't it unbearable being in love with a girl a foot and a half taller than you, who also happens to be your best friend's girl?'

'Answer one – I'm glad there's so much of you for me to feel.'

'A hippo would be your ideal, I suppose.'

'I'm into boys, not animals. Answer two – why do you think I want you? Because you are Cyrus's girl. I can't have him so I'll settle for next best.'

'A profound psychological truth – would you be easy to murder?'

'I'd make a hell of a clamour – Amy, why d'you have to wear so many clothes?'

'Remember what a knight had to fight through? Why do your ears turn red every time I kiss them?'

'They're embarrassed.'

'My marvellous moron.'

'Amy!' said a voice.

'That's the P – I mean your mother.'

'Yes, Mama?'

'I know it's cool in the bathroom dear, but the guests are getting ready to leave.'

'I'm coming.'

'But I wasn't even touching you.'

'I love your juvenile wit.'

'I adore your left-handed compliments.'

'Brit — you'll never let me down, will you?'

'Not as long as I'm me. Now, will *you* let me down gently so we can go back to the world.'

We went to the verandah, proud as winners. 'I'm sorry,' said Amy. 'I wasn't a very good hostess this evening.'

'You weren't a hostess at all,' said about six of the guests together. Amy laughed and flung her hair over her shoulders. I took a deep breath and put my arms round her bottom which was as high as I could reach comfortably. The file of departing guests froze. Some smiled shyly, others frowned in puzzlement and one girl dressed in a black lurex jumpsuit drawled, 'Wow! That's what I call guts.'

I didn't know if she was talking about me or Amy or the way we were that night.

23

'Brit, why did that Amy bring you home last night?'

'Because Cyrus left early.'

'How did she bring you – by car?'

'No, we walked. She doesn't live far – at Wodehouse Road.'

'She is Cyrus's girlfriend, isn't she?'

'She was.' Should I? Should I not? I remembered something Cyrus had told me about swimming. Shut your eyes when you get in. After that it's too late to wish you hadn't.

'She is my girl now,' I said, my voice sounding as if there were a hole in my windpipe.

'Bloody rot and poppycock!' she said, mindlessly rearranging the magazines on the coffee table, tossing out the new issues, keeping back the old. I waited like Marie Antoinette for the storm to pass. But, like hers, it blew my head off. 'Get this very clear, Brit,' said Sera, turning her attention to the bookshelf now that the magazines had been put out of their place. 'You are not going to have any girlfriend. Not Amy, not Freny, not Hilloo, not – '

'I don't know the last two,' I said.

'You know that's not the point – don't act cheeky. That girl is a rotter teaching you to talk like that. And to leave one man and make false promises to you. Which you believe like an innocent lamb. And sure enough, you'll be led to – '

'To the slaughter,' I said, less in anger than irritation at seeing Ayn Rand being pushed into a slot next to Marx.

'Yes; and you know how it will feel when your heart breaks – as if, and I'm very sorry to say this, as if both your legs had broken at the same time. And break your heart she will, when she leaves you. She's not going to marry you – she wants a

214

handsome wealthy man who can take her to the beach and the discothèque, chauffeur her round in a car, carry her over the threshold. Can you do any of these things? You haven't thought of that. You think love is sweet words and having a girl to show off to your friends.'

I was trying my hardest to go deaf to her roaring which only made me hear every word as if I had ear-phones on. Not only that. She was being more convincing than she knew.

'And think how Cyrus will feel, how much affection he has given you, how much you love him – is that how you repay a friend?'

'Sera, I know you are right – '

'Then leave her.'

'About a lot of things.'

'Everything.'

'And it would be so easy for me to agree with you and let Amy go,' and I think I'm having a heart attack. Because there are things you don't say to your mother or school teacher or boss even if you are having your nails pulled out slowly. And I was about to say them now. 'But, Sera, I've got to grow and get my heart broken if it must. You know that. You could have kept me safe in a soft bed all my life. But you didn't. You let me go around and break my bones and become as much like other people as was possible. And you took the pain every time I broke my legs.'

'Don't talk rubbish!' screamed Sera, sweeping off a shelf-ful of poetry in a great typhoon of swirling paper to the floor. 'Where did you get these mad notions?'

'They aren't mad – you are brave and that's true. But, Sera, be a little braver for me.'

'Shut up, Brit, I'm warning you, shut up.'

'Let me love Amy. Maybe it isn't fair asking you to go on supporting me – but I want to live like everyone else, feel the things they do – '

'Please, stop it,' she sobbed, lifting the poetry books back into their places.

'And if you've done it all these years, why should you give up now?'

'Who says I'm giving up? I just wasn't prepared for this and

215

it pushed me off-balance.' Sera took half a dozen short breaths to clear her head. 'You go ahead and court that girl. And I hope you are as happy as Sam and I are, were.'

I stared at her. She was beaming and the tears had evaporated from her cheeks. What a mother, I thought, even while the bastard-half of my mind was saying: Offer an actress a good part and she'll live it.

'Look who's here!' said Amy, and I wished I could see her face, but as usual she was behind my chair. We were strolling along the concrete jetty that thrusts itself like an impudent cock into the wetness of the Arabian Sea at Nariman Point. At the tip stood Ruby and Cyrus, their hair flying like twin banners in the breeze.

'Cyrus needs a hair cut,' said Amy, 'and you'll get a crick in your neck if you keep staring at my face like this.'

'I'm dying,' I squawked.

'You should take lessons in voice.'

'And speak like you in that frightful stagy manner.'

'Much as I love you, I think I'll tip you into the sea.'

'See what a glimpse of Cyrus does to you.'

'Hi!' said Ruby, turning round so that the wind made her hair stand up like a brown halo around her head.

'Hello,' said Cyrus, smiling a small lonely smile. I could've killed myself. This was the first time we had met since that bathroom scene a month ago.

'You must be Amy,' said Ruby, clutching her bright-pink dress between her knees. 'I've heard an awful lot about you from Brit.'

'And I've heard tons about you and Cyrus.'

'Cyrus? You know Cyrus?'

'Well, if you know Brit, you've got to know Cyrus.'

Cyrus gave a sort of strangled laugh and turned to gaze at the sea.

'Let me go,' I said to Amy who left the handles of the chair. I wheeled over to where he was standing. My chair was shaking in the wind and the sea waited on three sides of me. 'Feel like tossing me in?' I said.

Cyrus grinned and sat down cross-legged on the cement. 'Talk,' he said.

'I'm sorry.'

'Sorry you have Amy?' he grinned.

'You were the last person I – '

'Maybe not. Maybe you never forgave me for making you lust.' His white cotton shirt flapped in the breeze.

'Love,' I said, sure for that moment.

'I knew it was going to happen the moment you got together.'

'You knew?'

'Sure; anyone could have told us you and Amy were two of a kind.'

'But the two of you looked alike.'

'What's that got to do with it? You know something? I missed your weirdness.'

'Thanks.'

We laughed as if we'd got through the last exams of our lives. 'They're dying of curiosity,' he said, watching the girls watching us.

'Are you glad you've got Ruby?'

'Does Amy know?'

'No, I saw to it that she didn't.'

'Didn't want to catch a rebound?'

'No. But you didn't have to tell her Ruby was mine.'

'I wanted to spoil your chances.'

'Really? Really?'

'Yes. You don't know how crazily jealous I was those last days.'

'You feel you deserve it?'

'Because I kept Ruby on the side? But I didn't keep her for sex.'

'Not the whole thing.'

'Nothing. I kept Ruby because I was never really sure about Amy. Then I kept throwing you together. It was a sort of test. And that is why I didn't tell her everything – about the violin, and my mother and stuff.'

'Maybe that's why – '

'She left me? Perhaps. I never felt safe with her the way I felt with you.'

'And even I let you down.'

He smiled. 'Let's keep that for another day,' he said.

'Let's go back to the girls,' I said.

'But you've got such gorgeous hair,' Ruby was saying. 'How do you keep it like that?'

'Brit calls it a nylon shower curtain.'

Ruby gasped. 'What sort of lover are you?' she demanded.

'No one knows better than you,' I laughed.

'See those rocks?' she threatened.

'We must be going,' said Cyrus quietly. 'See you, Amy, bye, Brit.'

'We'll meet again?'

'Not at night,' sang Ruby. 'His nights are mine now!' Three faces turned to watch the sea crinkle into the horizon. 'Did I say something wrong?' cried Ruby.

'Of course not!' we said together.

'Something is fishy,' she said, a frown between her arched eyebrows.

'The sea,' said Cyrus, grinning abstractedly. Amy smiled at him lovingly.

'Is there something I don't know?' cried Ruby.

'The nights,' I said. 'It sounded suspicious you talking about nights like that.'

'Oh, that!' said Ruby. 'You are so stupid. If I were jumping into bed – as if I'd talk about it!'

'Brit,' said Amy, bending over my chair, 'shall we go?'

I nodded and we rolled away. 'What were you feeling then?' I asked nonchalantly, watching the rain clouds rising like grey mountains from the sea.

'Nothing, darling; I'm sure you love him more than I do.'

'But he's so much more beautiful than I am.'

'Don't! You sound like a queen. Oh! don't blush, darling. I'm going to kiss you.' She squatted on her heels.

'Not here, please, Amy, no – '

'Why all the protest?'

'The stares.'

'Don't care.'

'I do.'

'You can't stop them.'

'When anyone stares I become Osteo Brit again.'

'That sounds like a malt – Osteo Brit.'

'Shut up. I'm going to kiss you.'

A snigger. A gasp. More laughter. There were four urchins topless in ragged shorts, hooting, making obscene sounds with their fingers in their mouths. Amy went pale so that her skin looked like Madame Manekshaw's at the Tower of Silence. I shook my head. 'They'd do this to anyone,' I said. 'Anyone who kissed.' She smiled and her smile went out. Half a dozen more people had stopped in front of us: two men, one in a muslin *dhoti* through which you could see his scrawny thighs, the other nondescript in grey hair and grey pants; and four women, middle aged, plump in saris.

They were discussing us, as if we were the clouds or the sea or the rocks. 'What does she see in him?'

'Pity?'

'God will reward her.'

'Maybe he is rich.'

'I wouldn't take him if he were rich as the Birlas.'

'This is how the Christians must have felt in the Colosseum,' I whispered to Amy. We were sitting with our backs to the sea; there was no escape.

'Such people,' said someone, 'are often God's favourites: that is why he makes them different.'

'You are wrong, wrong. He is punished.'

'You mustn't laugh,' someone said to the urchins. 'Or the next time you are born, you will be unfortunate as him.'

'At least they should not come out, such people. Then loving in public – it's too much.'

Amy was gazing at the sea and crying without a flicker on her face. I thought: If I'm good enough for her, what does this matter?

Then the man in the *dhoti* said, 'Maybe something is wrong with her inside, we can't see it. That's why she has to marry this cripple. She can't find anyone else.'

'It's difficult for you,' I said in a loud and deep voice. They stepped back together as if it were a dance.

'Don't!' said Amy. 'Don't explain us. It's obscene.'

I whispered from the corner of my mouth, 'I must, because it's true and they don't understand.' I was almost booming. 'I know it's no fun looking at me. Because I don't like looking

219

at blind or lame people either. But try to believe that people live inside themselves; they aren't their bodies only.'

'The *atman*!' exclaimed a pious-faced woman. 'The body is only like clothes we wear. Bhagvad Gita tells us that.'

'And no, I'm not rich and this girl has nothing wrong with her. We're just happy to be together.'

They were shaking their heads from side to side in wonder and admiration, even the urchins who hadn't understood a word of what I'd said because I was talking in English. 'Long life, to you,' said someone.

'Thank you,' I said. 'And now, may we go?'

They hurriedly made way for us and Amy, like a queen, wheeled me through. We walked home. Everywhere we went we went walking, or rather Amy went walking because she wasn't strong enough to lift me into the cab. And both of us thought it was unfair to ask the driver for help.

'Why were you crying?' I asked, afraid of her answer.

'For you. As if . . .'

'Yes?'

'As if you were a black in South Africa. Oh! Don't make me talk about it or I'll miss one of the traffic signals.'

'I can deal with it, Amy. As long as you don't hurt.'

'But I can't help hurting if I love you.'

'You can if you see it like it is. If you just say I know what Brit is like, these people don't, so what they say or do is water off a duck's back.'

'You know,' she said, her voice pitched curiously high, 'the first thing you're going to do when we get home is make love to me.'

I took her palm from the handle of my chair and kissed it. 'Sera's out tonight,' I said.

It wasn't until we reached home that I remembered that Amy hadn't seen my legs, ever. I felt sick and icy with the temperature at thirty-five Celsius outside; my stomach churned as if I were going to shit and throw up all at the same time. If she saw me, she'd leave me. Not at once, but gently when she could without hurting me too much. Maybe she would go back to Cyrus and his hard long limbs. Maybe she would find someone like me, only his body would not be mine.

'Are you one of those weirdos – like Marlon Brando in *Last Tango in Paris* – who make love with their clothes on?' said Amy, swinging her nude legs as she sat down on the sofa. 'It's a good thing no one can see us.'

'Yes,' I said, 'the Causeway is a wide street.'

'I wish we didn't have to dress at home – I love being like this.'

So would I if I looked like some picture gone crazy with beauty. 'You've seen this *Last Tango in Paris*?' I asked.

'Yes; on video. It was awful.'

'I don't know.'

'Brit,' she whispered, leaning forward, her lips hardly moving, 'you don't find me attractive?'

I held her in my arms – as much of her as I could manage. 'Of course I do, darling. Especially the you inside you.'

'And the me outside?' she said mischievously. My shirt was slowly coming off my shoulders. My arms were OK, all muscle and hair – I could swing on them whenever I got tired of sitting.

'Shall we go inside?' I pointed to my bedroom.

'I like it here, with the moon looking in on us.'

'The yellow voyeur. No, we'll go in where it's darker.'

She wheeled me in, parting Sera's white lace curtains. I shifted to the bed and all three lights were suddenly on. 'The better to see me,' grinned Amy. I couldn't look away. She was silky and peachy and firm and soft and I was breathless.

'Saw you,' I said about fifteen minutes later. 'Now turn the lights off.'

'Why?'

'It's more romantic.'

'But I want to see you.'

'Believe me, it's lovelier this way.'

'How do you know? You said you'd never made love to a girl.'

'I haven't. Even if I had, it wouldn't matter, would it? I mean, I don't mind about you.'

'What about me?'

'You not being – '

221

'But I am!'

'What about the night after you and Cyrus dropped me off?'

'We listened to music – Mozart. If I remember right! Brit, don't you believe me?'

'Because how could you not?'

'You mean if you were me . . .'

'Didn't *he* want to?'

'Of course he did. But he was always saying sex had nothing to do with love, so I said why bother, let's just enjoy being in love.'

I rolled over with laughter and then she was on top of me. 'Who are you trying to fool?' she said. 'Lights off and romance? You're afraid I'll see your legs, aren't you? Oh, Brit! Why can't you – '

My eyes were shut so I wouldn't have to see the look in her eyes while she took my pants away. Then her mouth was between my legs. 'So this is what you were afraid I'd see,' she said. I smiled and felt her silky head against the insides of my thighs. Then she lifted her black eyes and said, 'Brit, you are the sexiest man I've ever met.'

For some time after that I couldn't see her face too well because I knew she was telling the truth. We didn't turn those lights off till the monsoon broke at dawn.

'I love your little growls of pleasure,' she said.

'That's thunder, Amy.'

'Oh!' she giggled. 'I'm feeling drunk.'

'Semen intoxicated.'

'Don't be porny.'

'I love that smell.' I breathed so I'd never forget.

'My hair?'

'The rain, darling, can't you hear it?'

'Is it raining? Then what are you doing sleeping here?'

I moved over to my chair. 'Let's go to the window,' I said.

'Put something on first.'

'I ought to be saying that to you.'

'What can I put on? Nothing of yours will fit me.'

'Take the blanket – the pink one. Hurry, I want to see the lightning.'

'What about you?'

'Sheets are too big for me – I use these.' I pulled out my one-yard-square of mustard-yellow flannel and threw it over my shoulders.

We crossed the room. The windows were fighting their stoppers, egged on by the wind. The temperature had dropped about ten degrees. I shivered. 'Don't die on me,' said Amy, cuddling up close.

'It's better to have loved and lost – '

She shook her head. 'I'll never lose you because I'll always feel you deep inside me.'

'Don't be obscene.'

'You have a filthy mind.'

'You mean what we just did was filthy?'

'Oh, you should've stuck to law!'

The lightning was turning our room into a disco with thunder for music. And the Causeway glistened like a slow black river in the moonlight. 'What does it remind you of?' asked Amy.

'What?'

'The moon – watch it slink like a thief behind the clouds.'

'Watch it float like a balloon some happy child has let go free.' Amy smiled and came closer. 'I feel like that moon right now,' I said.

24

ONCE UPON A time, there lived a giant called Zuhaak, a pillaging ogre, whose idea of fun was to destroy everything he could lay his huge hands on. They captured him and bound him with a massive chain to the Elburz mountains, where he still lives.

But every night, under cover of darkness, he begins to lick his chain with his tongue, which is as rough and powerful as a saw. Then when it's just about to give way and he's thinking of all the mean things he'll do, a cock crows and hey presto! the chain grows chunky once again. And if one day there are no cocks left on earth, Zuhaak, have pity on us.

I'm not out to get the world but I think I'm like Zuhaak. Because every time I think my chains are off I find myself in an unholy tangle again. It used to happen when I was a kid. I wouldn't have a fracture for months on end and I'd know I'd outgrown osteo, given it a proper kick in the pants, when crack! and you know the rest of the story. And then just when I thought everything was tickety-boo – I had Cyrus next door and Ruby below me and Dolly blissfully unmarried – you know the rest of that story too.

This time the cock crowed when Jeroo came waltzing in one morning just as I was putting the finishing pen-strokes to the summary and opening chapters of a novel Amy was sending to the literary agent in London for me.

'Look what I have,' chanted Jeroo, holding aloft a large green bottle of Vat 69.

'Vat!' yelled Sera. 'How Sam loved Vat! It's ages since I've had any.'

'Ha! Ha!' said Jeroo. 'I knew I'd fool you with that. It's just that when Swamiji came over I didn't have anything else handy so I filled it in this.'

'What did you fill?' said Sera, and I knew the same horrible liquid thought was in both our minds.

'Guess!' challenged Jeroo.

'Something that's best left in the toilet,' said Sera.

Jeroo put down the bottle carefully on the glass-topped coffee table and struck her cheeks in substitute penance for Sera.

'Pick it up from there!' screamed Sera. 'How dare you bring your Swami's *su-su* to my house.'

'Smell it!' cried Jeroo, unscrewing the cap and waving the bottle under Sera's nose. Sera pushed it aside crossly and some of the contents splashed on the speckled-tiled floor. 'Look what you've done!' cried Jeroo. She bent down, dipped her fingers in it and touched them between her eyebrows.

'You clean up that mess,' said Sera. 'My *bai* has finished her work and left.'

'Ignorant one!' intoned Jeroo, sounding like one of the ancient *rishis*. 'This is Gangajal, water from the holy Ganges. Your floor has been blessed and now I will proceed to bless your walls and furniture and – '

'Let me see it,' said Sera suspiciously. 'Here, pussy! Smell it and tell me.'

I wrinkled my nose; it didn't smell too good – sort of sweet and rotten.

'Ugh!' said Sera. 'Just look at his face. I'm not letting you sprinkle this slime all over my house.'

'Slime?' shrieked Jeroo indignantly. 'Do you know Holy Ganga is descended from Lord Shiva's head?'

'Poor chap. He must have needed a shampoo,' said Sera blithely. 'The river floats with corpses and sewage. Don't you know? Haven't you read about it? Don't you ever read the papers?'

'Never!' said Jeroo stoutly. 'Who knows what I may find? A picture of Tina?'

I hugged her shoulders; they were soft and warm. 'Let's get on with that sprinkling!' I said gaily. She jumped up, poured a little Gangajal into her cupped palm and started going round the drawing-room, tossing drops with finger and thumb as if she were playing carrom.

Sera stood at the window, her eyes turned up to the ceiling. 'You've missed that, Jeroo,' she said, pointing up. Jeroo smiled serenely. She went into my bedroom. The curtain was open and I saw her sprinkle my desk, the chair Amy called my Ferrari, the piano at which I could only play snatches of Bach because my feet couldn't reach the pedal and most of Bach doesn't need pedalling. Then she climbed on to a big waist-high wooden stool that stood next to Sera's Be Prepared cupboard.

Sera pounced, in one long leap from the drawing-room window to where Jeroo was gingerly making her way to the stock, shrieking like, well, Sera. 'Don't you dare touch my stock! You'll ruin it with your filthy water!' She shook the stool and Jeroo swayed like a statue.

'You wouldn't say that if this were water from Lourdes,' she mocked from her eminent position. 'Why? Because it's foreign. And my poor Ganga is the Mother of India.' She tilted the bottle she was holding.

Sera clutched Jeroo's hips and, using them as a lever, hauled herself up on the stool. 'Now, I'll see how you dare to!' she challenged, flinging her arms between Jeroo and the stock as if she were playing basketball.

'Mine is a holy task,' said Jeroo, 'and I must complete it.' She began dodging Sera's arms, aiming her bottle like a flashlight.

'Stop it!' I sopranoed in my best osteo voice.

'This is a fight to the finish!' declared Sera in her famous martial tones. 'I've bought all this with Sam's sweat and I'll never allow its defilement with these dregs from a septic tank.'

Jeroo gasped and flung the water into Sera's face. Sera lost her balance and reached out. Her hand caught hold of a steam iron which was jammed between two lanes of boxes. For a second it steadied her, then the whole lot slipped, teetered on the edge and went crashing to the floor.

Sera lay there in her pink housecoat as if she were in a junk-yard. Around her bloomed red and yellow boxes of Complan and bright brick cans of baked beans, rolls of cellophane-wrapped toilet-paper, pink-and-blue-candy-striped boxes of talcum powder, soaps gay in their wrappers. A bottle had broken and the smell of Dettol punched the warm air. At Sera's head, like a tombstone, lay the gleaming iron.

Jeroo's high, sweet voice began chanting the mantra of life, '*Om trayambakam*', as she lifted high the bottle of Vat 69 and poured its contents over Sera's stomach making a dark sash of colour round her waist.

'Do you think?' I asked, beginning to shiver.

Jeroo shivered and began her descent from the stool. We stood there; glass shards – a dozen shattered light bulbs – glittered on the floor in the soft monsoon sunshine. 'Isn't it beautiful?' whispered Jeroo. 'I feel we should leave her here. I can't reach her: I'm barefoot.' She sat on the stool and began to swing her long pink legs. 'You can't reach her either – you'll puncture your tyres.'

'Go, phone the doctor,' I said, my teeth clenched.

'Or the police? I've killed her, haven't I?'

'It was an accident – and she isn't dead.'

'It wasn't an accident – it was *karma*.'

'Maybe *karma* is an accident. Oh! Why are we having this crazy conversation? Jeroo, go and phone!'

She twirled round on the stool and slipped off and glided away. I kicked a path through the minced glass to where Sera was lying. I bent over her face – she looked pale and Roman, her nose was proud, her mouth stoic. I touched her forehead; she opened her eyes. 'I lost my balance,' she said slowly as if her mouth were stuffed with cotton wool.

'Are you all right?' I felt the relief-polio in my muscles.

'Of course. You?'

'Perfect.'

'Goody. I was terrified I was going to smash you. Sure you haven't broken a thing?'

'Sera, I don't break any more.'

'What if you never had?' She shut her eyes and I knew she was seeing those days when everything was chocolate and swimsuits.

'Then you wouldn't have been – ' I saw her mouth fill with blood, the level rising slowly till it reached her teeth. Twice she gagged, tried to draw a breath and failed. Then she flung her head back and threw open her eyes. They were not the slightest bit afraid.

Amy was sitting next to me at the funeral while the priests chanted. She looked like a bride in her soft white silk sari. That made me smile.

'Will you feel ashamed if you cry?' she asked.

'I guess so.'

'Don't,' she whispered, throwing a kiss in the air above my right ear. 'You laugh when you're happy, don't you?'

I saw Cyrus walking straight and handsome in his white *dagli* to Sera's body, bending beside it with a quick lithe movement and getting up with his dark head bowed, his face silent. Sera should've had a son like that. They could've had a marvellous time, done great things together. I watched him walking back to his place on the verandah till I had to shut my eyes.

When they took Sera away, up the green hill to the well of death, I couldn't go along. It was too steep, they said. I was glad to be left with only Amy for company. Because I was crying like a rain cloud, thinking of my mother's dark brave eyes in a vulture's beak.

I got down to licking my chains again.

One October afternoon, about a month after Sera had crashed out of the scene, Amy and I had taken off our clothes because it was so warm, and ended up in bed, when the doorbell rang once and once again. 'The postman always rings twice,' mumbled Amy with my tongue between her teeth.

'Oh, for a letter-box,' I moaned.

Amy went to the door, peeped through the magic eye and slid one bare arm through the safety-chain. Her arm came back with a glossy white envelope – definitely not Indian. 'Open it,' she said. I took it from her and put it under the pillows. If it said what I didn't want it to say I wasn't going to be in a mood to make love.

I took as long as I could. 'Darling,' moaned Amy, 'I love this but I'm not sure it's very good for my heart, it's beating at something like four hundred a half-minute.' I shut my eyes and let her tachycardia subside. Mine went on. I had Iris Murdoch, Chopin, Amy, perhaps Cyrus, my home above the Causeway, Ruby, Jerry, the sea at Apollo, Dolly's letters, bridge, Housman – my cup was running over. Why would I want to open that envelope and empty it? Slowly, I pushed my arm under the pillows and found the letter. I felt the cold paper in my palm, and I crumpled it up fiercely like it was a bad school report.

'It might just be good news,' Amy mumbled into my chest.

'Just might – only we'll never know.'

'I'm in love with a coward.'

'A writerly coward,' I corrected.

A couple of hours after Amy left, I was buying bread from the *powwallah* when the lift door clanged open and I dropped the bread at my feet.

'Now you'll have to buy another,' said a voice. 'No, make it two, I'm staying for dinner.'

Suddenly I was enjoying a bird's eye view of the Causeway as Dolly hoisted me in her arms the way she used to whenever things got too crowded for my chair. I held her and hugged her and she squeezed the breath out of me – it felt good being so close to someone without a hard-on in the way.

'You're getting heavier,' she groaned, letting me down. 'Bet you must be seventeen kilos by now.'

I giggled. 'Where's Salim?' I asked. She shook her head. 'You mean, you mean you've – '

'No, I haven't left him. He's at the airport with our baggage. He was going to this medical conf in Hong Kong so I came along.'

'Just like that?'

'Uh-uh. When you earn dollars it's easy.'

'When Salim earns dollars.'

'I do, Brit – I've got a new job with – guess?'

'A bawdy house in Brooklyn.'

'Oh, Sera, oh, I miss her . . . The job's with Pan Am. Isn't that great? I'll be seeing you so much more often when I start getting my free tickets.'

'Wow!' I swear I felt my heart dancing and I would've whirled Dolly in my arms. She was looking beautiful, almost as lovely as Amy. With her soft dark curls shaped to look as if she was born with a hairstyle, and her chutney-green-and-white-striped dress with a sash at the waist. If I wasn't me I'd be whistling at the sight.

'So you're all by yourself, Brit – how is it?'

'Super! I'm not all by myself. You know Amy and I – '

'I don't know Amy and you. You didn't tell me – Sera wrote something like Brit is involved; hope all goes right, and I had to make do with that. What is all this about – you mean you've stolen Cyrus's girl?'

'I took what was my own,' I said, sounding like one of those parliamentarians you hear over the BBC.

'Brit, how she must love you.'

'What d'you mean?' I asked so I could see her blush.

She did, pink as a prawn. 'OK, you're the most wonderful man I know – after Salim and Sam. But you know how lucky you are? You don't ever have to wonder if a girl loves you just for, you know what.'

'Dolly, you have Sera in your blood.'

'Brit, Brit – I have to go at ten. Can we have dinner? Who cooks?'

'Defarge does right now but I'm getting the kitchen refitted – everything at chair-level – only when Amy's here it's going to be difficult.'

'You mean you want her bending over all the time so you can look down her – '

'You're sounding like Jerry; I told you about Jerry?'

'Oh, yes – has he found a girl?'

'I don't know – he's in Davier. I got a post-card from his mother that said "Brit, we miss your chattering".'

'Did you shiver a lot?' And I chased her down the long passage all the way to the kitchen. 'I'll do everything,' she said. 'You can take a break.' So I sat back and let her serve as I used to do in Sera times.

'Can't you find another slave?'

'But I have. He's a part-timer, he takes me out when I want to, the rest of the time he goes around cleaning houses for people, and anyway when I'm with Amy I don't need anyone.'

'You need Amy.'

'Yes, yes, I need Amy.'

'I need Salim.'

Not the same way, but I let it go – we didn't have the time.

Defarge didn't serve very large portions so dinner didn't take very long. 'Go brush your teeth,' said Dolly. I had this thing about brushing my teeth, those that I still had, like balding chaps are always combing their scalps.

'What have you been doing in this bed, Brit!' sang Dolly. 'Passion Unlimited, I perceive.'

I was blushing, and foaming at the mouth with toothpaste, when she screamed. 'You've sold your book and you didn't even tell me! Brit, are you my brother or – '

I couldn't hear anything she said because there was this huge noise in my ear where a massed choir was singing and I was dripping tears into the wash-basin together with the toothpaste I was trying to flush out of my mouth.

Optimistic. Such a lovely word, so English, Jerry's mother would've said. I had a contract and the publishers were optimistic about my book. I had an advance, in British pounds sterling, as Sera would've said, and it felt as good as – it really was.

'Brit! You've made it,' exulted Dolly.

'Long way to go,' I said, not believing a bit of what I was saying.

Then it was time for Dolly to leave. I hugged her like I wouldn't let her go. Till she did.

The next night I took Amy to the Rooftop Rendezvous to celebrate. We settled down into the claret-velvet seats, and drank in the atmosphere – delicately gilded ceiling, the glass walls with the city and the sea gleaming far below us. Amy was wearing a soft silk dress with a tiny waist and a flared skirt; the silk touched her skin the way I wanted to whenever she was close to me.

We ordered some champagne, the first time I'd done anything like th t and it cost as much as I paid Defarge for a monthful of meals. But what the hell, it didn't add up to much when you converted it into British pounds sterling.

We drank the bottle between the two of us and I don't know if that's a lot or not but we certainly started acting strange. I kept seeing Cyrus's face where Amy's was and I kept stroking her hair which was heaven because I was doing it to Cyrus and I knew I wasn't.

'You know,' I said; my voice was new and quite un-osteo, 'Cyrus and I came here once. We had a wonderful time, a gorgeous time. I've never had a time like that before or after. Or after, Amy.'

Amy looked up with Cyrus's face and she said, 'If you go on like that, so will I. About how we danced – there, right there.' But she was pointing at the glass wall behind me. 'We were dancing, Brit, as if his body was, I mean were . . .' she giggled. 'Were mine and mine his. We'll never dance like that, will we?'

'Never, Amy. Not if you beg me to.' When we'd stopped laughing, she said, 'When I was with him there was nothing else for me.'

'And when you're with me?'

'There's him, there's Cyrus,' she said, smiling beatifically.

'I'll tell you a secret – when I'm with you he's with me too.'

'How I wanted him,' groaned Amy, doubling up as if her tummy hurt, 'and how I fought it – '

'You shouldn't have, you know,' I said, feeling genial. 'I wouldn't have minded.'

'What did you have to do with it?' she said. 'It was that girl he had and I was never sure how he felt.'

'What other girl? He only had me.'

'Dear chuck,' she said pityingly.

Amy brought her hands in front of my face and donkey-clapped. That reminded me of Dolly. 'My sister's gone,' I said.

'Good riddance, I say. You love her too much – no wonder you're gay.'

I glared. 'You were telling me about Cyrus's other women?'

'Correction. Other woman. They call her Ruby.'

'Ru-by? You knew about Ru-by?'

'So did you, didn't you? And you didn't tell me – you were too busy protecting your Princeton fucker.'

That was too huge to field – I let it pass.

'Brit,' she said, holding my hands, looking almost as beautiful as Cyrus in the golden light from the candles. 'Oh, Brit, it was awful never being able to trust him; but it's different with you, isn't it? I mean, I never ever have to worry – '

'Of course you don't. Is that why you wanted me, you insecure little bitch?'

'Brit! that's not a nice thing . . . where's the food we ordered? That's not a nice thing to say.'

'Amy, what have you and the champagne got in common?'

'We bubble,' she said and turned down her empty glass.

'The champagne tastes tart, you are one.'

'Well,' she said, picking up a bread stick and snapping it in two. 'This is brittle and so are you.'

Her *coq au vin* arrived together with my Charlemagne Châteaubriand. 'Whirrr!' I went, 'Whirrr!' The waiter was deaf. 'I've got a tape recorder inside me,' I told Amy. 'I remember everything; I've got it down – whirrr!'

'The least you could do,' she said, 'is get one of those silent models.'

We began to eat. The steak was delicious, better than it was the last time I had it here. Suddenly Amy raided my plate with her fork. 'You didn't get much,' I crowed, watching the shred dangling from the tines.

'You think you've got a lot, don't you?'

'But I have – look!'

'You think you've got a lot because you've got me.'

'More than you've got because you've got me. We just have to look into a mirror to confirm that, Amy.'

We started laughing as loud as the band was playing; we went on and on until we started aching, I before she. 'You don't love me,' she said.

'Now, wairr a minute – '

'You're no good at Hollywood dialogue – you should stick to Mills and Boon. And you don't love me, you only want me to push-push-push-push-push.'

'What are you saying, darling? You are crying, you are crying at my celebration. I've sold my novel.'

'And I push-push-push; that's all you want me for – to push-push you to Apollo and – '

'I thought you liked it, being with me without the servant along.'

'Only if you love me; not because you want someone to get the cash from the bank and bread from the bakery.'

'I have a *powwallah*,' I said haughtily.

'You just want someone now that they're all up in heaven.'

'Dolly isn't.'

'Wish she was – no, I don't, maybe I do. You want someone so you won't be alone. You don't want me; Cyrus would have done just as well – '

'Better,' I said. 'Remember, he can lift me.'

After that I heard a funny noise. It was that tape getting snarled up in my head.

The next thing I knew, I was in my bed with my shoes on. Someone had rewound that tape and it was playing in my head through a two hundred-watt amplifier. I opened my eyes to drown the sound but it didn't make any difference. Because everything was dark, black.

25

THE NEXT TWO days were good. I had the workers renovating
the kitchen and I had to be there watching them all the time,
explaining, giving instructions, because they'd never created a
kitchen at knee-level. This was going to be very expensive but
that was all right. I had money – Dolly's, Sera's, Sam's, and
now my own.

At least, I didn't have to worry about a split-level kitchen.
All I had to worry about was getting through the next few
days; I mean, you can only play a tape over and over that
much. After that it's got to wear away into silence.

When the workers left, it wasn't so good because I discovered
I'd got one of those untreatable diseases, writer's block. There
I sat, morning after morning, with the white sheet in front of
me daring me to deflower it while I waited till the impotent
pen wilted in my sweaty fingers. I thought: If I make a mark on
the paper things will roll. I planted a dot on top of the page.
Then a dash, then another dot till it looked like a message in
Morse I couldn't read.

I didn't give up; that would have been like putting all four
of my wheels over the edge of the cliff. As it was, I had two
of them hanging there.

So I sat down to write at ten every morning and I waited till
lunchtime. After lunch, I counted the pages I should've written
that day and I laid them aside in a little heap. I counted the heap
one day. I stopped at one hundred and one. Those tigers.

My doorbell rang in a familiar fashion. Too soon, I thought.
A few more days and I'll be ready. But the ringing went on
and I knew I couldn't open the door.

'Hi! Feel like a walk?'

'I'd like that. But what about this?' I said, looking at my blue poplin shorts.

'Fucking shit! You haven't learnt a thing from me, have you?' His nose crinkled as he put on his doleful look, the one he had that morning he needed the safety-pin.

I grabbed my key and shut the door. I thought I heard another one open. I smiled; my mouth felt strange.

'What's the time?' said Cyrus.

'It doesn't matter. I don't have to get back before midnight any more.'

'Tomorrow I'll be gone,' he said. I heard the flick of a match and smelt his cigarette.

'Where?'

'To Delhi.'

'New Delhi,' I said with that bit of mind that goes on like a lizard's tail.

'Yes. I'm not coming back, Brit.'

'Oh.'

'I'm getting a job with a law firm there.'

'Is that why?'

'I could've got a job with a law firm here. I'm sorry, Brit, I didn't ask where you wanted to go – now we're here. Quite appropriate, wouldn't you say?' We were at Apollo on the promenade opposite the Taj. He stopped. 'Hey! What's wrong?'

'I can't talk to you like this, sit down.'

'OK.' He swooped through the gap in the sea wall. I was too scared to scream.

'Talk,' he said, sitting down on the landing-stage for boats. The sea lapped sadly against the stone, the tide was going out.

'Don't go,' I said.

'I have to.'

'You don't.'

'Brit.' I turned and looked at him though I knew I shouldn't have. He looked very young and very dangerous. 'I've been going crazy,' he said, 'thinking of you and Amy and everything up in flames.'

'Nothing is,' I said. 'Amy and I are finished.'

He brought himself closer and knelt in front of me. 'Why, Brit?'

'You.' And I smiled quickly.

'Yes, but now I'm gone things'll be easier, won't they?'

'It's not you, as you, it's what you mean to us – '

'OK, don't go on, I get you. You mean,' and he laughed so I could see his teeth gleam, 'none of us got anything out of the whole thing?'

'We learnt,' I said, and winked so I wouldn't sound stupid.

'I have to go tomorrow,' he said. I watched the sea which was like the back of a huge zebra striped with moonlight.

'Forget the idea, you don't have to see Amy any more. If you don't go we can save something out of – '

'It's not you as you,' he said smiling, but not really. 'You and Amy are bits of me I've got to leave behind.'

'So you can get on with – '

He looked at me and I gulped. 'It's like your violin, isn't it?'

'That wasn't half as hard,' he whispered, and I saw the moon bobbing in his eyes.

After a long time, he lifted his head from my chest and said, 'Promise you won't write to me.'

'I promise.'

Sometimes, the weather turns and my legs ache in the places where they once broke; it's a funny kind of pain, quiet yet sharp, and I can feel the fracture as if it happened last week. He would've called this sentimental shit but there are other times when I smell a certain brand of cigarettes that the ache begins. Not in my legs. Somewhere in my pigeon-chest.

'You'll never believe who rang me today!' sang Ruby standing at my door, prettier than ever. She was wearing a tiny pink blouse and a skirt, fresh as a garden with green leaves and pink roses strewn all over.

'Who? Come in, first.'

'Jerry.'

'Really? You mean he's back! But why did he phone you – how?'

Ruby made a face that said she couldn't explain all the magic in the world. 'He asked if I'd go out with him.'

'Silly man – anyway, he's better than a snub.'

'I said yes.'

'What?'

'Why not? It'll be a change from . . .' Her eyes filled. She looked out of the window and said, 'This glare!'

I grinned and hugged her. She felt lovely – somewhere between Dolly and Amy. 'Tell Jerry to come and see me. I need a change too.'

'Do you realise, Brit Kotwal, this is the first time in our whole crazy lives that you've hugged me.'

'Here's to the next time.' She giggled; I blushed.

'See my kitchen,' I said.

She saw. 'I don't understand,' she said. 'How is Amy ever going to manage?' She saw my face. 'Oh! You're going to manage – that's super. C'mon! I'll give you your first lesson – let's make a chocolate cake.'

'What d'you need?'

'Milk, butter, flour, eggs, cocoa.'

'Got it, got it, got it.'

'I should've known. Sera's son.'

We giggled and began, Ruby bending over the table so I could look down her front. 'Looks gorgeous,' I said.

Ruby wrinkled her nose. 'You crazy?' she squealed, stirring the mud-coloured mess. 'This looks gorgeous to you?'

'I was talking of something else,' I said loftily.

'I can imagine what,' said Ruby, narrowing her sparkling brown eyes.

'Give that to me,' I said as gruffly as I could manage. I began to fold in the flour holding the bowl in the crook of my left arm; bubbles winked and stretched and burst in the dough.

'It's ready,' said Ruby. 'Put it in the oven – want me to do it?'

'Certainly not.' I slid it in and shut the door.

'Monopoly?' said Ruby. I nodded. She beat me really soon because I kept leaving the game to see how the cake was doing; it was my first time. When I saw I'd lost Mayfair and Park Lane, I resigned. Besides, the cake seemed to be ready. 'Test it with a knife,' said Ruby. I plunged it in – it came out clean.

'Let's eat it,' I said. It smelt like the smell you got every time you passed the bakery at the Taj – then you just had to go to the pastry shop and exchange all those notes for a boxful of croissants and cakes and tarts.

'You've got to wait till it cools,' said Ruby. 'Then we turn it out, we take a mouthful.' I sat there willing it to cool but the waiting was like that tachycardiac afternoon I knew I shouldn't be thinking about.

'I think,' said Ruby, 'I'll try a morsel before you risk injuring your tongue.' Then we were all over the poor cake like a pair of tigers mauling a sleeping deer.

'Delicious to the last crumb,' said Ruby, putting it in her mouth. We looked at each other and grinned as if we were at a grinning contest. I didn't have to worry about my lantern-jaw – she was used to it.

'The healing things,' breathed Ruby, holding her tummy that looked as if she were a bit preggers. 'Chocolate cake – '

'And Jerry – '

'And you,' we said together, kissing the crumbs off each other's mouths.

I knew I was ready.

I thought of Cyrus and the violin and I knew he wasn't the only guy who was trying to grow. Ruby had talked of the healing but I knew you had to stitch a wound before it healed. I picked up the phone and dialled Amy's number.

'Good afternoon,' yapped the Peke.

'Good afternoon – is Amy there?'

'She's at the library – they're open on Saturdays, Brit.'

'Yes, I forgot. Do you know if she's free this evening?'

'She is. Every evening.

Hell. 'Will you tell her I'd like to see her? Just for this evening.'

'I'll tell her. Goodbye.'

'Yes.'

By half-past six I had all my armour on. That still wasn't enough when I saw her toss her head to fling the hair out of her eyes, when I saw her crooked canine. I knew that stitching hurts and I didn't have any anaesthetics left.

'You called, sir?' she said and I took her hand.

'Sit down,' I said. I'm always saying that to people – it's awful talking with your head thrown back as if you were hollering at a skyscraper. She sat down; she was wearing a sea-blue dress that loved her, you could see it in the way it held her.

'You were right,' I began.

'So were you.' She inclined her head graciously.

'I wanted . . . I loved you because I needed you. Not to push-push, but to feel – '

'To feel you didn't have osteo.'

'Yes, yes, that was very clever.'

She smiled and I saw that infernal tooth again. 'I was happy because I knew you wouldn't have too many opportunities with other girls. As for what I felt about . . .'

'He's gone,' I said, and it was as if I'd hit her with the back of my hand.

'I suppose,' she said, 'you looked like I just did when he told *you*.'

'I don't know, it was too dark.' We laughed, badly, like at a funeral.

'We both felt something for him that we couldn't use.'

'Yes, yes, oh, you are very clever today. Do I sound nasty? I don't mean to.'

She shook her head. 'But we had something outside that, didn't we?'

She left her chair and knelt in front of me. One of these days I'm going to get a sword and start dubbing. 'We had something outside push-push and Cyrus and insecurity. Something huge and very good. Am I clever about that too?'

'No.'

'No?'

'No.' I wasn't going to argue about this.

'You mean, you can't separate the strands and you don't know if there's anything left after push-push and all that.'

'Yes.'

'Can we try?'

'No, Amy. I've got to be alone. I have to be Osteo Brit and not mind.'

'But you aren't Osteo Brit really; I mean, inside you are six feet tall.'

'That's a lot!'

'All right, five feet–six.'

'Make it seven.'

'Done. And you want to live like you're four feet tall. That's dwarfing yourself.'

'I want to be what I really am, no more acts, no more reaching for things I'm too short to reach.'

'But I told you, you aren't short.'

'Go, please go, Amy.' I was beginning to feel very strong; and that was something new.

'I love you,' she said, her Arabian Sea-eyes wide open. I nodded, a bit absently. She rose from her knees and touched my cowlick.

Then she went away.

I had never felt so good in my life. Not in the I-could-go-out-and-kiss-the-first-girl-I-see kind of way. But solid and calm and right. Then something strange began to happen – like a singing army, sentences, paragraphs, pages began pouring into my head. Up from my toes and knees and cock and stomach they came: fluent and clear and correct.

I shivered with pleasure and went to the window, more out of habit than for a last glimpse of Amy. She must have walked away really fast. The Causeway snaked, dry and deserted, into the distance. But I knew if I could see to the end of the road, I'd catch the moon in the white dome of the museum and the copper-pod and the flame trees shouting colour to the serene sky.

But things didn't work out quite that way. For one thing, I saw Defarge coming up the Causeway after her Saturday visit to the movies and I saw her see Amy in the entrance downstairs and I heard her exclaim. For another thing, I thought: If I can do without Amy, why should I?

I opened the door and rang for the lift and wished like a madman it would stop level with the ground so I could wheel in. It halted about four inches above. I flung open the collapsible doors. Without a blink I fell out of my chair, sharing my weight between the stronger bits of my legs and my arms. I looked like a funny kind of antelope balanced on spindly fours – the lift had a full-length mirror at the back; maybe Sam's mother used to watch herself, slinky in a ball-gown, when she stepped out with her English lover.

I eased myself to the floor of the lift, listening carefully for the smallest crack. Then the lift stopped with a bump and I bounced. In the mirror I saw Amy, her head bowed, pinned against the wall by Defarge who was grilling her. 'Amy,' I called into the glass, 'd'you think I look a few inches taller?'

She lifted her head; then her hair's silk hid her face from me. I saw her arms going around Defarge's plump back. I watched myself, sitting on the polished wooden floor with my legs stretched out. I blinked once. I blinked again.

There are some things we just can't believe. I liked the way I looked.

CLIVE JAMES

Brilliant Creatures

£5.99

'The brilliant creatures of the title live in a world of lost innocence and vast incomes; publishers, writers, media men and consultants, they belong to a charmed circle where everyone knows everyone else's business . . . Clive James doesn't miss a trick' THE TIMES

'Nearer to Wodehouse than to Waugh. He is not setting out merely to raise laughs. He takes vigorous swipes at most of the unacceptable faces of society' LISTENER

'Romping satire of London literary life . . . the writing sizzles off the page with a rare merriment' ILLUSTRATED LONDON NEWS

'The wittiest novel of the year' BOOKSELLER

'Clive James writes one-liners the way John McEnroe wears head-bands' FRANK DELANEY

MARIO VARGAS LLOSA

Aunt Julia and the Scriptwriter

£5.99

'Mario, 18-year-old law student and radio news-editor, falls scandalously for his Aunt Julia, the 32-year-old divorced wife of a cousin, and the progressively lunatic story of this affair is interwoven with episodes from a series of radio soap-operas written by his friend Predro Comacho, a scriptwriter of prodigious output and hysterical imagination . . .'

'Llosa's huge energy and inventiveness are extravagant and fabulously funny' NEW STATESMAN

'Pulls off that South American rope-trick with unprecedented power and skill' SUNDAY TIMES

'A high comedy of great warmth and masterly control of form . . . tough, tender, funny, tactfully erotic, with moments of bitterness, despair and farce' THE TIMES

'Will confirm the opinion of all those who think that the Latin American novel is the most vigorous contemporary form at present' LITERARY REVIEW

JULIAN BARNES

A History of the World in 10½ Chapters

£4.99

'Frequently brilliant, funny, thoughtful, iconoclastic and a delight to read. Barnes is . . . like a worldly, secular reincarnation of a medieval gloss-writer on sacred texts, and what he offers us is the novel as footnote to history, as subversion of the given, as brilliant, elaborate doodle around the margins of what we know we think about what we think we know' SALMAN RUSHDIE, OBSERVER

'With imaginative craft, and using a whole flotilla of historic and symbolic ships, this wittily individual book surveys human existence buoyantly, but never lets you forget the dark depths beneath' PETER KEMP, SUNDAY TIMES

'You will want to read it again and again, and why not? – there's nothing around to touch it. At last, the English novel seems to have got its balls back' ANNE SMITH, LITERARY REVIEW

'There is a boldness at work in his novel that deserves anthems of approval' THE TIMES

All Pan books are available at your local bookshop or newsagent, or can be ordered direct from the publisher. Indicate the number of copies required and fill in the form below.

Send to: **CS Department, Pan Books Ltd., P.O. Box 40, Basingstoke, Hants. RG21 2YT.**

or phone: 0256 469551 (Ansaphone), quoting title, author and Credit Card number.

Please enclose a remittance* to the value of the cover price plus: 60p for the first book plus 30p per copy for each additional book ordered to a maximum charge of £2.40 to cover postage and packing.

*Payment may be made in sterling by UK personal cheque, postal order, sterling draft or international money order, made payable to Pan Books Ltd.

Alternatively by Barclaycard/Access:

Card No.

Signature:

Applicable only in the UK and Republic of Ireland.

While every effort is made to keep prices low, it is sometimes necessary to increase prices at short notice. Pan Books reserve the right to show on covers and charge new retail prices which may differ from those advertised in the text or elsewhere.

NAME AND ADDRESS IN BLOCK LETTERS PLEASE:

....

Name——————————————————————————

Address——————————————————————————

——————————————————————————

——————————————————————————

——————————————————————————

3/87